MW00878274

SILO
Summer's End
A Post-Apocalyptic Survival Thriller

Extinction Series
Book 1

ISBN: 9798556434769

Published October 30, 2020
by BookBreeze.com LLC
Second Edition
Written by: Jay J. Falconer

This is a work of fiction. Names, characters, places, and incidents are the product of the author's imagination or are used fictitiously. Any resemblance to actual persons living or dead, or business establishments or organizations, actual events or locales is entirely coincidental.

Foreword

Admit it. As a reader, don't you just love that pulse-pounding, leave you breathless kind of science fiction story?

You know the one I'm talking about. The one with the rich characters, deep mysteries, and endless action. So much so, that when you're done reading, you can't wait until the next book comes out so you can see what happens next.

You're about to experience all of that and more when you jump into *Silo Book 1: Summer's End*.

Imagine what life would be like on our planet if the entire world was hit with a mini Ice Age and frozen over after a swarm of dark clouds filled the sky with volcanic ash, choking out the Sun?

Then, one day in the future, the Sun makes a comeback, peeking out from the heavens and warming the Earth once more.

What would it mean for the survivors when the great thaw began?

How could anyone have lived that long without sunlight?

What would the Frozen World look like after all that time?

Would the rules for society be different?

Get ready for a thrilling saga that takes off right out of the gates, and won't let you rest until the end, when you'll be left begging for more.

Welcome to *Silo Book 1: Summer's End.*

ML Banner

CHAPTER 1

Summer Lane tore down an abandoned alley with her stainless steel necklace bouncing off her chest. She glanced back to check her lead. It was down to half what it was a few minutes ago. Somehow the hunger gang had closed ground, increasing their foot speed as hers started to wane.

Faster! Faster! she convinced herself, pushing her feet close to their tripping point. Good thing she was young and in shape, her thighs still able to drive her rail-thin legs, even after a mile of this unexpected chase.

She tucked the keepsake inside her sweatshirt, not wanting it to shake loose. It was all she had to prove who she was and where she belonged, both of which might just keep her alive, depending on who might capture her or check her allegiance.

Trash from the abandoned metro area seemed to be everywhere, crowding her path like roving anti-personnel mines, if that was even a thing. She didn't know. History wasn't her strong suit; neither was following the rules.

The refuse blew around in clumps, nestling around other objects she had to dodge. Yet despite its abundance, its stench was long gone, as were the flies and maggots, much like the horde of citizens that used to occupy the city.

Summer made a hard left, angling her body to fight the inertia of her sprint as she raced across the frozen landscape, dodging the snow flurries smacking her in the face.

The sting in her legs grew with every step she took, but it still wasn't as wicked as the pain in her chest. The frigid air seared her lungs with each gasp, burning with the force of a Titan II Missile.

Right then, her mind flashed a video from her childhood—something that stuck in her memories all these years—a fiery missile launch from an underground silo, shooting high into the sky to deliver its devastating payload on some poor, unsuspecting target.

When this chase first began, Summer only needed to take in air every three steps, adding distance between her and the gang on her heels. However, now her breaths were down to a single stride, meaning her speed would continue to fail. The uphill jaunt wasn't helping either, not with a backpack strapped on and Mother Nature's unrelenting howl thrashing her face.

Right on cue, the hoodie across her head blew back from another gust of wind. Her hands went up, yanking it back into place for the third time in the last minute.

She made a sharp right, turning down another corridor she'd never trekked before, her mind changing its focus to the neon scarf atop her head.

What a total screwup. Who in their right mind would choose a bright red bandana on a day like today, with a hunger gang in the area? There were plenty of choices in her backpack, all different colors and styles—what was she thinking?

Just bad luck, she thought to herself as she vaulted over a soiled cardboard box with the word U-Haul stenciled on it. The airborne feeling didn't last long, but while it did, she felt like an Olympic hurdler, clearing the obstacle with precision.

Some might have plowed through the container, landing a shoe on its exterior, but she knew better. Any kind of object could be hiding inside, leaving her with a twisted ankle. An injury like that would mean death, as would most other failures that might occur during one of her Seeker Missions.

Summer peered back over her shoulder, catching a glimpse of the pursuers. Only a few hundred yards stood between her slender frame and those with knives drawn and bellies empty.

Experience had taught her that when starvation fuels adrenaline, a hunger gang's speed and endurance increase, mostly out of necessity, but also from desire—two closely related motives.

Sure, some of her cohorts in the silo thought the 'Scabs' chasing her were no longer human, simply because frostbite had taken the ends of their noses. Yet they were, even with their ravenous eyes leading the charge.

Somehow, they'd locked onto her tracks. She'd gotten careless. Downright lazy. There were rules and those rules existed for a reason. Seekers like her must never assume an area was clear of predators. But yet, she had.

She knew those chasing her would eventually catch up. A slip away point was needed, and fast, just like she'd been taught. Something to conceal her escape and slow them down. Her eyes scanned the area ahead, looking for an advantage.

After two quick lefts and a long right, she scampered out from behind a string of abandoned homes. They were stacked together like clones, built only a few feet apart.

No privacy, she thought, her mind flashing a snapshot of her lumpy mattress in the storage room of the old missile silo she called home, just wide enough to lie on her side with her knees bent to sleep.

A chain link fence waited for her at the end of the decaying asphalt. It had to be at least twenty feet tall, with barbed wire across the top. It stood just beyond a frozen patch of prickly-pear cacti—part of some ancient landscaping plan, she figured—an entrance to a sprawling salvage yard, one that formerly welcomed paying customers on a daily basis.

Dozens of scrap metal piles towered beyond the fence, most several stories in height and capped with ice from the overnight drizzle and freeze. They were statuesque reminders of a civilization gone extinct. A wasteful civilization. So many cars. So many people. So much junk. All of it useless or dead. None of it relevant any more.

She scanned the barbed wire as she shuffled in a fast step. It looked intact and formidable. Not something she had the time or desire to defeat.

The owners obviously thought it prudent to protect the now-defunct business from would-be trespassers, but she scoffed at the idea, her eyes continuing their hunt for an entrance point.

She wondered if the owners back then had only known what the future would hold for them and everything else that drew in air for life, would they have changed their minds and spent their money on an underground bunker instead? Something formidable. Something buried deep and unmarked. Something to help them withstand the Frozen World that would come soon after.

Probably not, she surmised, just as she spotted a vertical slit in the metal lattice near its base. It was on the right—in the same direction she was trotting—ten paces away.

There'd been a breech. But when? No way to know. At least the gap was partially hidden and low to the ground, like her. Maybe the Scabs might miss it.

"Gotta chance it," she mumbled, bringing her feet into a full skid, feeling like some soon-to-be-dead cartoon character running from Wile E. Coyote.

A quick peek behind told her she still had time—nobody there—but it wouldn't last long. The hairs on the back of her neck were on alert. They were close. She could feel it. Closing fast.

Summer took off her pack, then bent down and pried the two sections of fence apart, making sure the sharp edges didn't tear into her hands. Her tattered wool gloves only provided limited protection, especially with the cutouts for her fingertips.

The passage was only a few inches wider than her shoulders, but she was able to squeeze through after a couple of attempts. It took longer to slip inside than she'd hoped, but maybe she'd done so in time.

Another glance back told her the answer. The gang had eyes on, their faces locked onto hers.

Shit! They'd seen her.

Her legs were exhausted and so were her lungs, but she couldn't give up. She put her hand back through the fence and grabbed her pack, then yanked it through and slung it on. Her sprint resumed, tearing around a rusted ambulance lying sideways in the road.

If she had to guess, she figured it had been rocked by a starving horde until it tipped over. Then whoever was inside became that night's dinner. A bloody dinner, one filled with tissue tears and bones breaking.

That visual brought a whole new meaning to the word "crunchie," a gory term she'd heard Krista Carr, the silo's Security Chief, use many times.

It usually meant *death by tank treads*—an old military term, something that no longer had meaning in the new world. Neither did *rules of engagement*, another phrase Krista had mentioned during Seeker Training.

The back door of the ambulance was splayed open with a wind-blown collection of ice resting inside the threshold, protected by a northerly shadow. Summer wasn't surprised. The burn of the sun hadn't melted it yet after the nightly freeze, its surface just out of the sun's reach.

The ground used to be perpetually covered in snow, but then the thaw started. Almost like magic. That change in temperature seemed to bring out the Scabs from wherever they'd been hiding after The Event took out most of the planet. The string of sightings since meant the cannibal problem wasn't going away. In fact, it was getting worse—a problem that her boss, Professor Edison, said he pondered daily.

The next street took her into an old warehouse district, the kind that used to make assembly line stuff. Stuff the world needed back when it actually had a population.

Normal life, she thought, sifting through her memories as she ran. Populations need food, water, shelter, families, and governments. Summer still remembered what all that was like, even if the others in the silo couldn't or wouldn't.

"You can't change the past" was the motto in her group. It was an optimist's attitude—one she understood, even if she didn't believe in what it meant.

The next building ahead was a multi-story parking garage. The structure had collapsed along the front, its foundation and walls in tatters. She cruised past the damage, breathing heavily, pumping her arms like a jackhammer. Chunks of cement and rebar slowed her pace, but she was able to sidestep the threats to keep pushing ahead.

She was almost to the end of the building when she heard the echoes of death behind her. It was the Scabs closing ground, with metal clanking, mouths growling, and lungs screaming.

Her panic convinced her to charge right, ducking out of sight, just past the end of the garage.

She was now in a narrow passageway with four piles of dirt in her way. Huge piles—twenty feet tall. They looked like a soiled version of ski moguls on a twisted obstacle course, only these had patches of brick and rock mixed in.

Summer slowed, switching from sprint mode to climbing mode, one that involved hand grabs and knee bends. It took extra effort and time, but she made it over the mounds, draining more of her energy than she hoped, especially the last one—the tallest—its downslope side the worst, taking her careening forward with off-balance foot plants and wild arm swings.

She fell to her knees at the bottom, struggling for air, her eyes surveying the area ahead. At first, she didn't know what she was looking at, but then it came to her, from the deepest recesses of her mind.

An old skateboard park with curved ramps, rusted hand rails, cement dips and rises, and other useless inventions.

Before her next breath, she froze, hearing a clattering of noise behind, on the other side of the dirt mounds she'd just traversed. Damn it! The gang was close. Their gorilla-like grunts and heavy footfalls could be clearly heard.

Summer took one last breath to recharge her lungs, then got to her feet and brought her thighs into motion. It only took a handful of seconds to tear across the cement park, where she found a long corridor on the right. There was no light inside.

Nothing she could see, except a patch of light at the far end—at least two hundred yards away.

The hairs on her neck tingled out of control as her feet found their way into the tunnel. She knew the decision to enter was a tactical mistake, but there was no choice. A reversal of course would take her into the teeth of the Scabs.

The cement inside the tunnel had been invaded by a stretch of ice down the center. Her feet slipped a few times, but she managed to keep them wide to maintain traction. She emerged at the far end, feeling lucky. Unfortunately, that feeling vanished when the sun landed on her face and exposed the next segment of her route.

The tunnel had led her to a cavernous spillway, the kind that dumped into a giant cement canal. Trash, tree limbs, and other debris littered the area, the recess acting like a natural collection point.

"More like a garbage heap," she muttered, correcting her own logic. "At least there's no wind down here."

The left side of the spillway was awash in sunlight, its vertical walls standing fifteen feet tall and smooth. The few puddles of water were nothing to be concerned about, unlike the complete lack of ladders and handholds.

No easy way out.

The other side was angled, reminding her of the slope on an A-frame house, built high in the mountains somewhere. It was in the shadows, like the inside of the ambulance she'd passed earlier. No sunlight on its surface.

Damn it, more ice.

Summer ran to the slanted area and jumped. Her feet hit the surface exactly where she had aimed, but they flew out from under her, twisting her body around as she fell. Down she went, on her butt, like a grade-schooler on a water slide, hitting a puddle at the bottom of the canal with a plop.

She needed a new plan before the Scabs caught up. She got up and ran to the collection of tree branches piled next to the bank. They'd probably been blowing around for days, coming to rest here. She snatched a thick stick and broke it in half over her knee. The ends were jagged—hopefully sharp enough, she prayed.

Summer took a run at the angled bank again, this time launching herself headfirst with a broken tree limb in each of her outstretched hands. The pointy ends slammed into the ice. So did her stomach, taking her breath away.

The pain was tolerable, but the downhill grade wasn't. The sticks she'd made couldn't penetrate the ice deep enough to act as icepicks, sending her zipping down the bank once again, this time landing on her knees in a crack.

The Scabs tore out from the tunnel behind her, their feet pounding at the cold cement covering the spillway's expanse. It only took seconds for them to arrive.

"Stay away from me!" Summer yelled, holding the sticks out in a defensive position as they formed a semi-circle in front of her.

CHAPTER 2

Summer hoped the Scabs would heed the spear-like branches in her hands, seeing them as a threat. In truth, they weren't much of a defense against this many Scabs, but she had to pretend they were.

One of the Scabs, who didn't have a knife, took a step forward, his breath deep and purposeful. He was younger than the others, who had decided to hold back in watch mode, as if this encounter had been planned in some way.

"Probably a junior cannibal," she quipped, keeping her eyes locked on his nose-less face. There wasn't much to the meat-eater—his gaunt, pale skin hung from his bones.

Two of his fingers were missing on his free hand—more frostbite, she assumed, or someone in his group had needed a snack, munching on younger flesh.

Or maybe his digits were considered expendable, depending on how the cannibals viewed others in their gang. A gang of all men, if you could still call them that, their gender and their humanity slipping away with each course of flesh.

Her mind drifted off topic as the gang moved in concert with each other, stepping another foot closer. She wondered why nobody had ever seen a female Scab. Maybe the male Scabs had eaten all the women, and not in a good way, she pondered, wondering if she was going to die a virgin. She flushed the random thoughts from her mind, bringing her focus back to the throng of teeth aimed at her.

Despite his lack of size, Summer knew the junior Scab's hunger would make him difficult to stop, if he decided to—

That's when he came at her in a snarl, arms out and mouth open. Summer brought her hands together, then swung the pair of sticks like a baseball bat.

Her swipe landed on the mark, catching the attacker in the side of the face. His skin ripped open in a bloody tear, but the blow didn't stop his advance.

His chest slammed into hers, driving her back in a stumble until she hit the wall of the spillway. When the cement met her spine, the sudden force stung her, taking the strength from her legs. She fell. So did the Scab, sending both of them slamming into the ground in a tangle of arms and legs.

Summer tried to stab the attacker but couldn't bring the pointed tips around, not with him on top of her. There wasn't enough room. She dropped the branches, then tried to wriggle free. He had the advantage, his leverage greater than her strength, their faces now eye to eye.

A glob of drool hung from his mouth as his teeth came into view. Summer turned her head in a flash as the dollop dropped, the putrid-smelling saliva landing on her cheek instead of her lips. Her throat convulsed, wanting to throw up, but she held it down.

When she brought her eyes back to his, his head exploded in a spray of red, as the sound of gunfire ripped through the air.

She watched his brain matter fly apart in what she could only describe as slow motion, her mind taking in every detail one frame at a time. It looked like a rotting, blood-filled cantaloupe had been destroyed by a bazooka, all of it captured on high-speed film in some old Hollywood movie.

More gunshots rang out, only this time they weren't aimed at the Scab lying dead on her chest. She rolled her neck to the side and watched the bullets tearing into the rest of the Hunger Gang, their bodies flying apart like balsa wood.

Tissue went one way, blood the other, as round after round hit its mark. It was both a massacre and a miracle—someone coming to her rescue just in the nick of time.

Summer pushed the corpse off, grabbed the sticks, and rolled to her feet. When she looked up, she counted seven men—all up on the bank, high above her position. Each was bearded. Most were burly and none of them wore sleeves, despite the near-freezing temperature and constant wind.

Her eyes found their way to their high-powered rifles and tactical vests stuffed with ammo magazines. When she looked a few inches higher, she noticed what looked like grenades attached near the top, though Summer couldn't be sure. She'd never seen one of the explosives in real life, only in the books she read at her secret library.

Camo pants completed their outfits, along with black military-style boots. Two of the men had something in their mouths, their jaws in constant chew and spit mode, looking the part of grizzled hunter—ready to kill.

"I thought they had you there for a minute," a bald, dark-skinned man said, his face glistening under the sun. The towering brute was ultra-handsome and had the deepest voice Summer had ever heard. Every word was smooth and commanding.

"Almost," she said, unable to take her eyes from who she assumed was their leader.

The black man pointed at the sticks in her hands, his shoulders as wide as a silo's missile bay. "You don't need those anymore."

She dropped the branches, figuring it was best to follow his suggestion and not appear threatening to the gang who'd just saved her from a painful death.

Summer ran the standoff through her mind, deciding that if the situation spun sideways, her would-be saviors would have to scamper down to her position, allowing her a chance to grab her sticks and make a run for it. If that happened, she'd need to head out the same tunnel she'd just come through.

Of course, if they decided to just open fire, she was dead already, regardless of whether or not she still had the makeshift weapons in her grasp.

"Good thing we came along when we did," a second man said. He had white, cherubic cheeks and huge bulge around his middle. He, like most of the others, had long, out-of-control hair and was loaded with guns and ammo.

A fat Rambo, Summer thought, holding back a smile. "Thanks for the save," she said in her most genuine tone, noticing each man had a tattoo stenciled along his neck—the same tattoo—just below the ear on the left side.

She recognized the symbol: interlocking chains, a sign of unity and strength. The facts led her to only one conclusion. This band of mouth breathers was a security patrol. One sent out by their leader, Simon Frost—a blonde Neanderthal who ran the south side of town. Rumor had it that every man under his command was branded with the same mark.

Some sort of sick control issue, she decided, changing her tone to one of confidence. "You guys aren't supposed to be here."

"Neither are you," the black man said, his eyes intense and penetrating. "I'm sure you know this is the No-Go Zone."

"Oh yeah, I know," she said, flashing a look at the dead cannibals littering the area around her feet. "But I had to run somewhere. I really wasn't worried about where I was at the moment, only that I didn't want to be there, if you know what I mean. A girl's gotta act when the creatures attack."

The dark-skinned hunk snickered, a smile taking over his mouth. "Frost sent us out, wondering if we'd see more of them after last week."

The fat Rambo guy spoke next, looking at the leader. "At least we know our sights are zeroed in. I don't know about you, Fletcher, but I wish there were more of them. We could certainly use the practice."

Summer wasn't sure about those comments. Killing was killing and it was all wrong. However, she was thankful these men showed up when they did. Otherwise, she'd be part of some cannibal's all-natural granola breakfast. One filled with bones instead of nuts. "Nobody seems to know where they come from or how they survived."

"I guess it's true, like Doc says. Life finds a way. Whether it's cockroaches, coyotes, or Scabs," Fletcher said, his tone comforting in some strange way. His hawk-like eyes turned soft, peering deep into her soul. "What's your name, girl?"

"Summer," she said, her lips responding before she could stop them. Maybe it was his striking looks, or his tenor. She couldn't be sure, but she wanted him to know her real name. She could have made up an alias, like a wayward stripper at a seedy club in the red-light district she'd read about in one of her books. But for some reason, she wanted to stay legit and play it straight. At least part way, until she knew more.

"We should take her with us," Fat Rambo said, interrupting the conversation. "Probably get a good price."

Fletcher pointed at Summer's chest. "You see that, Slayer? We can't."

Summer peered down and realized her Infinity Chain had popped out from her sweatshirt—again. She tucked it away.

Fletcher continued his explanation to Slayer. "She's one of Edison's group."

"Ah, fuck that. Nobody will know. Let's take the necklace and sell her for supplies. Then get some chow."

"Slayer's right. We should sell her," a third man added, nodding in Fat Rambo's direction. He looked Hispanic, his skin weathered and bronzed, with a hint of redness. Probably from the lack of sleeves. Or the relentless wind. "I'm starving."

Summer glanced at Slayer's belly hanging below his beltline. *Fat Rambo is obviously hungry a lot*, she mused, her eyes tracking the hands of the men standing above her. All it would take was one flinch, she figured, to bring about what she decided to officially call Summer's End.

Fletcher sent a steely-eyed stare at his men. "We all are, but nobody here is breaking the treaty. Frost would have our heads."

Slayer's face flushed red, filling his oversized cheeks. "So . . . we just let her go?"

"Roger that. We have our orders."

"Then why did we waste all the ammo?" the Hispanic man asked.

"Should have just let them eat her skinny ass, though it does look yummy," Slayer added with a twisted mouth, his eyes scanning her figure.

Summer was about to say something to the pervert, but Fletcher beat her to it. "Nobody takes a step. That's an order."

None of the men answered, which Summer took to mean Fletcher's orders ruled supreme.

Her apprehension melted away. So did her nervousness.

Fletcher pulled a pistol from the holster on his hip and held it by the barrel, aiming the grip in her direction. His eyes locked with Summer's. "Here, you should take this. Just in case."

"What are you doing, boss?" Slayer asked.

"I'm not getting blamed if something happens to her out here. That's a good way for your insides to end up on the outside."

Summer shook her head, holding her hands up in a stop signal. "Thanks, but I can't."

Fletcher flared his eyebrows. "Why? Because it's against the rules?"

She shrugged. "Something like that."

"I don't understand why Edison sends you out here without a gun."

Summer shot a look at the corpse closest to her feet, then at Slayer. "Normally, it's not an issue. At least, not until recently."

"Still, Edison's a smart guy; why would he not arm his people? Doesn't make sense."

"Because he hates guns. Especially in the hands of those of us with no training. It's pretty simple, really. Unless you're former military, like Krista and her men, you get squat. At least we have food and a roof over our heads."

"Well then, he's a hypocrite."

"Why? Because of Krista and her security force?"

Fletcher nodded. "Edison's not afraid to use force when it suits him. Or protects him."

"It's not like that at all. They're only a last resort."

"I doubt that. I've seen her kind before. Krista is a ticking timebomb. I hope you know that."

Summer laughed. "Yeah, well, you should talk. You cruise around with enough guns to start a war."

"Or save young girls from the Scabs."

She smirked. "Well, there is that."

"Why did you let them corner you here?"

"It wasn't my plan, trust me."

"Should have headed for the Trading Post. Heston and his crew would have protected you."

"Was thinking about it, but everything happened so fast. Didn't exactly have a lot of options. I'm sure you know Scabs don't send out a warning bark to let you know they're closing in."

"That's why everyone needs a weapon. You never know what's out here."

"I appreciate your concern for me and all, but it's really none of your business."

"Apparently."

Slayer cleared his throat.

Fletcher peered at him.

Slayer pointed at the top of his wrist, where a watch would have been if the world hadn't ended, rendering batteries and other technology a luxury.

Fletcher nodded, looking annoyed. He holstered the pistol. "All right, let's move out. We've got a meet-and-greet to cover in the morning and I want everyone frosty."

With that, the men disappeared from view.

A few minutes later, engines roared and tires squealed as they peeled out. Summer decided they must have parked a distance away, probably to sneak up on the Scabs. Maybe they'd been tracking the Hunger Gang for a while. That's how they followed them here. It was the only explanation she could muster, given their perfect timing.

"White knights," she mumbled, remembering a book she'd read a few weeks ago. Only today's saviors were anything but the good guys. Normally, that is. Plus, some of them weren't white. They were a mix of races and skin tones, actually—a hodgepodge of brutes.

Summer closed her eyes for a few moments as her mind latched onto an image of Fletcher floating inside her memories. She couldn't believe how the black man's eyes seemed to dig into her soul, reaching down to a place that had been hardened like stone. She'd never felt a sensation like that before. It was both scary and reassuring at the same time.

What she'd just visualized and felt didn't make sense, but it filled her heart with hope. Not only had he saved her from the Scabs, but he'd kept her safe from his own men.

He didn't have to do either, but yet he did.

She smiled, tucking a lip under.

CHAPTER 3

Simon Frost finished his trek across the warehouse and shoved the door to Ben Lipton's lab with a forearm shiver. It flung open and smashed against the wall.

He knew barging in would piss off the fifty-five-year-old scientist everyone called Doc, but Frost didn't give a shit. In fact, he enjoyed it. Sometimes the boss has to push back, especially when he can't gut an insubordinate like Doc Lipton. "Where are we with those upgrades?"

Doc looked up, holding a soldering gun in one hand and a spool of wire in the other. He pried the magnification goggles loose from his face, looking annoyed as usual.

The bags under his eyes were pronounced, matching his wide nose that cast a strong shadow across his face. The man hadn't used a comb on his brown, shaggy hair, looking as though he'd slept in his office all week. "Seriously, would it hurt for any of you grease-heads to knock once in a while?

Constantly breaking my concentration is how accidents happen."

"You mean that's how design flaws happen."

"Same thing."

"Need a status report, Doc."

"Same as yesterday. Still retooling. If all goes well, our refinery will be back online sometime next week, with something north of double the capacity, depending on how well the welding crew did its job with the refab. Still have a few bugs to work out, so don't get pushy."

Frost fumed, his blood pressure skyrocketing. "Look, last week you said it would be ready today and that's what I need. Patrols are due back any minute and they're gonna need fuel. Supply tanks are almost empty."

"I'm working as fast as I can, but you need to be patient. Not to mention reasonable. Genius takes time. So does inspiration."

"We don't have time, not with the recent string of perimeter breeches. I need to keep the patrols out 24x7 and that takes fuel. Lots of it."

"Maybe if your men would quit pushing the limits all the time, we wouldn't have all these breakdowns. I'm not exactly working with the best equipment here."

"Then you need to do a better job of improvising. We bend over backwards to get you what you need, usually at the expense of something else, so suck it up and do your frickin' job."

"Or else what? You gonna fire me?"

Frost sucked in a breath, holding back a punch. Doc knew exactly how to push his buttons. Plus, the scientist didn't seem to care how often he did it, or where he did it. "Look Doc, your safety is on the line, too. Same as ours. We all rely on each other to keep things operational and secure."

Doc laughed, shaking his head, sending his stringy hair into a wiggle. "Gotta love the logic. Or lack thereof," he said in a mumble, fiddling with the hunk of machinery on his desk. "Do I need to remind you that you need me significantly more than I need you? This is not anything close to a symbiotic relationship. Without me, you and your crew would've been history long ago. You know how this works, so don't stand there and pretend you don't."

Frost knew the man was right, but it still didn't lessen the anger swelling within. He paced the room, working the situation through in his head.

It was one thing for Doc to disrespect him in private, but when the man's insolence reared in front of the other men, it took another chunk out of Frost's foundation as a leader. And that was something that could not be tolerated. It was all he could do not to take his blade out and rip open the Brainiac, but he kept his hand clear of the Ka-Bar knife strapped to his hip.

Doc continued, almost as if he had a death wish. "I know you and your band of street crawlers barely graduated high school and all, but if it weren't for me and my skills, you wouldn't have all your toys. And by toys, I mean advantages. Technological, that is. By the way, in case you forgot, I'm still waiting for that new mechanic. Can't do it all by myself, not after you gutted the last one."

Frost sneered. "Shaw left me no choice."

Doc rolled his eyes after a snicker. "Yeah, where have I heard that excuse before?"

"Rules and discipline must be enforced. Otherwise, we have anarchy."

"Spoken like a true caveman," Doc said, putting his goggles back on. "I thought you were going to trade for one with Edison."

"The meet is tomorrow, so hang tight. The plan is set."

"Okay then. That settles it. If I have to wait, then so do you. Just make sure it's a man this time. No more Annettes. Or Bettys. Or Veronicas. I can't deal with all those emotional swings," Doc said, motioning at a red and white satchel sitting on a table four feet away. "Your compound is ready."

Frost snapped out of his funk. "The thermite?"

"Four batches, as requested."

"Excellent."

"I also included a propane torch."

"Why?"

"It takes intense heat to ignite. Not like all that C-4 you've been stockpiling."

"So no det cord?"

"Correct. I know instructions are not your thing, but try not to melt your legs off when you use it."

Frost sucked in his lower lip, his gaze never leaving Lipton's face. There were too many words on his tongue at the moment—all of them energized but none of them lining up correctly.

Lipton didn't wait for a response, waving his hand in a rush, looking as though he just lost interest in the rest of the world. "Move along now. We're done here."

Frost hesitated for another beat, then decided to let it go as a dozen flashes roared through his mind. Each scene showed a different way to kill the former physicist.

"Oh, and one more thing," Doc said in a matter-of-fact tone.

Frost clenched his fists, waiting for the man to speak.

"While you're out there, bring me some chow. An empty stomach is quite the distraction. And make sure it's none of that mystery meat this time. Bring me something I recognize. And can stomach. That smoky flavor is getting old."

Frost couldn't believe the nerve of this guy. He spun to face Lipton, switching to his most sarcastic tone. "Is that all, Doc? Is there anything else I can get for you? A massage, perhaps? Or some fine wine? Chocolate mousse? Hand job? Stripper?"

"Now who's being an ass? Just bring me some real food. And a mechanic like I asked," he snapped, holding up the tools in his hands. "I have work, in case you hadn't noticed."

* * *

Summer Lane took a hard right to duck out of the whistling squall, taking refuge behind the corner of an abandoned 7-Eleven that bordered the frozen river. Its windows had been smashed long ago, leaving only a set of deteriorating walls and a hanging sign to mark the edge of the No-Go Zone. Unofficially, that is.

The frigid air stung her cheeks, even with the sun shining. It was almost as if the weather gods had taken notice of her course correction, deciding to punish her with a vengeance. Not that Summer could blame them; she'd deviated from her designated search grid—again. Even after the run-in with the Scabs and Frost's band of deviants.

There were things to do—personal things—before she headed back to the silo and Professor Edison's version of Nirvana, most of it buried deep underground and all of it laced with rules and consequences.

Summer pulled back the hoodie of her drab sweatshirt, removed the bandana with a single finger pull, and ran her fingers through her hair. The strands needed to be set free, much like she felt at the moment.

Freedom is measured on a sliding scale, she decided, thinking of her tiny bunk in the cramped storage room of the silo. It wasn't much, but it was all hers—the only place where she could enjoy a modicum of privacy.

The numbers in the silo seemed to grow each week, taking up more and more space. Bunks, bodies, and bare feet seemed to be everywhere, banishing her to the storage closet when she couldn't take it anymore.

Life after The Event didn't afford many grooming options, certainly not any personal items that the head security stiff, Krista, would let her take from the complex.

Summer's fingers would have to serve as a brush, trying to control the frizz of her shoulder-length hair. Always jet black. Always out of control. She knew it was a fruitless endeavor to fight the flurries whipping about her face, but she tried anyway.

It didn't matter how many layers of clothes she wore, either. A shiver always seemed to be lurking just below the surface. And it wasn't only when she was outside amidst Mother Nature's fury. The cold was everywhere, even deep inside the silo with its eight-foot-thick walls of reinforced concrete.

Cold is cold, more so with the sun struggling to restore its dominance over the planet. She'd tried everything, but there was little a skinny girl could do to stay warm. She didn't know what was worse—

running around hungry all the time or being cold every minute of every day.

Before she could decide, her mind slipped into memory mode, dreaming of a hot soak in a tub. All she needed was a quiet moment to rid herself of the endless chill. A single hour. That's all.

Was that too much to ask?

Then she'd be good—for the rest of her life. She'd never want for anything again, other than perhaps a bottle of anti-depressants.

It had been at least ten years, maybe longer, since her last real bath. She'd lost count of the days—heck, even the years. So had most of her cohorts, she figured, everyone's stench mounting between the weekly one-minute shower rotations.

Let's face it, it's tough to clean all your parts when the line behind you is long and time is short. But you had to make do. For everyone's sake, not just yours.

Collective stink just adds to the misery of it all. More so in a hardened military bunker where the air is circulated from one floor to the next. It's funny what you learn when you live underground. Like the fact that BO doesn't vanish on its own, growing like a plague inside your nostrils.

Summer planted a gentle kiss on her stainless-steel necklace, her lips landing in the center of the number-eight-like symbol that had been soldered horizontally to the end of it. "Keep me safe, June. From here to infinity and beyond," she whispered before tucking it under her shirt.

Right then, her eyes caught a glimpse of someone standing atop a broken-down structure—one that used to house an old Chevron gas station, its blue trim and company sign faded, but still visible.

The man wore an ankle-length leather coat. It was open down the middle, with what could only be described as military-style body armor underneath. Or maybe it was some old hockey pads, like what her dead brother Blaze used to wear in his pick-up games. Either way, she figured the shielding was to help stop the teeth of a hunger gang.

His deep-set hoodie looked like it was from medieval times, masking his head in a blanket of secrecy. It reminded her of something she'd seen in one of her books—an eighteenth-century monk's cloak, except it was all black, not the typical one-piece outfit of all red. The two swords in his hands finished his ensemble, hanging from his hands in a sweeping curve of each blade.

"The Nomad," she mumbled, recognizing his wide, two-legged stance, reminiscent of a warrior from centuries past.

She couldn't see his face, mostly because it was covered in a shadow from the hoodie. However, she knew the legend well, knowing there was a mask covering it. One designed to conceal every inch of his skin.

Summer had seen him twice before. Each time he'd been standing a distance away, observing something she'd been involved in. For some reason, she got the sense that he was always around, hiding in the shadows to watch her from a distance. Even so, he never came across as a threat. More of an observer, gathering intel or something along those lines.

Nobody knew his real name, but he had gotten involved in a couple of altercations, assuming she chose to believe the lore that had swept through the silo over the years.

One of the skirmishes took place at the Trading Post, during a heated barter exchange. It had something to do with rescuing a group of wanderers who'd been surrounded by a gang of thieves.

Everyone had their theories as to his identity, but Summer chose to ignore them. She didn't care who he was, as long as he stayed in the shadows. The man could observe all he wanted, as long as he never came any closer.

Summer watched him turn and disappear beyond the edge of the building's roof, vanishing in a blur of leather.

She swung the knapsack from her back, plopped it on the ground, and opened the zipper.

Inside was a folded piece of paper. It was buried under two sticks of marker chalk, a rubberized caster wheel, extra scarves, a stick of beef jerky, a water bottle, a church key can opener, 100-feet of paracord, a well-used fork, four strike-anywhere waterproof matches, a six-inch candle wrapped in a sheet of bubble wrap, a metal container the size of a cigar box with three dozen crayons in it, a small roll of cotton twine, and two cans of tuna. She was almost done for the day but needed to score one more item.

Summer snatched the map, then turned her body at an angle to block the next blast of wind. The skin on her fingers opened the fold, protruding through the tattered wool holding the gloves together.

"Gotta be quick," she told herself, scanning the highlighted areas of her duty map. The blue outlines told her where she'd been assigned, while the red X's told her the grids she'd already cleared.

So far, twelve successful recovery missions this hunting season. At least in this section of town.

Like the days since her last bath, she'd lost track of the number of areas she'd cleared over the years as Edison's "Worst Seeker"—the unofficial title given to her by the gruff, pain in the ass Security Chief, Krista.

Krista was an almost forty-year-old woman who wanted to be a man, Summer guessed, based on her endless sense of duty to all things rough and tumble. Even Krista's ultra-short crewcut factored into that assessment, as did the girl's daily regimen of pushups and other strength-building activities.

Not that any of that mattered; Summer had her own agenda and that alone drove her actions. She really didn't care what the others thought of her, certainly not Krista.

They couldn't kick her out of Nirvana nor raise a finger in anger. She was untouchable—a benefit of being one of the charter members of Edison's compound and what she assumed was Edison's favorite.

This Seeker assignment was the closest she'd been to this area of town in weeks—a sector controlled by Edison's rival, Frost. A real peach of a man.

Simon Frost fit the mold of a zealous mutant exactly. His long blonde hair was trimmed back, fading into an out of control mullet. His six-foot-five frame demanded attention. So did his abundance of facial hair—seemingly unkempt since the dawn of man.

Yet none of that compared to his hulking at the seams. He had the kind of physique that pushed the limits of human muscle and bone, all of it meant to intimidate.

She'd only seen him a couple of times from a distance, but his abundance of scars and tattoos was more than memorable. She figured he was in love with his bulging arms since he, like his men, never wore sleeves, even when the cold reigned supreme across the land.

Granted, from what she'd seen, the muscles were impressive but that was the end of his redeeming features. Someone had smacked the dude in the face too many times with the ugly stick.

Summer took in a deep breath and let the air drift across her lips, her exhale billowing out in a cloud of white vapor. Time was short and she was already running late. "Just stay low and move fast. You got this, girl."

After a quick scan of the area, she folded the map, stuffed it back into the pack, yanked the zipper closed, and then slung the bag over her shoulder.

Moments later, she was off with purpose in her step. Her destination: the bridge that would take her across the river and into the forbidden Frost Zone.

A smile took over her lips. It came out of nowhere, pushing through the stress of the day.

Only one more block to go.

Then she'd be inside the abandoned building across the way. A building that protected her favorite place in the entire world—an abandoned bookstore called INFINITE READS.

CHAPTER 4

"Damn it, Summer. I don't have time for this," Security Chief Krista Carr muttered to herself, her military boots pounding at the metal floor of the silo.

Her brisk jog continued, taking her around the outside of the circular, eight-story hydroponics bay. The lights inside the underground chamber beamed on all levels, blinding her vision with brilliant, momentary flashes as she passed a string of observation windows around its circumference.

The lights inside the bay fed an array of hanging garden beds from top to bottom with UV light, something Edison said all plants needed.

Rich garden soil was a tough find, so they'd rigged the system to produce food using sand and gravel—or whatever else they could scavenge or acquire at the Trading Post.

Fruits, vegetables, and herbs hung over the edges of the various platforms, cascading down under the force of gravity. There were also a few dozen cannabis plants being cultivated—for medicinal purposes, of course.

A good fifteen years earlier, her boss, Stuart Edison, known to most as simply The Professor, began his quest to retrofit this Titan II Missile silo for his new society.

Krista didn't understand the science behind everything inside the old launch bay, but it was impressive. It seemed logical to assume there weren't many scientists on the planet who could have turned a subterranean military facility into something useful and life-sustaining. But the Professor had, elevating his world-renowned genius to a new level.

Edison's new underground society, codenamed Nirvana, was top-secret—not because it had been deemed 'classified' by a government or some military branch, but rather because Edison himself declared it so.

He wanted its location kept a secret from the outside world, a world that had become desperate and lawless after The Event ended society a decade before.

Krista made it to the central freight elevator, but the platform was already in use, the hydraulic gears of the fifty-year-old wire-mesh lift clanking away. A change in plan was needed.

She reversed course, passing one of the spring-loaded platforms that formerly supported a fuel control station for the nine-megaton warhead back in the day.

A pair of metal ladders waited just beyond the station. She passed the first and went to the second, where her hands made quick work of the rungs, taking her upward.

Experience had taught her to ignore some of the ladders on this deck. There were several. Some went nowhere, leading a climber's head into the bottom of the next floor.

The first time she noticed the goof, she laughed so hard she couldn't breathe. Initially she thought the government contractors messed up, misreading the schematics during the build.

However, that's not what had happened.

The mistakes were a result of what the Air Force called "concurrent engineering," an old term used during the construction of the silo.

The phrase gave the impression of something sophisticated and well-planned. But in reality, it meant the facility was built from bottom floor up, one level at a time, all while the rest of the complex was still being designed by the engineers.

Plans are usually complete and vetted before a project of this scope is started. But not this place. It had been built using a hasty "design on the fly" approach.

She imagined some of the conversations that took place in the logistical meetings, focusing on one statement . . . "You work on sublevel 8, while I design the next floor up. It'll all work out. Trust me."

The concurrent processes had led to sudden plan changes, yielding ladders that went nowhere, useless beams sticking out of the walls at odd angles, and spring-loaded contraptions serving no purpose.

Krista stepped onto the deck two levels up and cruised past a parade of bunk beds with sheets and pillows in disarray, then found the long cableway that connected the missile bay to the control complex.

Two of her guards stood at the entrance, their faces tight and eyes fierce. They gave her a quick salute, pulling their trigger fingers free from their rifles to do so.

She skipped her half of the response, passing the men clad in full tactical gear.

The paint in the tunnel gave off an eerie green hue. It was almost a neon lime color, something she'd never expect the Air Force to choose, not with its official color palette revolving around some vainly-named version of blue.

Wild blue yonder was her favorite.

Oh, and *air superiority blue* was another.

Yet, the green did offset the heavy runs of black cables stuffed into the recesses of the ceiling. Each was a couple of inches thick and tucked beyond the metal struts and steel support beams, maximizing the space available to thread them from end to end.

Perhaps the offset nature of the paint was the reason for its use. Not that it mattered anymore. Nearly everyone involved in the military was long gone after The Event. Starvation, resource shortages, and Ice Age level temperatures can wipe out even the stoutest of armed forces.

Every time Krista walked this tunnel, she felt a sense of awe. The sheer amount of work that had gone into constructing the straightaway was impressive.

There had to be thousands of miles of electric and hydraulic cables across the silo, all of them flowing through this central point in the complex.

Unreal was a term she'd first used to describe this section after factoring in the hefty number of pipes and endless electronics. Fifty-four heavy duty shock absorbers hung evenly along both sides of the cableway, each responsible for keeping the tunnel intact in the event of a nearby nuclear strike.

In fact, the entire installation had been built on huge springs to cradle everything that might be sensitive to shock. Even the former occupant of the missile bay—a 330,000-pound liquid-fueled monster, capable of obliterating a thousand square miles clear across the globe in the blink of an eye.

The number fifty-four seemed to have a special meaning to the Air Force. Not only did it cover the number of industrial grade shock absorbers in the cableway, but it also represented the number of Titan II silos commissioned across the USA.

Silos had been built in three groups of eighteen, each cluster centered around a strategic city. She wished she knew the significance of the number 54, another one of those odd military designations, like her service specialty in the Army: 88K.

The multi-story Command and Control facility was just ahead, beyond a series of bank vault-type blast doors guarding the entrance from the surface. Nothing was getting through those mammoth bulkheads, not without a MOAB being dropped first to loosen the hydraulic hinges and crack the heavy steel security rods that locked into place.

Krista zipped past a metal placard that featured the same symbol she wore on her necklace—an infinity symbol. The sign also had the word NIRVANA stenciled underneath it.

The same community marker hung in every hallway and nearly every room, and had been there ever since Edison first transformed this facility. None of that surprised her. However, the handwritten sign next to it was new.

Tragedy lies in having no goal to reach. *~Benjamin Mays*

"Old men and their magic markers," she mumbled, recognizing the handwriting. It was the Professor's. "Looks like he found a use for all that extra cardboard."

She wondered why he wasted the time on useless shit like this. Only weak minds needed this crap. Not a trained soldier like herself.

Krista used the auxiliary stairwell to head down, the rubber tread of her boots plinking against the mesh of the metal steps. She preferred to keep her descent in rhythm, the sound of her foot plants acting as a PT cadence of sorts. It reminded her of her early days in the Army. Back when her eyes were bright and her heart remained filled with honor and hope.

Thirty seconds later, she passed the last of the community information boards with the words NO INJURIES IN 502 DAYS. The tally had been written with a messy hand and in white chalk. The other two boards hung in the mess hall and crew quarters, each of them kept in sync by Rod Zimmer, Supply Chief.

The last accident cost a life—a gruesome fall down the missile shaft. Some thought it was suicide. Others figured a misstep. Nobody knew for sure.

Krista took a right and proceeded until her trek stopped at Professor Edison's lab. She knocked three times on the solid metal door, her knuckles landing just below the fancy infinity symbol welded to its surface. She held her position, waiting for the man in charge to confirm entry.

"Door's open," Edison said, his tone light and welcoming.

Krista walked in, moving to the right to make her way around the tables and other clutter. The place was a mess, much like the bunks she'd passed on her way to this meeting. She didn't understand how people could function with such disorder in their lives.

Four heads turned to greet her, their pre-teen smiles a welcome respite from the stress of the day.

Krista sent a smile to one of the kids, then brought her eyes to Edison. "Professor, I really need to speak with you. In private."

"Sure. I think we can arrange that," Edison said, his wire-rimmed spectacles sitting at a slight angle across his nose.

His hair was all white and combed back into an old hippie-style ponytail; his white beard was freshly trimmed into a ZZ Top style look. The bags under his eyes looked more profound than normal, drooping like soggy noodles. She figured he hadn't been sleeping well, probably more so than normal.

Edison's attention went to a list of words on the grease board hanging along the front wall of the room. He wrote another item at the bottom, adding the number ten in front of it. Above the list was the title *Ten Uses for Organic Solar Cells*.

The Professor turned to the kids, who were busy taking notes at their stations. "Children, Security Chief Carr and I need a few minutes of privacy. Why don't you head to lunch? I'm sure Chef Watson has something yummy waiting for you. We'll resume study tomorrow. Same time. Okay?"

A series of "Yes, Professors" were sent back as the kids gathered their belongings and scampered out the door.

Before Krista could speak, Edison beat her to it, grabbing a stack of cardboard tear-offs from the credenza behind his desk. "I'm glad you're here, Krista. I need you to take these down to Mr. Zimmer. He's expecting them."

Krista took the signs in hand, reading the topmost inscription: *Put your future in good hands — your own. ~Mark Victor Hansen*

"Is there something I should know?" she asked, wondering how long it had taken the sixty-eighty-year-old to write all these messages. The black ink from the marker seemed to be fading a bit the farther down the stack she checked.

"I'm getting a sense that morale is dropping a bit. I'm hoping these motivational quotes will help restore equilibrium in our ranks."

"You mean help with some of the depression."

Edison gave her a single nod. "I hear the rumblings. Not everyone is comfortable living here, especially some of the new folks."

"I'm not sure that's it exactly. I think it has more to do with the feel of the place. I know some think it's depressing. But I don't mind the whole industrial look. It's comforting, knowing we are deep underground and protected by eight feet of reinforced concrete."

Edison held his arms out, like a preacher giving thanks. "And the genius of the men who designed this place."

She cleared her throat, not wanting to sound insubordinate, but the Professor's statement needed revision. For accuracy's sake. "Men and women, sir."

"You're absolutely right—the men *and women* who designed this place. I stand corrected. Just as my lovely wife June would have done if she were still with us."

"Yes sir. She was a great lady," Krista said, feeling compelled to say those words. For some reason, Edison had this overwhelming desire to have others validate his sense of loss. June had died a long time ago. It was time for him to move on already.

She decided to jump ahead and change the subject. "When I walk these corridors late at night, sometimes I think I should have joined the Navy as a submarine specialist. That's what this facility reminds me of—a boomer," she said, her mind running through the facts: numerous tunnels, endless pipes and gauges, heavy grates and scaffolding, and miles and miles of cabling and electronics. All of it close, and all of it filled with people. Too damn many people.

"I can see why," he said. "But I'm afraid not everyone loves this place as much as you."

"Can't really blame them," she said, skipping the other words she wanted to say.

"No, I suppose not. But I wish they would realize that sometimes, *out of tragedy comes hope.* One of my wife's favorite sayings, God rest her soul."

Krista didn't want to debate the man who'd built this place and saved the lives of everyone with his foresight, but if Edison brought in any more new members, the impenetrable concrete walls might just explode outward and bury them all in an earth-filled grave. Greater numbers meant greater problems, usually of the personal nature.

She let the silence in the room linger a few seconds more before she decided it was time to move the conversation forward. "I saw the new sign in the hallway."

"What do you think?"

"Worth a try, I guess. But not everyone is allowed down here."

"That's why I need you to take those signs to Zimmer. He'll hang them where they need to go."

"He agreed to do it?"

"Been doing it," Edison said, nodding. "It took some convincing, but in the end, I usually get my way."

She smiled, wanting him to know she was onboard with whatever he needed. Well, most everything.

"Navy, huh?" he asked, taking a seat in his chair before bringing his hands together. "Why the Army, then?"

"Seemed like the best fit for me at the time. I wanted infantry, where all the action was. Imagine my surprise when they assigned me to Watercraft Operations."

"You didn't have a say in the matter?"

"No, sir. Just told me my MOS was 88K."

Edison looked puzzled.

"MOS means Military Occupational Specialty. When I found out that it was 88K, I had to look it up. Didn't even know the Army had boats."

"Or soldiers who operated them, I'm sure."

She nodded. "You never know what the brass is going to assign. Sometimes a MOS is pre-determined by special arrangement at enlistment, but for everyone else, they get doled out by the thousands. Usually randomly, but in my case, I think they may have looked into my background."

"Your father. The mechanic."

"Muscle car rebuilds, mostly. That's where I learned my skills with a wrench. Never knew those days as a kid would help me score off the charts in the mechanical maintenance section of the Armed Services Vocational Aptitude Battery Test."

"Everything happens for a reason. Only sometimes it takes a while to understand why."

"Little did they know, I only helped Dad to spend time with him. Not because I was into classic cars or anything. I did it so I wouldn't be alone in the house after Mom died."

"That cancer is nasty business."

Her heart sank, thinking of the last days with her mother. "Every spare minute he was out in his workshop, tinkering on something."

"It's hard to lose someone close," Edison said, reaching across his desk and picking up a photo of his wife, his eyes flooding with tears. "When my June was gunned down in that robbery, I thought my heart was going to implode. This day of the year is always hardest for me."

Right then is when a new revelation rose up and sucker-punched Krista in the gut, reminding her that she'd forgotten something important. Something that explained the professor's sudden need to revisit the pain associated with his dead wife. "I'm sorry, sir. I totally forgot. Today is the anniversary, right? Please forgive me. I should have remembered."

"It's okay, Krista. We're all a little busy these days."

"Still, sir. No excuse. My deepest apologies. I know how important today is."

His eyes dropped to the desk, his tone low and full of emotion. "I still miss her as much as I did the day it happened."

Krista didn't respond. None of the words in her mind sounded appropriate, not after disappointing the one man she admired the most above all, even if he tended to always see the bright side of everything.

Her thoughts turned to the metal necklace under her clothes. She could feel it dangling with a purpose as the infinity symbol swayed back and forth, brushing against her skin with every movement.

It was a copy of the original necklace made by June's own hands right before she died. Edison had one made for every member of Nirvana. It was to be a constant reminder of the woman whose death had become the catalyst for the silo and all it stood for. Somehow Krista had forgotten all about it. Shit.

If she didn't have her hands full, she would have taken it out from below her camo-colored muscle shirt and kissed it as a sign of respect.

Edison's look of grief vanished as he brought his eyes to Krista. "Your father must have used those classic car rebuilds as a therapy of sorts."

"Yeah, probably," she said, realizing something she hadn't thought of before. She held the stack of signs higher in her hands to draw attention to them. "Like your new signs."

His tone changed again, this time sounding convinced his words were true and on the mark. "Different patients require different therapy. Sometimes that means it must come in a form nobody expects."

"I'm sure you're right, sir," she said, even though she wasn't convinced the trite sayings would help with morale. Despite her doubts, she wasn't about to argue with the man she'd just disappointed. "I'll get them to Zimmer right away."

Edison raised an eyebrow. "You said you needed to speak to me about something."

Krista hesitated to choose the proper words, then let the words rip. "It's Summer, boss."

"Don't tell me she's late again?"

"Roger that. Third time in a row. This can't continue. We have rules and they apply to everyone. Even her. It's time for disciplinary action, sir. And hard. Otherwise, she'll never learn. We simply cannot continue to let her keep putting all our lives at risk."

CHAPTER 5

Summer turned sideways and squeezed her lean frame between a brick wall and the side panel of an abandoned delivery truck. She inched along until she made it past the rear bumper of the vehicle and into an open recess not visible from the other side of the truck. A door stood in front of her, one she knew well. It guarded the rear entrance of her favorite destination in the world—a store called INFINITE READS.

The door appeared to be in worse shape than the last time she visited. The two dents near the bottom hinge looked recent, but she couldn't be sure. Haste and hunger can cause memory to become unreliable, even unstable.

The sudden twinge in her stomach acted as a trigger, sending her mind into search and recovery mode. A vision of the metal door flashed from her memories, showing her the previous state of its surface.

The answer was yes—the dents were new. Of course, there was no way to know what had smacked into the door. The routine gusts of wind could have driven something heavy into it.

She hesitated, thinking it through as her eyes began to scan the area around the back of the truck and her feet. There didn't appear to be anything that might have caused the damage, but that didn't mean it didn't happen. The wind could have blown the evidence away.

Summer wedged the door open with her arm and slipped through the opening and headed inside, where a cascade of smashed glass, torn boxes, and soiled clothes stood in her way. It was evidence of a break-in, though not a recent one. She'd seen this same disarray before—each time she'd broken the treaty to cross the No-Go Zone and enter Frost's territory.

The first time was years earlier, during one of her routine Seeker Missions. A pile of human popsicles in an old schoolyard sent her into a panic, the sudden fright fueling an unplanned sprint across the No-Go Zone.

That was when she stumbled onto this place—a used book store that doubled as a clothing and food donation center for the homeless. Of course, the store's charity work vanished along with the population, the displaced perishing first after the sky filled with ash and the sun went into hiding.

Had she not lived it herself, she may not have believed it. But it was true. All of it. Her own history had proved everything she'd read in her fiction books correct.

When the world ends and society faces imminent death, the less fortunate are the first to be abandoned. Or sacrificed, depending on the author's viewpoint.

Those authors way back when were correct. Social causes may have been in vogue before The Event, but when the end came, social justice warriors and their moral outrage became extinct like everything else.

Summer continued past the clutter, then changed course, avoiding eye contact with the broken-down counter that used to contain a cashier and a register. The blood stain along that wall behind it was her primary worry, not wanting to bring up an old wound.

The splatter belonged to her one and only Seeker partner, Avery. He was one of the initial victims of the Scabs when they first showed up, focusing their attention on the stocky twenty-two-year-old while she ran for safety.

Her knees went weak, but she pushed on, ignoring the pain in her heart. Avery wasn't the only Seeker to die that day. Eleven more of her friends met the same fate—all of them in the same area of town, less than a block apart from each other. Nobody was prepared for what happened, decimating the silo numbers.

Summer knew from her readings that mass tragedy often leads to kneejerk decisions by those in charge, causing swift and radical changes, usually in the name of safety, or to address some misplaced agenda. Sometimes the reactionary changes were for the better. Often they were not.

The massacre that took Avery was no different. The Council acted quickly, decreeing that Seekers would no longer be sent out in pairs, nor would they be assigned to the same sector of the city. Risk had to be mitigated, they ruled, even if that meant making any one Seeker expendable in order to protect the majority.

In truth, Summer didn't mind the risk. It was worth it—anything to get out of the silo and do her own thing for a few hours. It wasn't easy living in cramped quarters, where everyone watches everything you do and does so every minute of every day.

She imagined silo life was akin to being confined to a prison cell, the time between seconds growing longer with each new day. For some reason, Tuesdays were the worst. She didn't know why, but it didn't change the fact—she hated Terrible Tuesdays. They simply felt wrong in some way. Not for any particular reason. They just did.

Yet, the slowness of time wasn't the worst problem. It was the utter lack of privacy, and the fact that she was forced to wear the same damned clothes over and over.

Both can make a girl crazy. Or desperate, willing to take chances she wouldn't normally take. Like wearing a bright red bandana during a Seeker Mission for food and supplies. Anything to change things up.

The storeroom in the back greeted her next, its floor littered with castoffs. Stuff was everywhere—*a junkyard for the damned,* she called it, bringing about a twisted smile on her lips. The grin was not out of a sense of amusement. It was in reference to her little home away from home.

Someone had gone through the store long before she'd found it. That much was obvious.

They'd skipped whole groups of items: trinkets, flip-flops, hand-carved elephants, kids' toys, and board games, tossing useless possessions about during their frantic search for something life-sustaining.

Desperate citizens have their priorities, just like young girls who are in search of an escape. While a mob went on the hunt for food, supplies, or ammo, Summer had a different need—one that would feed her desire for a different life.

What the throng missed, she'd found by mistake. It was hidden along the back wall, behind the built-in shelving unit. Summer bent down and found the release under the loose baseboard and pulled it. The safety latch clicked, then the unit swung open on its hinges to let her inside.

The passage led to a secret room about ten feet across and just as deep. The blue paint on the walls had been sullied by handwritten scribbles, mostly in white chalk.

Random names and other doodles were drawn at random angles with dates underneath. To the left was a family of stick figures holding hands—two large and two small. Above them were the names—Hector, Silvia, Edwardo, and Marta—written in red.

What she found odd was the prevalence of three capital letters: I-C-E. Each time they appeared on the walls, the letters were crossed out with multiple lines, as if someone was angry at the time.

Summer hated the snow and ice, too, but wondered why I-C-E was such a focal point before The Event. She couldn't ask her mentor, Edison, because then she'd have to tell him about this secret room.

An old beanbag chair took up most of the space in the corner on the right. It was next to a wooden crate, with twelve piles of paperback books nearby. Each stack stood as tall as the crate—waist-high and sorted in alphabetical order by title.

The light fixture in the center of the ceiling didn't have a bulb and the toilet in the corner no longer had a supply of water in the bowl. The sink next to it was also out of order, but at least the knee-high pyramid of cans she'd scavenged was still intact. Peaches mostly, plus a good supply of chunky tuna. Her favorite.

Summer had decided years ago that not everything needed to find its way back to the others. They would never know if she kept a little in reserve, storing them here as she went. Besides, a little treat now and then was a fair and just reward for those, like her, who would go out and take the risk. She figured everyone would agree with that position as she walked to the crate.

She snatched her trusty board with an upturned nail and moved it to the center of the crate. It took a few seconds to scrape the remnants of melted wax from the base of the nail with her thumbnail.

Summer dropped her pack, opened it, then pulled out the wad of bubble wrap. Her fingers dug through the air-filled plastic and snatched the most prized possession she owned—a brand new, six-inch long candle. She held its thick base to her nose and took in a long draw of air. "Damn, that's nice."

It took a bit of force, but the virgin candle slid down the sharp end of the nail, spearing the length of wax by an inch. A strike-anywhere match came out of her pack next. She lit it, then applied the flame to the wick.

The room glowed in a random flicker, while the scent of watermelon filled the air. Summer smiled as she walked to the stacks of books she'd collected and began to sift through them. Most at the bottom she'd read, but she found two that she hadn't near the middle.

She thought about taking three books with her this time since her available reading time had increased in recent weeks due to the swarm of Scab activity, forcing the leaders of Nirvana to slow mission assignments. However, she thought it might bring bad luck to change her routine, so she decided to keep with tradition and only take two novels. No reason to chance it. Bad luck has a tendency to mount over time, especially when you egg it on and ignore the negative karma that comes with it.

The new books went into the pack and the old ones came out. Seconds later, they found their way back into her inventory, sorted by title, of course.

While she was in her knapsack, she snatched the church key opener and put it on the table, then grabbed a can of peaches from the reserve stack she'd built.

The label said *Del Monte Sliced Peaches*, four of the most delicious words in the entire world. Well, those and *Sugar Added*. The printed expiration date was long in the past, but she wasn't worried, not after the deep freeze that ravaged the world for almost a decade. In effect, the entire planet had become a giant freezer unit, keeping her bounty safe until she found it.

The weather had done the same with all the human popsicles, at least until the thaw began. That's when the Scabs and coyotes took care of the meat.

She couldn't wait any longer, using the can opener to cut around the lid and give her access to the powerful rush of sustenance she knew waited inside. Her head went back and the can came up, pouring the sugary sweetness into her mouth.

It was nectar from the gods, racing down her gullet toward the promised land. She couldn't imagine a more fulfilling sensation than that, other than maybe finally having sex, with some hot guy no less, and then soaking with him in a bubble bath.

Summer let her mind hold on to that sudden vision of nakedness, warmth, soap, and complete and total satisfaction, then flushed it away as she used the fork from her backpack to finish off the bits of food remaining in the container.

After tossing the can into the corner with a plink, she spun around and flopped her butt into the beanbag chair with her head back and arms flying out to the side like a dead body.

"Now this is what I'm talking about!"

* * *

Doctor Liz Blackwell adjusted her backside in the office chair next to Krista Carr, wondering if the Security Chief would ever soften her stance—on anything.

Dr. Stuart Edison finished his most recent statement from behind his desk, motioning with his hands as he spoke. "I understand how you feel, Krista, but we can't start ousting members simply because they break a rule here and there. It happens. People are not perfect."

Krista's tone intensified. "Yes, mistakes happen, Professor. But our community can't survive without law and order."

"I understand why you feel that way, especially with your military background. I used to believe the same as you, but my beloved June always believed in compassion for everyone, even those who make mistakes. Her convictions changed my mind and I think over time, they will change yours, too."

Liz decided to add to the conversation, figuring it was wise to help sell the professor's viewpoint to Krista. "He's right. June gave her very life for that notion. It's something we all need to do—have empathy for everyone. Even those who screw up."

Krista snorted a quick breath, clenching her fists. "Look, I get the whole kumbaya approach. I really do. But it's not that simple. Laws exist to maintain discipline and keep order. Summer keeps breaking them. We simply don't have a choice anymore. Her selfishness is putting everyone in danger."

Edison leaned forward in his chair, looking both the part of leader and listener. "I take it you want to punish her in some fashion."

"That would be my first choice. If nothing else, we should at least send a strong message. Maybe we can get through that thick skull of hers."

"How exactly?"

"I'd leave her out there. For one night, at least. It's the only way she'll learn."

Edison didn't hesitate with his response. "No, I'm not in favor of that approach at all."

"Neither am I," Liz added.

The professor continued, "We're going to send out a search team like before and bring her in. Safely. It's just too dangerous with the Scabs in the area."

"She could already be hurt or in trouble," Liz said. "We can't just leave her to fend for herself."

Krista folded her arms across her chest. "Which is exactly why she needs to follow the rules. They exist to help keep her safe. And us by extension."

Liz felt the heat rise in her chest. "Well, I don't know about that. Not after The Council decided to send out Seekers alone. In retrospect, that decision was wrong and never should have happened."

Krista threw up her hands. "Well, it did. They really didn't have a choice, now did they? Not after the massacre. Again, those are the rules. They exist for a reason. Everyone has a designated search grid, a quota to fill, and a time due back. How hard is that? Seriously? Otherwise, everything breaks down."

"I get what you're saying," Liz said, needing to let the tension wane a bit before she continued. She knew that if she pushed too hard, Krista would only dig in more with her stance on Summer. "I think the Professor would agree with me on this, that we do understand the need for rules and discipline. They are both important like you mentioned. But in the end, we must protect our own. Seems to me the best course of action is to send out a search team to bring Summer home, like the Professor suggested. Then we deal with her. I'm sure she'll listen if we sit down and explain it all to her. Calmly."

Krista shook her head and glared at Liz for a few beats before she responded. "Why should I be surprised? You always side with the Professor."

"Because he's usually right. Don't forget, he built this place. If it weren't for him—"

"Yeah. Yeah. Yeah," Krista said. "That's all beside the point. We have rules and we need to enforce them. That's the deal we all signed up for. Decisions must be fair and equitable. No special treatment. The rules apply to everyone. Equally. No two-tiered rules of justice. We know from history that only creates anarchy."

"Can I ask you something, Krista?" Liz said, her tone turning soft and gentle. She'd learned during her years of medical service that a properly worded question of introspection usually helped calm an angry parent. Or a patient, depending on the situation.

Krista shrugged, looking frustrated as she sat up in an attentive posture. "Sure, fire away. Ask me anything. I've got nothing to hide."

"Why do you hate Summer so much?"

Krista leaned back with eyes pinched, taking a moment before responding. "I don't, really. I'm just sick and tired of her doing her own thing and putting everyone at risk. My job is to keep everyone safe and I can't do that by enabling rule breakers."

Liz touched a soft hand on Krista's forearm. "She puts her life on the line, just like everyone else who goes out there. Remember, it's a voluntary mission, something most of our people would never do. That has to count for something."

"It does, but she never follows the rules. This has to end before something tragic happens."

"Never is a strong word," Edison said. "I'm sure you'll agree that's not entirely true. Summer doesn't always break the rules. Deep down, she's a good kid with a big heart. She's just lost at times, like we all are. Living here isn't exactly easy."

"Yeah, maybe, but you get my point. We have to take steps."

Edison's eyes grew tight. "The first of which is sending out a search team."

"Well, I disagree. And since security is my responsibility, I'm not putting my teams at risk. Not again. She's lazy, undisciplined, and unfocused."

Edison shook his head, his eyes turning lower while he hesitated. Then he brought them back up. "I guess we're at an impasse, then."

"Come on, you two. Work it out," Liz said. "We all want the same thing here."

"No," Krista said. "I'm not budging this time. No more free passes for that little snot."

"I'm sorry, I can't sign off on that," Edison said.

"Neither can I," Liz added, wishing she didn't have to take sides.

"Then I guess there's no other choice," Krista said, standing in a flash with her back straight and shoulders firm. "I demand *Committee*. It's my right as Section Chief."

Liz looked at Edison to get his reaction. As expected, he didn't look happy about Krista's demand for a ruling by The Council.

"Are you sure?" Edison asked, his tone obviously trying to sway Krista's decision. "You may not like the result. There are never any guarantees during Committee. Trust me."

"Yes, I'm sure. Once the rest of The Council hears me out, they'll agree. The rules are the rules."

Edison stood from behind his desk. "All right, as much as I hate wasting everyone's time, call a meeting. Let's get this over with. We have a missing member to attend to."

CHAPTER 6

A deep, rattling snort startled Summer awake in her beanbag chair, yanking her from a wonderful dream involving her long-lost sister, Hope. Blaze was there, too, beaming his big brother smile. A smile she hadn't seen since his tragic death.

When her eyes came to bear on the new candle she'd lit, she sat up in a lurch. The wick had burned down half an inch. "Damn it!"

She hopped out of the chair, sending the book in her lap flying into the pyramid of food cans. The paperback hit the middle of the bottom row, knocking the pile down like a perfect strike in bowling.

The room filled with random clanks and thuds as the cans spread out in a mess of directions. The strange thing was, the peaches all seemed to go left, while the tuna cans went right.

They must not like each other much, Summer mused, thinking of her and Krista. They lived in the same space, but that was the end of their relationship. Sometimes you just had to go your own way.

If Summer had to choose a side, she'd be the peaches because of their sweetness.

Krista would be the smelly tuna, all protein and gung ho.

Summer laughed as she grabbed the backpack, deciding to restack the food cans on her next visit. It was time to jet back to the silo. However, before she did, she needed to grab one more item on the scavenge list.

A quick blow of air took care of the flame, sending it into a tuft of rising smoke. She licked her fingers and applied a little spit to the wick, then stuffed the candle back into her pack.

She let her eyes adjust to the darkness, keeping one eye open and one closed, precisely how Krista had taught her and the other Seekers during training. Pupils adjust faster that way.

Summer grabbed the bubble wrap and went through the hidden door with her backpack in hand, closing the secret entrance behind her.

Once the latch engaged, she covered the release handle with the baseboard, then turned and headed for the far corner of the main retail area.

Her target was the tallest of the cardboard boxes. Specifically, the one sitting next to a crusty pair of pink flipflops and a smashed electric pencil sharpener, about ten feet from the board-covered windows protecting the front of the store.

Sunlight streamed in through the cracks, penetrating the dark with streaks of light, allowing her to avoid most of the shards of glass on the floor. A few crunched underfoot, but nothing broke through the soles of her shoes.

The scent of candle wax and watermelon had made its way to the outer room, giving her another minute of pleasure, while her hands dug into the box. The container was full of old picture frames, crammed in at odd angles, as if someone was in a hurry.

Most were made of fake wood, rectangular, and designed for a single photo, but one was perfectly square. It was fabricated out of metal and twice the size of the others, the kind that was designed to hold a number of smaller shots around a central image—a family portrait arrangement, she guessed.

Summer put them aside and kept rummaging, pulling out one after another until she found one she liked: a stainless-steel picture frame—oval shaped and glass included—with a frilly lace pattern glued around its edges. It was beautiful. Even the prop-up stand on the back was intact.

"She'll love this," Summer mumbled, covering it in bubble wrap before stowing it in her pack, which she then slung over her shoulder.

She turned to walk away but froze when a loud BANG rang in her ears. It sounded like someone had punched a dumpster somewhere outside, not far away.

Summer kept low and moved behind the dilapidated checkout counter, peering through the slats of boards covering the end of the window. She was now standing in the same location where Avery died, a spot her feet had never been.

A shadow outside cruised past the window, blotting out the sun for only the briefest of moments. Then another shadow came into view with the same direction and speed. Then another. Eventually a total of nine scampered past the store.

Scabs?

Summer turned an ear and listened. She didn't hear any of the expected heavy breathing or groans. Only the clatter of boots and equipment.

Frost's men, she decided before moving her feet back several steps, hoping they'd keep on moving and not stop.

So far she thought she'd been pretty quiet, except for the crunches of glass and the noise the cans made when the book flew off her lap and took out the pyramid. She didn't think the patrol could've heard any of it. Not unless they were standing right outside and listening.

"Fan out," a man's voice said. He sounded older, but definitely in charge. It wasn't the deep tone of Fletcher's voice from before. This one was different, breathier and light, almost nasal.

"Roger that. Team One, with me," another man said, his voice set in a thick mire of gravel.

She saw something out of the corner of her eye after the movement outside changed the lighting in the room. There was an object she hadn't noticed before. It was attached to the rear of the counter, hanging in the murky light by a clasp. Maybe two inches in size. Reflective.

Summer didn't know it was there, probably because she'd always avoided this area behind the counter where Avery took his last breath. She snatched the object and held it in a streak of light.

It was an intricate piece of stained glass. Pink mostly. A pretty tulip design, with a unique inlay near the base where it curved into the stem. The inlay's shape matched the symbol on the end of her Infinity Chain. June's symbol. A sideways number eight.

Did she make this?

Regardless of whose handiwork it was, Summer couldn't believe this delicate keepsake had survived all the damage to the room. The odds had to be astronomical.

Perhaps it was like Edison said, *things work out how they are supposed to, even if it takes a while to understand why.*

Right then, she knew she had to keep it.

Out came the bubble wrap again, and so did its contents. The stained glass was much more delicate than the frame inside, needing special protection. She unwrapped the frame and replaced it with the stained glass, its smaller size allowing her to triple wrap it.

Summer opened the metal box from her pack and removed the forty or so crayons she'd found and put the fragile trinket inside, compressing the bubble wrap in order to work the lid closed. Both the frame and the bubble wrap went back into her pack and so did the loose crayons, then she zipped it up and slipped the straps over her shoulders.

She couldn't believe her luck today—what a haul. Everything she needed and then some. Plus, an unexpected nap, some delicious peaches, and a quick read of something new.

A grin crossed her lips when she realized that life after The Event wasn't all doom, boom, and gloom. It had its moments, like now. Simple pleasures. If only this place had a working bathtub and hot water, she'd never leave.

Unfortunately, Summer had to get back to the insanity of the silo. Sure, that concrete prison kept her out of the cold, but it certainly wasn't home. Not her idea of it, anyway. There was no privacy, no quiet, no place to read, and certainly no place where she could ever fire up the candle and enjoy its aroma. Everyone would smell it, then they'd swarm to take it.

She took one more whiff of air, wanting to remember the watermelon scent. It might be a couple of weeks before she could make it back here, depending on the weather and the Seeker assignments.

"Goodbyes suck," she muttered, letting her eyes scan the room. Who knew she could get so attached to a place? A rundown place with crap everywhere. Her little slice of heaven.

Summer put her hoodie on and made sure her clothes were ready for the temperatures outside. She pushed the rear door open and began to squeeze through the opening. First her shoulder, then her torso went through. However, her backpack was fatter than before, getting caught on the edge of the door frame. It took a second try, but she was able to work it free and finish her exit.

Once the door was pushed shut, she slid alongside and stepped out from behind the delivery truck. That's when she saw them. Rifles and pistols, all pointed at her face.

"Hold it right there, missy," a man's voice said as the ratcheting clatter of charging bolts forcing rounds into their respective chambers landed on her ears.

"See Slayer, I told you I smelled watermelon. Must have been this chick," another man said, his index finger moving in and out of the trigger guard. "They all love their scents. It's like a religion with them."

"Hello, Summer. We meet again," Slayer said, his eyes scanning her from head to toe, just like he'd done earlier. "Only this time, Fletcher's not here to save your sweet little ass."

Summer didn't hesitate, climbing onto the hood of the bread truck, then up the windshield and onto its towering cab. She took a running leap toward the roofline of the store and grabbed the fascia wall, pulling herself up and over in a heartbeat.

Summer spun around, then leaned over the wall and looked down at Slayer and his men. They stood there with their mouths agape and rifles flat against their chests.

She brought both hands up and flipped them a pair of birds. "Suckers!"

Slayer waved a hand signal at some of his men. They broke into action, their boots hitting the metal bumper of the delivery truck, then its hood.

Summer turned and took off, wondering if any of the brutes could make the leap she had just made, then manage to pull their heft over the fascia wall. Probably not many, she decided as she raced across the flat roof and down the exterior pipe that led to the ground.

Sometimes it pays to be small and wiry.

And hyper-motivated.

CHAPTER 7

Security Chief Krista Carr stood behind the podium, shuffling through her notes as she prepared her opening statement for her meeting with The Council. She'd rarely been on this side of the process, taking a moment to admire the symmetry of the circular Committee Room.

The white paint along the walls was spotless, as was the polished surface of the Council's Ruling Bench—a half-moon-shaped oak table in the middle. Everything had been cleaned and polished to perfection for this all-important summit, including the equally-spaced positions of the three chairs tucked under the table.

Ten rectangular placards hung along the curved walls, each with the silo's name, Nirvana, stenciled in the center. Above the name was an infinity symbol that stretched from one end of the letters to the other.

The signs had been installed in precise 36-degree increments around the room to symbolize the purity of logic and the balance of order.

Edison always had a specific agenda in everything he did, deciding that this room was the most important area of the silo.

He'd also written famous quotes on white posters placed between each of the logo signs. It wasn't clear if he thought they were needed for decoration, or to further his idea of motivation and symmetry.

Krista scanned a few quotes, taking in their wisdom:

Honesty is the First Chapter in the Book of Wisdom. ~Thomas Edison

Truth is Rarely Pure and Never Simple. ~Oscar Wilde

Truth Carries the Weight of the Victims, While Justice Frees the Soul of the Damned. ~Jack Bunker

The First Duty of Society is to Uncover the Truth. ~Frank Cartwright

A raised platform stood a few yards beyond the Ruling Bench, much like a judge's stand in a court of law. It featured a simple wooden desk and high-back leather chair, both of which belonged to the curator of Nirvana: Dr. Stuart Edison.

He'd designed The Council's Ruling Process to be quick and efficient, allowing the various Section Heads to handle complaints and other matters needing a leadership vote.

All decisions were final.

There were no appeals.

No stays.

No objections.

No procedural logistics to trip over, either, like warrants, probable cause, witnesses, or cross-examinations.

It made the need for lawyers obsolete, and the same could be said for the need of a jury of your peers. Or the need to face your accuser. Everything was timed to keep the process moving and reach a decision quickly among those standing in judgment.

Each Section Chief voted for their respective rank and file. Normally Krista was seated in one of the three chairs, hearing the complaint and whatever summary evidence was available before making her decision.

Now she was on the other side of the tribunal, bringing charges against a young girl. A girl who ignored the rules, pretending she was immune to their reach.

The side door to the chamber opened and in walked the remaining members of the Ruling Committee, each wearing an ankle-length ceremonial robe to denote their status. The robes featured a rainbow of primary colors, vertically striped in six-inch increments. Edison had designed the garments, including the infinity symbol sewn across the chest in honor of his slain wife, June.

Fifty-one-year-old physician Dr. Liz Blackwell sat down first, her slender frame nestling into the center chair with precision. She leaned forward to adjust her position, bringing the legs of the chair farther under the bench in a screech. The sudden weight shift sent her black hair into a wiggle, jostling the subtle wave of curls that reached the top of her shoulders.

Despite Liz's age, her hair hadn't begun to turn gray. Good genes, Krista figured, admiring the porcelain shine across the doc's smooth cheeks and her perfectly white teeth. Not a wrinkle in sight. Everything about the woman screamed she was in control.

Liz adjusted her glasses, touching a finger against the bridge of her slim, rectangular frames, then brought her hands together on the wood surface, as if a famous teacher was about to walk into the class and demand her attention.

Krista respected Liz, not only for her intelligence and good nature, but also for her accomplishments in the world before The Event. It takes something special inside to push through life with a clear plan in place. In truth, anyone who sets out to become a doctor and does so in record time has that drive.

However, Krista never understood why the brilliant woman seemed to defer to whatever Edison wanted. Certainly, the Harvard-educated doctor had her own opinions. She couldn't possibly agree with Edison every single time. Yet she did. It wouldn't be easy gaining her vote.

Supply Chief Rod Zimmer sat down next, taking the seat on Liz Blackwell's right. His salt and pepper hair, mustache, and beard were a bit unruly, but their distinctive look made him distinguished. His handlebar mustache extended out well beyond his cheeks, curving upward at the ends.

Nobody knew his true age, but if Krista had to guess, Zimmer was in his late fifties or early sixties.

He reminded her of a distinguished Confederate General from the Civil War era. His accent and mannerisms screamed Southern gentleman—probably from Alabama or Georgia. Again, nobody knew for sure. He wasn't the kind of man to share tidbits about himself or his background.

His keen eyes were like those of an eagle, always locked on target, taking in every fact while searching for the next kill. His wrinkled skin sagged around his slender nose with equal balance on each side, giving him a look of both predator and prey.

Engineering Chief Alexander Morse entered the chamber next, laboring across the floor with the aid of a walker. He shuffled the unstable device a foot at a time until he was able to sit down in the remaining seat with a grimace. The ebony-skinned scientist sent a gentle smile Krista's way, then a head nod, his chest pumping for air in recovery.

His wide nose was his most distinctive feature, breaking up his round cheeks and sun-damaged complexion. He kept his hair short and temper long, measuring every syllable before he spoke, as if he were running out of words. Morse was the oldest of the Council, clocking in at north of seventy.

The final attendee was the man himself: Dr. Stuart Edison, Professor and Chairman. He, too, wore a ceremonial robe, only his was all black instead of a mix of colors like the others.

Edison walked past the Ruling Bench and climbed the steps to his perch atop the raised platform in the back of the room.

He sat in his chair and spun it slightly to roll himself behind his desk. The only item missing from the scene was a white wig sitting on his head, reminiscent of colonial days—long before the United States spun off on its own, in a flurry of bullets and death.

Edison cleared his throat, then made eye contact with Krista. "By order of the Nirvana Code of Conduct, I, as Chairman of the Ruling Council, hereby declare this meeting open. We have a series of complaints to hear today, all of which are being brought by Security Chief Carr. Established rules and procedures dictate that we hear the grievances first, then the facts of the case will be submitted and rebuttal heard. Each phase of the process will be delivered by Chief Carr and Chief Carr alone, with ten minutes allocated for Q & A thereafter. Judgment will then be reached by those in attendance today. Since I stand in opposition, I will abstain unless the ruling process ends in a deadlock. Security Chief Carr, you now have the floor. Please read your complaint, then begin outlining the facts and deliver your prepared rebuttal. You have fifteen minutes to complete testimony. The clock starts now."

Krista nodded, then began her delivery, choosing her most sincere tone. "Thank you, Chairman Edison and distinguished members of the Ruling Council. I stand before you today with a conflicted heart. As you know, Nirvana is primarily a community of hope and compassion for all those weary souls who request entry. But in order to survive in a world that's been decimated and nearly extinguished by man, Nirvana must also stand for law and order, both of which must apply equally to all those who choose to live within her walls," Krista said, taking a moment to fire down another breath.

She made eye contact with each member in the room before she spoke again. "When someone joins our group, they take a solemn oath to live by the terms and conditions as outlined by the Nirvana Code of Conduct. To achieve peace and harmony, each of us must respect not only our neighbors, but also the NCC. If any provision is breeched, each member agrees to accept summary judgement as ruled by The Council."

Krista took a sip of water from a glass on the podium before continuing. "Today, I bring formal charges against one Summer Lane, an adult we all know and love, but a young woman who has repeatedly broken rules and shirked her responsibilities. This, my fellow council members, can no longer be tolerated. For too long, we have turned a blind eye as her transgressions continued. It is my opinion as Security Chief that Summer has now exceeded the overindulging tolerance of our good nature. She is putting all of us at great risk. It is therefore imperative that we act now to preserve that which we all hold dear—the safety and security of our community. By the end of this testimony, it is my firm belief that you will agree with me on all counts. The defendant, Summer Lane, must be banished from Nirvana. Without delay."

CHAPTER 8

Summer ducked in behind a deteriorating brick fence to catch her breath after giving Slayer and his band of miscreants the slip, at least temporarily, thanks to the massive pile of rubble from a collapsed movie multiplex blocking the path for their vehicles. She knew eventually they'd abandon their rides and come at her on foot. It was their only option, assuming they were still hungry for her ass, as Slayer had mentioned.

The masonry fence marked the exterior of an old apartment complex that had burned long ago. Portions of the multi-story housing had fallen in on itself, piling in clumps, leaving whole sections of the building's foundation exposed. A network of exposed water pipes stood vertically where a wall used to be, looking more like the framework of metal scaffolding than plumbing.

She figured she only had a few minutes to rest, despite her cleverness. Eventually, they'd find the crawl space she'd used to get through the wreckage of the destroyed theater. The passageway was small and partially hidden, but they might stumble across it like she'd done several months earlier.

Home Field Advantage was an old term she'd heard Security Chief Krista use a few months ago, and now Summer understood what it meant. It was all part of a Seeker's skill set, identifying secret tunnels and hidden rooms, then remembering their location in a time of panic.

Before her next breath, four men entered her field of vision at the far end of the alley, about five hundred yards from the farthest end of the apartment complex. They were headed her way, walking in standard two-by-two formation, sweeping the area from left to right with their rifles in firing position.

Damn it! Already?

Summer couldn't believe her luck, all of it bad lately, as she kept low and moved in the opposite direction. She worked her way along the inside of a fence, her feet sinking into the slush, compliments of the thaw turning the earth into mud.

The sucking sounds made by her shoes each time they penetrated the muck and came out again might get her caught. A different plan was needed—

one that wouldn't alert Slayer's patrol to her position as they drew closer.

A spray of 2x4 studs with nails sticking out of the wood held promise since the lumber was mostly intact, except for the sections that had been burned.

She stepped onto the end of the first board, tip-toeing with her arms out for balance against the uneven wind as she navigated the sharp tips of the nails. The boards weren't parallel to each other, nor were they connected end-to-end like railroad tracks, but they were close enough to allow her to hop from one to another and keep moving.

A minute later, she worked herself up a pile of crumpled drywall, broken furniture, and rusty appliances, where she spotted a long section of sheet metal. It was dead ahead, at the bottom. The obstacle was shiny and rectangular, maybe six feet wide on each side, with a snake-like twist along its length.

She figured it was ductwork that used to supply air to the gaggle of apartments. There didn't appear to be a way around it since it stretched across her path, covering every inch of width from the brick fence to the base of the housing structure.

There were only two choices: traverse the mess on her right to see if she could navigate through the remnants of the destroyed building, or she could climb over the ductwork.

Her eyes went into survey mode, calculating the odds of safely entering the remains of the apartment building. Some of its towering walls were badly burned. Yet somehow, they remained standing, even with the wind pushing at them. Maybe it meant they were stout enough to let her pass.

However, if she was wrong and she disturbed their delicate balance, they'd collapse and she'd be crushed. There'd be no way to run fast enough to avoid the cave-in with all the crap in the way.

That left only option two: the sheet metal ahead. It wasn't a better option, but at least she wouldn't be buried if something went wrong. Plus, it would take her in the right direction—away from Slayer and his men.

A shadow came out of nowhere and washed over her from above. She stopped and knelt down, her neck craning up in panic. She saw a man three stories up on a wooden beam atop the wreckage like a cat without fear, wearing a leather coat and standing on a beam. It was the Nomad, his pair of swords together and pointing ahead. He wanted Summer to choose the second option, so she did.

Summer waved him a quick thank you, then finished her trek forward before putting her hands on the metal obstacle. A sting of cold shot through the exposed tips of her fingers, but she didn't stop. She hopped up and crawled across, feeling the unstable ductwork below her knees.

Just then, her hands felt the metal give way near its midpoint, sagging downward at an angle. She froze after the ductwork groaned, wondering if it might continue to fatigue under her weight and end up creasing down the middle into a deep bend. If that happened, it would make a much louder sound that might give away her position.

Summer turned her head and looked up, hoping for more guidance from the Nomad.

He wasn't there. Only her memory of him remained.

Summer ran the options through her mind. She couldn't turn back, not with the patrol hot on her trail, nor could she move, not without the metal alerting Slayer to her position.

Either way, she was screwed, leaving her only one choice: go for it. She crawled forward in a flash, making a horrible racket as the ductwork popped and pinged a hollow, metallic tune from impacts of her hands and knees.

When her feet hit the ground, she took off at top speed, hoping it would take Slayer some time to figure out what he just heard and where.

"That way!" one of the men chasing her said, his words pushing through the gusts of wind.

Summer wasn't about to look back. She kept her eyes locked on the path ahead—a path filled with boards, drywall, junk, and other debris.

There wasn't time to be careful, so she'd just have to guess where her feet needed to land to avoid a messed-up ankle. Stride after stride, she pushed her legs, praying she could put some distance between her and the patrol.

A path opened up twenty feet ahead. She took it, angling left, not stopping to think. Clear ground was good enough, she thought. It didn't matter where it led. She'd just have to make up the rest on the fly.

Her trek continued with a steady increase in speed, her chest pumping air. The loaded backpack smacked at her shoulder blades, but she ignored the discomfort. Speed and distance were her focus; getting back to the silo in one piece was her goal.

Thirteen more strides brought her to the back of another building. This one was intact and huge, stretching for what seemed like a city block. It was a warehouse, featuring a string of rollup style doors standing side by side, with cement ramps leading up to them.

A huge white sign with faded black lettering said *LaDean Co-Packing and Cannery*. The word *cannery* caught her eye—maybe there was food and other supplies inside. If nothing else, the immense building and all of its ancient equipment would have plenty of hiding places.

Summer tore up the first ramp and tried to lift the towering metal door. It wouldn't budge. It must have been locked, or it was too heavy for her arms to maneuver.

Back down the ramp she went, running past the remaining loading docks to see what might be around the next corner.

That's when it happened—she ran into a smear of wooden pallets. They were everywhere along the side of the building, tossed about in the wind like landmines.

Her feet tangled with the slats and down she went—hard and out of balance. Her elbow landed first, cracking a pallet in front of her and smashing into the dirt underneath. Her cheek hit the same location next, catching a nasty splinter of wood that tore open a chunk of skin next to her nose. The splinter missed her eye by only a couple of inches.

"Eeeeeooooww," she cried out before slamming her mouth shut. The stars in her vision multiplied, as did the blood pouring out from her face.

Summer ignored another round of pain as she pulled herself free from the impalement, then slapped a hand on the gaping wound. It took a few seconds for the blobs and specks to vanish from her eyes, but her vision finally cleared.

She rolled over and worked her feet loose, then stood up and took off running in an awkward stumble, this time avoiding the rest of the pallets.

The next corner wasn't as dangerous as the last, bringing her to a neatly-stacked collection of propane cylinders, some wider than tall, while others were round and almost symmetrical. There was also a side door to the cannery not far away. The combination of the two gave her an idea.

Summer put her free hand on one of the smaller tanks and tried to pick it up. It was heavier than expected and wouldn't move. She took her other hand from her facial wound and latched onto the cylinder with both sets of fingers.

Blood dripped from her cheek as she grunted to pick the tank up and haul it to the door. After a deep breath to charge her lungs, she took a roundhouse swing at the doorknob.

CLANG!

The reverberation from the impact stunned her hands, making her drop the tank. It rolled downhill, coming to rest several yards away against an electrical transformer box.

When Summer brought her eyes to the door, a shriek almost shot out from her lips. The door was sitting open about an inch and moving back and forth under the control of the wind. She'd done it, and on the first try. Maybe her luck was turning.

She pressed her palm to her cheek to stem the flow of blood as she ran to the entrance, pulling the door open. A second later she was inside, standing in a modest work area with walls stretching from floor to ceiling.

The room was cold but it wasn't completely dark like she expected. There was a swatch of light emanating from somewhere off in the distance— around the wall running parallel to her right.

She figured the light originated from a window in the next room. The light itself wasn't a surprise, but the air movement landing on her face was. The same window must have been smashed, she figured, allowing an offshoot of the wind to find its way through the cannery and to her.

Since the doorknob had been bent out of position, the door behind her wouldn't stay closed on its own. Slayer and his men would notice. They'd come inside, seeing it as a roadmap to follow. Something else was needed. Something to use as a weight or as leverage. Or both.

Three feet away was the answer—a red handled dolly sitting by a ten-foot long stainless steel worktable that was covered by pieces of industrial equipment. This was clearly a maintenance room, where some ancient grease monkey used to stand all day and repair whatever was broken.

The hand truck was vertical in design, much like the one she'd seen Edison use in the silo to move a stack of boxes, only this one was twice the size of the Professor's and had a pair of flat rubber tires.

Summer drug it to the door, figuring the beast weighed over a hundred pounds. Next, she took off her backpack and fished around inside of it for one of the scarves.

The first to come out was yellow in color, with a mosaic pattern. She twisted it lengthwise into a rope design, then used a square knot to secure the handle of the dolly to the broken doorknob. There wasn't enough length to make a second knot, so she pulled the two ends as tight as she could, hoping it would hold.

A quick review of the makeshift anchor told her it wouldn't keep the door closed, even with its massive weight and flat tires. The door was acting as a sail, moving as the wind pounded the area. She needed to secure the other end of the dolly somehow.

Her eyes made their way to a leg on the workstation. It was made of steel, the heavy-duty type, and was bolted to the wall behind it.

Perfect!

Summer's hand went back into her pack and found another scarf, a solid red color, then bent down and used the cloth to tie the axle of the dolly to the leg.

"That should hold," she mumbled, pushing on the door. Nothing moved. "For a while at least."

When she took one last look at her solution, she noticed the yellow scarf on the handle had a red stain on it from the blood on her hand transferring from the wound in her cheek.

The red cloth tied to the other end didn't show the blood. A better choice. Color mattered.

She checked her backpack again, looking for more red scarves. There weren't any. They were all light colors. Shit. Nothing she could do.

A quick turn of her heels allowed her to scamper deeper into the warehouse, her hand once again covering the gash on her cheek. It was time to dress the wound, assuming she had a few extra minutes.

The source of the light drew her forward, taking her around the corner and to the right. An open space greeted her. It contained a sea of equipment, wires, overhead pipes, and curved conveyor tracks that snaked from one end of the warehouse to the other.

Everywhere she looked, she saw a nameplate or placard that carried the name of the business: *LaDean*. Probably a family name, she figured, or it carried some sentimental value. Maybe it was the name of their pet wildebeest, she scoffed, letting her imagination loose for a second. Either way, someone was obsessed, needing the constant reminder.

The facility was massive, but like the rest of the planet, its life had run out. She imagined what the production line looked like before The Event, its tracks humming along with glass jars clicking against each other as they moved from one station to the next.

Her mind filled with visions of the food being sealed into the jars—everything from mama's homemade hot sauce to a sugary treat of canned peaches. Too bad the place was empty; otherwise, this would have been the score of a lifetime for any of the Seekers.

Light streamed in from above, finding its way through a hefty crack in the ceiling. There weren't any windows like she thought—only an overhead hole in the roof. A steady trickle of water dripped down through it, making a pattering sound when it hit the floor.

Summer made her way to the center of the room, taking a measured path around the equipment in her way. The floor started to creak as she neared the center where the sunlight touched bottom.

When the warmth of the sun landed on her face, it felt amazing—just what she needed, even though she could still see her breath every time she exhaled.

When she looked down, she saw her feet sitting in water. Just enough to cover the soles of her shoes—nothing more. The hole above must have been recent; otherwise, the water leak would have filled more of the room.

The throb in her cheek changed her focus. Time for some personal repairs.

Another search of her pack turned up nothing she could use to help stop the bleeding. All she had were the remaining scarves. Their cotton fibers would mop up the blood, but without adhesive help, they were useless as a dressing. Well, almost useless—she could tie the scarves to each other and wrap them around her head, like a giant pressure bandage.

However, given the location of the injury, she wasn't sure it would work. The laceration was too close to her nose, meaning pressure couldn't be applied directly, not with the size of her snout in the way.

Her eyes went in search mode, looking for a solution. That's when she spotted it—black electrical tape wrapped around a wad of the wires hanging from a tan-colored control box along the conveyor in front of her. It was in the sunlight, so maybe it wasn't frozen.

Summer bent down and pulled with caution at the end of the tape. It wasn't cold to the touch. In fact, it was soft and pliable thanks to the sun doing its job.

It took a few seconds, but she was able to work it free without it snapping in half. The liberated piece was about six inches long and it still had some of its stickiness.

Her teeth made quick work of a section of a scarf, tearing a hunk off about two inches wide. She pressed it against the wound, using extra pressure to close the incision, then used the tape to hold the bandage to her skin. "Not bad," she said, flexing her cheek muscle to test her solution.

BANG! BANG! BANG!

Summer snapped her head around, tracing the direction of the sound. It appeared to be coming from the door she'd anchored shut with the hand truck and the steel worktable. Someone was beating on the entrance. Probably with a closed fist, or maybe a boot.

BANG! BANG!

Wait, check that. The wall in front of her just cracked a seam down its drywall. Plus, a cardboard box fell from one of its attached shelves. This told her that someone was yanking on the door and shaking the attached worktable.

As the noise continued, she looked down at the water around her feet, seeing the vibrations from all the force making the pool shimmer.

Before she could react, the ceiling overhead caved in, sending an avalanche of snow and roofing material at her. She dove under the conveyor belt next to her, hoping it would protect her.

A moment later, she heard a loud clang above her, right before the floor gave way and she fell like a rock.

* * *

Slayer took a step back from the cannery's back door to let two of his strongest men continue their work. They had their hands wrapped around a bent doorknob and were yanking hard in unison. So far the door hadn't budged much.

A fresh blood trail had led them to this location. It started near the wood pallets and then took them to the propane tank lying next to an electrical box, and finally to this door.

"Hey boss, look at this," one of his men said, holding up his hand. It was Bird, the former helicopter pilot, standing among the pallets near the corner of the building.

"Bring it here," Slayer said, wishing he didn't have to walk his men through every step of the tracking process. It was like babysitting a group of infants. Well, infants who liked to party more than they worked.

Bird arrived in seconds with the item. "Looks like you were right."

Slayer took the find and held it up by its chain. It was an infinity necklace from Edison's group. "Gotcha now, bitch." He turned the pendant over and read the inscription: *Summer Lane.*

"Going to be easy to track her now," Bird added, pointing at the blood smeared on the chain. "Especially if she's hurt bad enough."

Slayer brought his eyes to the work being done at the door. "Enough of this brute force bullshit. Someone get the crowbar from my truck. She's not getting away this time."

"On it," Horton said, his second-in-command. The man never said much but always followed orders to the letter—usually without a moment of hesitation.

Slayer watched Horton run to the truck, his beard twisting around his neck as it fought against the nonstop wind. The man's facial hair was legendary, hanging down to his chest in a loose v-pattern, the interspersed gray speckles balanced against the dominating black.

Horton whipped open the rear door and put a hand inside. A moment later his arm came out, holding the crowbar above his head in victory. A quick sprint back brought the item to Slayer's hands.

"Make a hole," Slayer said to the men yanking on the door. His men moved away, allowing him to stick the angled end of the crowbar into the doorjamb next to the mangled knob. He worked it farther inside, wanting to maximize the leverage.

Once the bar was in position, he slid his hands to the very end of the steel and used all his force to pry at door. It took several tries, but he managed to wedge it open about an inch. "Tell me what you see in there," he told Horton, grunting to keep the pressure in place.

Horton leaned in, pressing an eye to the gap. "Looks like a hand truck has been tied to the door."

"Tied with what? Rope?"

"A cloth of some kind, it looks like."

"Hurry up. Use your knife. I can't hold this forever."

"You got it, boss." Horton pulled out a ten-inch pig sticker from the sheath on his hip and stuck it inside. He began to move it back and forth, sawing with abandon.

Seconds later, the tension on the crowbar released, sending the door flying open. The dolly's handle hit the cement floor after gravity took over, making a loud metallic pinging sound.

"Spread out. Search the place," Slayer told his team. "I want her found! If she resists, put a bullet in her."

CHAPTER 9

Security Chief Krista Carr finished writing the tenth attribute in favor of Summer Lane on the chalkboard in the Council Chamber. Summer's disciplinary meeting was coming to an end and Krista was thankful. It was almost time for a ruling—a long overdue ruling—a ruling that would finally rid her of her biggest headache in the silo.

However, Krista needed to finish her role as both prosecutor and defender and do so honorably, as prescribed by the Nirvana Code of Conduct. Rules were rules and she intended to abide by each one of them to the best of her ability.

She underlined the last item that read: *Loved By All*, then turned to face The Council, who were still seated at the Ruling Table. "As you can see, I've been rather thorough in my analysis of why Summer should be allowed to stay."

Krista moved the tip of her chalk to the other column on the board; its header read: *Reasons to*

Banish. "But it doesn't compare to the list of infractions."

Liz Blackwell interrupted. "I know you feel that you've been complete and balanced, but if you look at the two lists, they're a bit lopsided. Not exactly what I would call a fair representation of the facts. Or the accused."

Krista shrugged, flaring an eyebrow for emphasis. "That's exactly why we're here today. The list of violations keeps growing, outweighing the positive contributions by three to one. We have to do something before she gets someone killed."

"A little melodramatic, don't you think?" Liz asked, flashing a look at Edison, who was seated behind the judge's desk on the raised stand.

Edison held his tongue, appearing to be frozen solid, like many of the corpses in the city after The Event.

Liz's eyes came back to Krista. "I think we need to ask a few questions before a ruling is called."

Krista welcomed the scrutiny and cross-examination. She'd been planning for this moment a long time. "Sure, fire away."

"When you say *get someone killed*, do you honestly believe that her occasional tardiness will actually lead to someone's death other than her own?"

"Yes, I do. And it's not occasional."

"Explain, please."

"When she's out there doing whatever the hell she does, she runs the risk of getting caught."

"Wait a minute; that only puts her life at risk. A life she takes into her own hands every time she goes out there. A Seeker's mission is a very dangerous task. One she does out of the goodness of her heart."

Krista threw up her hands in frustration, her tone turning cynical. "Yes, we've all heard that same argument before. She risks her life for the benefit of Nirvana, but it still doesn't change the fact that she's chronically late. Plus, she's barely successful with her recovery efforts."

"What do you mean by that?" Alexander Morse said from his seat, interrupting. "From what I understand, she always brings back food and supplies. In fact, if my memory serves, doesn't Summer lead all Seekers in terms of success rate?"

Krista shook her head. "But it's always just two cans of food. Not one. Not three. Always two. Do you know what the odds of that are?"

Morse took out his pen and began scribbling something on the paper in front of him. "If you wait a minute, I'll give you the answer."

"That's not what I meant," Krista said, taking a breath to calm her nerves. "What I meant is she's lazy. If a Seeker finds two cans of food right away, then she can certainly find three or four. Maybe more on occasion. That, to me, would be helping the group. It's obvious she finds two cans, then stops looking. God knows what else she's doing with the rest of her time."

"Isn't that up to her?" Morse asked, sending a look at Liz Blackwell. "She's the one taking the risk."

Rod Zimmer broke his silence. "Technically, no. A Seeker's job is to find everything on their duty list, but not stop there when they have the opportunity to recover more."

"Maybe that's exactly what she *is* doing," Liz said with a heavy tone to her words. "Maybe that's why she's late, looking for more items that will benefit our community."

"I doubt that's the case," Zimmer said after a smirk. "We also have to take into account her character. She's not the most reliable member of Nirvana, or the most well liked."

"I appreciate what you're saying," Krista said to Liz, shifting the weight on her feet. The temperature in the room seemed to be about ten degrees hotter than it was a few minutes ago. "But Summer never does."

"Never does what?" Liz asked.

"Never excels at anything. Not once has she turned in anything other than what's on her recovery list."

Morse cleared his throat. "Has she ever returned without something she was sent to find?"

Krista didn't hesitate, having reviewed Summer's mission logs before this meeting. "Only once."

"When was that?" he asked.

"A while back. When Avery died."

Morse seemed to expect that answer, his retort unleashed only a millisecond later. "Yes. Every time except once, and that was under very unusual circumstances, wouldn't you agree?"

"Sure, if you want to make excuses for her."

"Otherwise, she's always been one hundred percent successful."

Krista had to agree, even though she didn't want to. "Technically, that's correct."

"But never more. That's the key here," Zimmer added in a matter-of-fact tone, his eyes scanning through a stack of paperwork in front of him.

Krista continued, appreciating Zimmer's vote of support. "Summer only does the absolute minimum required to get by and not be reprimanded, even when I go out of my way to assign her the best areas. Areas where she can achieve and be successful, but it doesn't change a thing. When I was in the Army, we called that *just marking time*. When a soldier does that, mistakes happen. Things get overlooked. Supplies run low. The whole nine yards."

"I hope you know this isn't the Army," Morse said in a sarcastic tone.

"Well, maybe it should be," Krista added, bringing her eyes to Edison sitting on his perch. "If we instilled more of a military approach around here, then maybe, just maybe, everyone would be a little safer. And happier. Not so depressed all the time."

Edison only blinked and didn't respond.

"I think things are regimented enough around here," Morse said, swinging his head around to look at Edison. "Normal people can only take so much.

Next thing you know, we'd have people saluting each other and marching in formation."

Liz spoke before Krista could respond to Morse. "Okay, let me get this straight. Summer goes out and risks her life and always, except once, completes her Seeker Missions with every item she's asked to find, and now you want to banish her from the community for it? On what planet is that fair? Or just?"

"Look, I get that you're all fond of her. So am I, but we have rules that must be followed. Every time she's late, we have to send out search teams to find her and that puts everyone's life at risk."

"Isn't that what the search teams are for?" Liz asked, her face flushing. "To go out and find missing members?"

"When needed, yes. But Summer's chronic lateness is a waste of resources and pushing the odds. Eventually, casualties will result."

Liz rolled her eyes. "It's all doom, boom, and gloom with you, isn't it?"

Krista remembered that exact phrase coming out of Summer's mouth, on more than one occasion. Obviously, the girl's attitude was spreading to the others. "That's my job, Doc. If I don't look out for the safety and security of everyone, then who will? You?"

"Well, I never—" Liz said in an angry tone.

"Okay, that's enough," Edison said, finally breaking his silence. "Our time limit has been reached. Testimony has been heard. Questions asked. Now we must move forward to a ruling. Let's take a vote."

Krista wished she had more time to rally support, but Edison was correct. The time allotted had been reached. "I agree. Time for a vote. The rules are the rules. They apply to everyone, even me."

Liz folded her arms. "Agreed."

Alexander Morse nodded.

Rod Zimmer looked at Krista, his eyes tight and focused. "I've heard enough."

"Then let's proceed," Edison said. "All those who find Summer guilty of repeatedly breaking curfew in violation of established rules, please raise their hand."

Krista put her hand up in an instant. So did Zimmer. There was a momentary pause before Liz and Morse did the same, though they looked tentative.

"Then it's unanimous. Summer is guilty on all counts and shall be punished accordingly," Edison said.

"It's about time," Krista said under her breath, her heart beating even faster than before.

"Now I need to see a show of hands from those who think Summer should be banished from the community."

Krista shot hers even higher into the air.

Zimmer did the same.

Liz and Morse pulled theirs down.

"Seriously?" Krista asked, not believing what she was seeing. Everyone just voted Summer guilty, yet they didn't vote to kick her out.

Edison stood from his chair. "Then we have a deadlock regarding banishment. By the established rules and procedures of the Nirvana Code of Conduct, I will now cast the deciding vote. It is hereby declared that Summer Lane will be given one more chance to conform before she is banished permanently."

Krista fired back at the ruling. "One more chance? This has to end, boss. We can't keep going down this path."

Edison banged his gavel on the desk, using added force with each strike. "The Council has ruled.

However, given the unanimous guilty verdict regarding ongoing rule infractions, some form of reprimand must be forthcoming."

Krista didn't hesitate with her response. "Since the violations involve curfew and security, then I invoke my right as head of security to decide on sanctions."

Edison nodded. "That is within your purview." He looked at the council members seated at the table. "Does anyone object?"

No hands went up.

"Then it is so declared. Security Chief Krista Carr shall render sanctions once Summer is found and returned. We shall reconvene at that time for adjudication."

CHAPTER 10

Stanley Fletcher kept his eyes low as he fast-walked a narrow trail through the mask-wearing team of welders in Simon Frost's compound.

On the left, the heat from a squad of torches warmed his skin. On the right, the high-pitched whine of grinder wheels rang in his ear, their friction sending a flare of sparks across his path.

The fabrication of new weapons and upgraded vehicle armor was well under way, and none too soon. Breaches had been mounting across their territory, sending the ire of his boss to an all-time high.

The last thing Fletcher needed was his short-tempered leader stepping closer to the proverbial cliff, but that's exactly what was happening.

Fletcher's primary focus would now be containment on all fronts, testing his ability as second-in-command. If he failed even once, he knew his job would be withdrawn with extreme prejudice. The kind of prejudice that begins with the tip of a blade and ends with a pool of blood. His blood. He'd been witness to such firings before and today might not be any different.

He closed the door behind him and walked through the next room, where two men sat at a counter covered in supplies and equipment. This area was all about powder, priming, dies, presses, and brass casings, bringing high-powered rounds back to life—7.62 rounds, mostly.

When Fletcher arrived at the closed door to Frost's office, he took a deep breath with feet frozen, wondering if Sergeant Barkley would be attending this meeting.

His mind ran through a flash of memories involving previous run-ins with the sergeant. Each instance zipped by in fast-forward motion, heightening his apprehension.

There was only one officer besides Simon Frost who was protected and completely untouchable. Beyond reproach. Sergeant Barkley was that officer. Fletcher needed to keep his temper in check and not let the sergeant get him off his game.

While Fletcher was tasked with carrying out Frost's orders, Sergeant Barkley was the only one Frost actually trusted, a scenario that Fletcher knew all too well, but one he accepted. It was better than not being part of Frost's compound, wandering the frozen landscape alone.

"I can see your shadow below the door, Fletch," Frost yelled from inside his office. "Are you coming in or not?"

Fletcher sucked in a purposeful breath, realizing he may have already pissed off his boss, simply for taking a moment to gather his thoughts. Not a good start. He turned the knob and walked in. "Sorry, chief. Got distracted for a moment."

"You really need to relax, Fletch. You're one of the few I don't have to worry about," Frost said from his refurbished barber's chair—red in color with white upholstered trim. Sergeant Barkley sat next to him on the floor.

Frost bent down and ran his hand across Barkley's back, just as Fletcher's eyes met the sergeant's.

Barkley's scar-covered snout went into a snarl, showing a bank of impressive teeth. Drool dripped as his growl went from low to high.

"Easy boy," Frost said to the blonde German Shepherd, who was now standing on all fours. Like his owner, the ratty dog hadn't had a bath in ages. Barkley's teeth were yellow, the same as Frost's, making them look related in more than one respect.

They say dogs resemble their owners. In this case, the old adage fit perfectly. Both were junkyard mutts with short tempers and a mean streak that could turn most men into mush.

Fletcher didn't know what was worse—a growling meat eater who never barked or one who drooled excessively. The animal could fill a water bowl in seconds with the foam oozing from his mouth.

Frost grabbed the sneering machine by the collar and yanked him back. The choker was strong and unbreakable, made of interlocking steel chains— the same symbol that everyone in Frost's compound had tattooed on their necks.

"Sit, boy! Now!" Frost snapped.

The dog followed the command, planting his haunches on the floor. The animal's eyes never left Fletcher's, but at least the growling had stopped.

Frost laughed. "I'm not sure what it is, Fletch, but I don't think Sergeant Barkley likes you very much."

Fletcher wanted to say something derogatory about the mangy animal but held his tongue. Dogs can sense changes in tone, mood, and intention, not just with their owner, but with guests. Guests that might end up as part of an unprovoked attack.

Fletcher swallowed a lump of saliva, forcing it down his throat. "You wanted to see me, sir?"

"Status report."

"Patrol three came up empty."

"I thought they had it covered?"

"That's what I was told as well. Apparently, they failed to contain the breach."

"Damn it. Another failure. This can't continue, Stanley."

"I know, sir. I'm on it," Fletcher answered, loathing the fact that his boss just called him Stanley. He'd tried to hide that name from everyone in the compound, but somewhere along the way, it leaked out.

"Who's running that team?"

"Slayer, sir. You put him in charge last month after we had those issues with Gronk."

"Oh yeah, that's right. My mind must be slipping."

"You're just busy, sir. It happens."

"Good thing I have you to keep the ship in order."

"I do my best," Fletcher said, knowing what his boss would want to discuss next. "Slayer is on his way. They just pulled up a few minutes ago."

Frost didn't react to the statement, his eyes pinched as he stared at the floor.

Fletcher wasn't sure if his boss heard the words. He was about to repeat them, but Frost spoke first. "Doc said the refinery won't be ready until next week, if you can believe that shit."

"Thought it was supposed to be today."

"You and me both, brother. I think he's slow-walking the upgrades just to boil my balls. He's still pissed about Shaw, I think."

"Well, you didn't have a choice with her, sir. She had to go."

"Yeah, maybe. Sometimes, my temper gets the best of me."

Fletcher could feel the tension rise in the room. So could the dog, whose teeth were showing again under a twitching upper lip.

Time to change the subject. "As for the meet tomorrow, boss, I figure two full teams ought to cover it."

"Everyone needs to be on their toes, Stanley. Edison might talk a good game about hating violence and all, but I don't believe that nonsense for a minute. Especially when it comes to Carr. She's just itching for a fight. I have a sense about these things."

"We'll be ready, sir. Count on it," Fletcher answered, holding back a grin. This wasn't the first time his boss had used that exact phrase.

Frost thought everyone was itching for a fight and did so every minute of every day. His one-dimensional thinking would eventually be his undoing, probably sooner rather than later. But in truth, it was simply Frost being Frost—projecting his true nature onto everyone he knew.

However, in this one case, Fletcher agreed. Carr was former Army and he'd run across her kind before. Proud. Focused. Duty-driven. Of course, that was back before The Event, when every country was prepping for war. Now the few who had survived needed to adjust to their new roles. And rules.

It's never easy being a warrior without a war. Sometimes, you have to start one just to create normalcy in your life. Or equilibrium. That's who Frost was—and Carr—warriors who'd rather bleed someone than shake their hand.

Just then, a triple knock came at the door.

Sergeant Barkley reacted, climbing to his feet, his eyes locked on the entrance like a hawk eyeing prey. The drool began again after the dog's ears angled back and his back arched.

Fletcher knew to take a step to the side and clear a path to the door, just in case the animal charged the entrance. It's never wise to stand in front of a fur-covered cheese grater that has a single mission on its mind.

Slayer walked in, his pace slow and measured. He swung his eyes to the dog standing at attention, whose gaze was locked onto his. Barkley interrupted his growl long enough to lick his lips, then returned to his low-pitched intimidation tactic.

For once, Fletcher wasn't the focus of the mongrel. He wasn't afraid of any man, even Frost. But a bark-less, snarling, drool machine—that was another matter altogether.

Nobody ever knew what the mutt was thinking. Then again, the same was true for Frost. Another beast that few could read.

Animals like the two of them reigned by terror but Fletcher knew those tactics would catch up to them. The question was, would Fletcher get caught up in their self-destruction or not?

"Slayer reporting as ordered, sir."

Frost ran a hand over Barkley's head, pausing to scratch the pooch's neck. The dog relaxed a bit, shifting its feet before planting its hind end on the floor.

"I understand we had a run in with one of Edison's," Frost said.

Slayer nodded. "Actually, twice sir. Once in the No-Go Zone, not far from the old skateboard park, and the other in sector two."

"I'm well aware of the first encounter," Frost said, shooting a look at Fletcher before returning his attention to Slayer. "What I'm interested in is the second. On our side of the No-Go Zone. What the hell happened?"

"We followed the target to an old cannery, where we found a blood trail leading inside. We breached the perimeter and swept the building, but our efforts turned up nothing."

"So . . . what you're telling me is," Frost said, supercharging his voice, "you lost her!"

"She's a clever girl, sir. All we found was this," Slayer said, holding out an Infinity Chain. "Belonged to the same girl we ran into before. Summer."

Frost took the chain in his hand. "What about the blood trail?"

"She must have dressed the wound. It vanished once we got inside."

"There had to be some sign of her. Somewhere."

"We checked everywhere. Twice. All we found was a section of roof that had caved in."

"Could she have been buried under it?"

"I doubt it. Everything was in the basement after the floor collapsed. Nothing but pipes and a ton of debris down there."

"Did you send a team down?"

Slayer shook his head. "We didn't have our gear, sir. Besides, nobody could have survived that. Not with half the roof on top of them plus all that equipment."

"There'd be a body at least."

"Didn't think it was worth the time, boss. If she's dead, then she's dead. What does it matter?"

Frost's reply was instantaneous: he flew out of his chair with his Ka-Bar knife drawn from its sheath. The blade entered Slayer's body before he could react, penetrating deep into his abdomen.

Slayer gasped as Frost yanked the knife upward, gutting the man from his navel to his chest. The man's insides spilled outward as blood shot out in spurts, spraying the floor with red.

Frost tore his knife from Slayer's body and stepped back as the man toppled over and hit the floor. Frost wiped the blade on his camo-colored pant leg, then stowed it back in the sheath. His tone turned resolute. "Respect. Rules. Results. Failure is never an option."

Frost sat down in the barber chair that Doc Lipton had restored, his face turning stiff like some barbaric ruler taking his perch atop a throne. He waved a hand signal at the dog.

Sergeant Barkley shot forward, tearing his teeth into the fresh meat on the floor. The canine growled as he twisted his head from side to side, tearing off a hunk of thigh meat.

Frost brought his focus to Fletcher, his tone harsh and direct. "Who's second-in-command of Slayer's team?"

"Horton, sir."

"Find him. I wanna have a chat. Time for some changes around here."

* * *

Krista Carr slipped on her tactical vest, then stuffed the pockets with spare magazines loaded with 7.62 rounds. The vest was a little snug around her winter camos, the same nearly all-white outfits her teams wore on most search and recovery missions.

She loosened the straps, adjusting where the rig landed on her hips. There was no doubt about it.

She'd put on a few pounds in recent weeks. More PT was needed. She couldn't afford to get soft around the hips, thighs, or anywhere else for that matter.

Softness equated to weakness and that was something she couldn't afford. Not when leading a security team of all men. Their eyes were constantly on her, judging her for both her command readiness and her figure as a woman.

She'd tried to downplay her sex, but she knew deep down the men would never see her as anything but a woman. A butch woman playing soldier. A woman with assets they craved nonetheless.

No more stress eating, she declared in her mind. Time for some steadfast willpower. And more running. Yet cutting back on calories wouldn't be easy, not with the sudden influx of meat in the silo's freezer.

The last Trading Post encounter with Frost had been a fruitful one for Nirvana. They'd traded battery tech for a few hundred pounds of beef—the type of meat that wasn't of the rabbit or goat variety, both of which took up residence in one of the lower levels of the silo.

It's not that she didn't like the smaller game. It tasted fine. At least they had meat on occasion, though it was rare. More of a delicacy, if she had to categorize it.

Her problem with their in-house meat supply was the lack of variety. Rabbits and goats all tasted the same to her. She didn't know why, but they did.

Krista had no idea where Frost was obtaining his beef, but it was a godsend, bringing some red juiciness to her lips. The flavor was unique and anything but gamey, each portion the same shape and thickness, roughly the size of a deck of cards.

Whatever the sweaty asshole across the No-Go Zone was doing, she wanted him to keep it up. There was nothing more satisfying than biting down on a juicy, delicious Frost burger after a long day of dealing with the crap that filled her duty roster.

Variety is the spice of life, she quipped to herself, appreciating the old saying.

"We can handle this, boss. You don't need to ride along," said her second-in-command, Nathan Wicks, a mountain of a soldier. He was former Navy and probably pushing the maximum height and weight limit for your average swabbie.

Of course, he was anything but average. He could break most men in half, hitting the weight room every day to feed his 6'6" frame with more muscle. He was already pushing the limits of the scale, but his quest for more body mass was unrelenting.

She figured some of his obsessive-compulsiveness was to cover up the nasty scar across his forehead. It ran from one side to the other and was very noticeable.

Even so, she'd never asked about how he'd gotten so disfigured. That would be crossing the line, whether she was the man's commander or not. Some things are best left in the past, especially if they are combat-related. He'd tell her if he wanted her to know the backstory.

Krista figured Wicks could chew glass and crap lightning if someone dared him to do it. That's why he was at her side in most things mission-related. A leader must have strong underlings—both physically and mentally. He never questioned her orders, until now.

Krista gave him her most intense stare. "Rest assured, my joining the mission has nothing to do with your command abilities. It has everything to do with the missing Seeker."

"Summer? Again?"

"Roger that. It's time for me to get my hands dirty."

"Pressure from above, ma'am?"

"More than I'd like. But it is what it is. We have a job to do."

Krista pulled her AR-10 from the weapons rack and inspected the chamber. No round inside. She took a magazine from the stack on the table and shoved it into the lower receiver, then pulled the charging bolt back and released it with a snap.

She thought about the six mags in her chest rig, wondering if they'd come out again while on mission, meaning contact with hostiles. Either a herd of Scabs or some of Frost's men.

If the mags did get deployed in action, then it would mean Summer's tardiness would probably cost someone their life. Whether it was on her side or Frost's, it would be Summer's fault.

CHAPTER 11

Supply Chief Rod Zimmer entered Edison's lab and held up a loose stack of paperwork. "We need to talk, Professor."

"Well, hello to you too, Rod," Edison said, standing near a two-foot wide pane of glass being held upright by a stand on a lab table. He waved a hand at Zimmer. "Come here. I want to show you something.

Zimmer didn't have time for another one of Edison's Show and Tells. He shook the paper in his hand as he walked to Edison's position. "This can't wait, sir."

Edison ignored his request, pointing an index finger at the center of the mini-window. "Does anything look out of the ordinary to you? Anything at all?"

Zimmer pretended he was interested, scanning the object with a quick swipe of his eyes. "Nah. Looks like glass to me, except for those wires sticking out the side."

"Exactly," the professor said. "That's the idea. Nothing but glass and electrical leads. But what you don't see is that I've applied nano-layers of polymetric solar cells. It's my own special blend of metallic hydrogen and liquid graphene. The layers are completely transparent, yet highly efficient at converting light into energy. And not just on one set of wavelengths, either. I call this invention HGS, or hydro-graphene solar. It's a roll-on application that produces electricity at levels never before thought possible. Its quantum efficiency is off the charts, Rod. Off the charts."

"I'm not sure what all that means, but it sounds amazing, Professor. But we do need to talk—"

Edison didn't wait for Zimmer to finish his sentence. "This new technology can turn any glass surface into an electricity-producing super array, the likes of which the world has never seen."

"What's left of it," Zimmer quipped, his interjection unplanned but perfectly timed in his mind. Sometimes, he couldn't help himself, taking subtle shots at those with a singular vision. And Edison wasn't the only one.

Edison let a smile loose before he continued. "Imagine what happens when we apply this to our surface mirrors that direct sunlight into the silo bay. Not only will they feed our hydroponics, but they would also convert a sizable portion of that light into power. The potential is endless."

"Yes, sir, it is," Zimmer answered, running through a number of scenarios in his mind. Edison wasn't the only senior citizen who still planned for the future, though Zimmer's version wasn't anywhere close to what Edison had in mind.

"Especially if I can somehow trap more of the light and process it multiple times through some type of refractive prism technique. Ideally, I'd like to split the sunlight into at least eight different wavelengths, then create nano-layers that are specifically designed to convert each of those wavelengths into electricity."

"Impressive. I'm sure it'll help with our power requirements."

"And then some. Our community needs to evolve in order to stay secure and survive, Rod. That means we need backups. You can never have enough backups. And by that I mean, multiple ways to generate power and store it."

For the out-of-control population increase you are pushing, Zimmer wanted to say, but didn't. "Of course, boss. Options are key. We all have to plan for the future."

"It would be the Holy Grail of solar power, Rod. Right here. In Nirvana. This new process would pass on the specific wavelengths of light the plants need, but also convert the rest of the spectrum into electricity. We'd be looking at close to eighty percent efficiency. Possibly higher. It would lessen our dependency on the generators when the storms swell, and that means less dependency on Frost and his diesel."

"Damn cool, sir. But can we talk? It's urgent."

"Right. Right," Edison said, moving to a lab stool. He spun and planted his rear end on the seat. "I'm all ears."

Zimmer gave the top sheet of paper to Edison. "Look at items four and eight. What do you see?"

Edison took the list and studied it. "Barbie dolls and a box of LEGOs."

"Toys. On a department's needs list. Those are not allowed."

"Technically, no."

Zimmer shuffled through three more sheets of paper, making his point visually by holding the paper up and pointing at it. "Plus, there's more. I see art supplies. Mystery novels. And a bunch of other crap. This is getting out of control."

"I understand your concern. But I don't see why we can't make an ex—"

"With all due respect, sir, the rules are the rules. Seekers need to focus their efforts on food and supplies. Items the community actually needs to stay alive. Not all this personal crap."

"I hear what you're saying, Rod. But some of our citizens are going to have special requests now and again. Especially the families with little ones."

"I get that, but not toys for their damn kids. This is ridiculous. Can you imagine losing one of our Seekers because they went after a bunch of useless toys? First, there would be an uproar across the ranks, then everyone else would flood our lists with even more stuff that just takes up space and doesn't help anyone stay alive."

"Yes. Yes. Of course, you're absolutely right. But a few toys here and there would help with morale. So would art supplies. Or books. I'm sure you've read the signs I've had you hang around the complex."

Of course he had. He wasn't blind. Or oblivious as to what was happening in the shadows. He could hear the whispers, like everyone else on The Committee. "Yes, sir. I have."

"Well, there's a reason. I'm sure you've heard your share of complaints from some of the newer residents."

He could have agreed, but chose not to, not for any particular reason other than he felt like it. "Actually, I haven't. But then again, I'm not out there chatting like you every day."

"I mingle to get a pulse on morale. It's an important aspect of life in our community. Happy members equal productive members."

"But does that extend to their kids? With toys?" Zimmer asked, wondering why this man never focused on the more pressing needs, like food, security, or sanitation. His myopic view of the silo was going to be his downfall. And everyone else's.

"Sometimes, yes. People have needs, Rod. Needs that are outside the norm."

"You mean outside the practical and tactical. Things that keep us all alive."

"Yes. We must always have compassion and be willing to make an exception or two. It's all part of tending to the flock. Like the Good Shepherd would do."

Zimmer held back his true sentiment about compassion—that it was for the weak-minded and unprepared. He needed to spin it a different way, one that wouldn't offend the founder. "Makes sense on paper, sir. But with all due respect, I disagree. Not in the long run. We have limited space and our Seekers need to produce. Hunting down personal items is a gigantic waste of manpower."

"And woman power."

"Of course, woman power, too. But it's a risk we just can't afford to take. We must stay focused every minute of every day, especially with the increase in Scab activity out there."

"Now you're starting to sound like Krista."

"Well, she's right. Everyone's lives depend on it. It's our job to keep this place running smooth and everyone safe. That's more important than a temporary boost in morale and certainly more important than toys. More so now than before, with our increase in numbers."

Edison hesitated for a good twenty seconds, running a hand over his chin. "Yes. Yes. I see your point. Maybe I'm the one who needs to adjust on occasion."

Zimmer was pleased he finally broke through the ideology of their leader. "Can you make an announcement to the ranks? They'll listen to you."

"Sure. I'll take care of it in my next public address. Thanks for bringing this to my attention."

"That's my job, sir."

"And we appreciate all your efforts, Rod. Is there anything else?" Edison said, giving the needs list back to Zimmer.

"No, that about covers it," Zimmer said, turning for the door. He walked out, organizing the paperwork in his hand, while his mind drifted into analysis mode.

The professor's new solar technology might change the balance of power so to speak, which on paper was a good thing for Nirvana.

Yet he wasn't sure if it was a good thing for his stake in the future, a future that might also need adjusting, depending on what happened next with Frost, Krista and the Scabs. So many variables, all of them adding to an uncertain future. A future in which he needed to have some level of control.

* * *

Edison waited until Zimmer closed the door, then sent the rolling chair back several feet toward his work desk with a shove of his feet. His body spun ninety degrees thanks to the swivel seat, bringing him around to face a picture of his wife, June.

The photo showed her standing next to her prize-winning rose garden with tattered jeans on, plus a tie-dyed t-shirt, work gloves, and trimming shears in hand.

It was his favorite picture, the sun glistening off her bob of short gray hair. Her infectious smile was sustenance for his soul, even in a two-dimensional photo.

Sometimes he'd sit there with hands folded, staring at her for hours on end, hoping for her wisdom to somehow ooze across the desk and fill him with insight.

Edison picked up the cracked picture frame and brought his face close to it. He moved his spectacles up to free his vision for a close-up view.

He loved the gentle wrinkles around her soulful eyes and her turned-up nose, even through the broken glass of the frame.

Her subtle beauty brought a warm feeling to his chest, one that he missed dearly. He knew the day he met her that he'd always feel this way.

His eyes wandered down to the Infinity Chain hanging in front of her shirt. She'd fabricated the necklace only a week before the picture was taken.

It symbolized everything she was about—an infinite   future   with   peace,   tranquility,   and compassion for all. The same ideology he'd built Nirvana on, hoping each resident would learn to embrace it as well.

Tears welled in his eyes as he brought his lips to the picture and gave it a soft kiss. He put the photo back on the edge of the desk, angling it toward him.

"I'm trying June. I really am. But I'm afraid I'm failing you. Things are starting to come apart and I'm not sure what else to do. I know I'm supposed to find a balance between the rules and compassion like you taught me, but it's not working. It seems like every decision I make backfires in some way."

He sobbed for a short minute, then collected himself after a blow of his nose into some tissue.

"I miss you, darling, more than you know. If only you were here. You're so much better at all this political stuff than I am."

CHAPTER 12

Summer woke up on her left side in a jolt. Even though her eyes were open, all she saw was black. It took a few seconds for her mind to catch up to what she was sensing.

Her legs were bent at the knees and her left arm was out straight, with her right hand draped behind her. The throbbing in her cheek was intense, but that was the only pain other than the sting of cold. The chill was everywhere, but even more so underneath her rib cage pressing against the ground.

A moment later, her memories came alive, showing her a series of events. The vision started with her feet tripping over the pallets. Then the faceplant and cheek injury. Her mind's eye flashed a view of the cannery and conveyor system, then it changed to show the hole in the roof with water dripping down through it. Then she remembered hearing the loud bangs from the building's door, right before the roof collapsed.

That's when the answer hit her—she'd fallen through the floor. Shit.

Now she was here—wherever here was. It must have been a basement below the cannery's production room. Somehow, though, she was still alive.

Summer ran it all through her head again and again, trying to understand how the collapse could have happened. It took several minutes of pondering, but one answer did come into focus—the water dripping from the roof must have weakened the floor, allowing it to cave in when the rest of the ceiling came tumbling at her.

It made sense, given the lack of deep water around her feet when she walked to the middle of the conveyors. Water must have been seeping into the subfloor ever since the thaw started, rotting the support structure over time. When Slayer and his men started banging on the door she'd leveraged shut with the dolly, it must have shaken the ceiling loose, bringing the rest of it down on her.

Summer twisted her body so she could slip off her pack and bring it around in front of her. She unzipped the main pouch and put her hand in, fishing around until she found the waterproof matches. They were next to the can opener and the fork she'd used earlier.

There were only three matches remaining, one of which she ran across the ignition strip on the side of the box. The flame roared to life, giving her a view of her surroundings.

When her eyes came into focus, so did a spread of colors above her—diffused white with a plethora of browns, grays, and blacks mixed in.

She looked down to see snow—lots of it. It must have cradled her fall. What a stroke of luck, much like the flat section of roofing above her. It was about four feet away and the size of a pickup truck, angling from high to low. It acted like a shield, keeping the rest of the debris at bay.

Just then, a rush of air came at her from the side, making the flame dance. She whipped her head around and peered into the darkness, moving the match farther away from her body.

There appeared to be a crawl space, but the light only extended a few feet beyond the flame. She couldn't see much else past that point.

Regardless, stiff air movement meant a possible means of escape. She needed to follow it.

When the flame burned close to her fingers, she blew the match out, then dug into her pack. She felt around for the candle and took it out, along with the fork. It took a bit of force, but she was able to jam the tines into the bottom of the wax, making a mini-torch she could carry by the handle of the fork.

Another match lit the candle wick, leaving only one remaining in the box. Four matches weren't enough, she decided, thinking of Krista's fixed allotment before every mission. Summer planned to raise a challenge to the limit, assuming she made it out of here alive.

Summer put the matchbox in the pouch, closed the zipper, then wrapped one of the straps on the backpack around her left foot, securing it using an over/under loop technique.

She towed the pack behind her as she crawled on her belly, the makeshift torch leading the way. The first few yards were easy, allowing her to slide forward a few inches at a time. If she were any bigger, her body would have gotten stuck in the narrow space.

The candle flickered when the air flow changed again, but it didn't stop her advance. The crawl space angled to the left, taking her to the first obstacle—a section of electrical conduit pipe, bent at the middle with wires sticking out of one end.

She grabbed it with her free hand and tugged. It wouldn't budge. She tried pushing it straight ahead—again no luck. Only one choice remained—sideways force.

Summer took a deep breath and let out a grunt as she sent all her strength into her arm, shoving the metal to the left. The pipe twisted as it rose up about a foot, almost as if it had been buried in such a way as to act as some kind of cantilever. She didn't care why it worked, just that it had, giving her the space to proceed.

The tunnel widened ahead, taking her past another section of conduit, only this one was lying free and didn't contain any wire. She pushed the bent pipe out of the way and continued, her path remaining clear for another ten feet or so.

That's when she came upon another obstacle—on the right this time. One of the control boxes for the canning equipment had landed there. It was still attached to a length of conveyer assembly, with a colorful array of wires hanging from it.

There was also a pile of boards with nails sticking out. It was on her left—2x6s mostly, crisscrossing each other in a random pattern. Yet that wasn't all.

Broken pieces of plywood stood a little farther to the left, acting like a dead-end wall. She tugged and pushed at the control box, the conveyor, and the boards, but none of them moved. It felt like they'd been cemented into place.

Damn it. So much for her luck. She was stuck like a sardine in the ice. At least the air was able to find its way through the wreckage. It felt fresher than before, though still cold as it entered her nostrils.

There was no doubt in her mind. The way out was dead ahead—through the obstacles and into the wind. Probably not far, either, but this part of the debris wouldn't let her pass. She'd come so far, only to fail a few feet from freedom.

Her heart sank. So did her head, coming to rest on her outstretched arm.

Was this it?

Summer's End?

She lay there for a minute, feeling the strength wane in her body. She didn't want to admit it, but the facts were clear. She'd done all she could but there was no way out.

Dread took over, screaming at her to make peace with the facts—death was coming for her.

She exhaled a breath, knowing that no one would ever find her body. She'd become one of those human popsicles she despised, doomed to languish here for all of eternity. Even the Scabs wouldn't find her. Not under a pile of debris and ice.

"Wait a minute," she mumbled, as a new idea tore into her mind. Her heart raced with energy. "Ice! That's it! A sardine under the ice!"

Summer rolled onto her back and brought the torch up, pushing it close to the ceiling above. All she saw was the color white on this side of the control box.

If the cannery's floor had collapsed around a central point, then maybe it fell into a mound. Mounds get thinner as you move toward the edge, like she had. If she was right, then perhaps the area above her was not very thick.

The flame from the candle began to melt the hard-packed snow, dripping near-freezing water onto her chest. A chill soaked through to her skin, but she didn't care, even if her new plan took a while. As long as the candle kept doing its job, she'd deal with the aftereffects.

Just then, a drip of water snuffed out the flame. "No! No! No!" she snapped as blackness took over, showering her in a void of nothingness.

Her mind reeled when she realized that only one match remained. It was all that stood between her living and dying. A single match. There had to be a better way to do this.

Summer pulled her leg forward, dragging her pack along with it. When the strap reached her hand, she tugged the backpack forward, unwrapped it from her foot, and opened it.

Inside, only a handful of scarves remained, each a different color. She pulled them out and held the soft cotton in her hand, working through various scenarios in her head.

The marker chalk, picture frame, rubber wheel, and half-full water bottle didn't give her any ideas. They seemed useless.

So was the Seeker Map. It was untouchable. Krista would demand that it be turned in when Summer returned from the mission. Failure to turn in your paperwork was a guaranteed way to get sanctioned—whether you were Edison's favorite or not.

That left her with only the can opener, a bunch of crayons, the paracord, a stick of beef jerky, the metal container with the bubble-wrapped trinket inside, some cotton twine, and two cans of tuna. Not exactly a wealth of tools. Or options.

What she needed was a way to melt the snow pack without risking the heat source being snuffed out by dripping water.

A more powerful torch was the only answer—something that would be impervious to an unexpected flameout.

The wide base of the candle would allow it to stand on its own, so she pulled the fork out of its base and put the candle aside in the dark. She took the lone remaining match and ran it against the side of the box. Her heart skipped a beat when it didn't light, sending her hands into a tremble.

Summer sucked in a deep breath and tried again, applying more force against the strip. The flame roared to life in a brilliant flare, then settled into a steady flame.

She cupped her hands around the tip to protect it from any unexpected air movement, then held the fire to the wick. When the candle sprang to life, she let out the breath she'd been holding.

She leaned back to admire the tiny flame dancing before her eyes. It was the key to everything. Nothing in her life had ever mattered more. Not even the precious memories of her long-lost sister Hope and dead brother Blaze.

Just then, panic set in when her mind flashed a vision of snow falling and burying the candle. Water drips weren't the only threat. She needed a secondary light source.

"A girl can never have enough backups," she mumbled without thinking, channeling one of Edison's favorite sayings.

She dumped the contents of her pack into the snow, then moved her eyes to the pair of tuna cans. Their labels were the same and read: *Chunk Lite Tuna in Sunflower Oil.*

The word *oil* brought a new idea to mind. She used her teeth to chew through a length of cotton twine, splitting it into two segments, one of which was two inches long.

Next up, the can opener.

She used its sharp tip to penetrate the center of the can, making a hole about twenty percent smaller than the end of the twine. She took the twine and stuck it into the hole, forcing it deeper and deeper into the tuna until only a half inch was visible. "That ought to do it."

Summer held the can sideways over the candle until the homemade wick took the flame. She watched the fire burn its way down the string and enter the hole she'd made. A second went by, then two, then ten and the flame held, thanks to the sunflower oil inside.

"Gotta love that shit," she said, feeling damn good about herself. She leveled the can and put it several feet away, separating it from the candle.

"Now for the tricky part," she muttered, her hands taking turns picking up each item from her pack and pondering its use. A few minutes passed before an idea sprang to life, bringing a smile to her lips.

It took some creative body bending to turn around in the tunnel with the candle in hand and then crawl back to the two-foot-long piece of pipe she'd passed earlier. But she made it happen.

She grabbed the pipe, flipped another U-turn, then headed back to the control box and conveyor blocking her path to freedom. The conduit she'd scavenged had a thirty-degree bend roughly three inches from one end.

Summer grabbed a handful of crayons and placed them next to each other around the end of the pipe, with their tips pointing up and away from the bend. So far so good—she just needed a way to secure them.

The paracord and twine were the most logical choices, but they'd burn when exposed to fire.

Likewise, so would the cotton scarves. Something noncombustible was needed.

That's when her eyes found their way to the electrical wires hanging from the control box.

She inched forward and brought her mouth to the longest of the shielded wires, biting down on the casing closest to the control box. Once her teeth hit the copper inside, she angled back and pulled the rubber off to expose the wire.

Since there wasn't a knife or pair of cutting pliers handy, she needed to liberate the wire the old-fashioned way—by working it back and forth until fatigue set in and the wire broke free. A minute later, that's exactly what happened.

She wrapped the wire around the crayons, starting from the bottom up, keeping the wraps close together and tight until half the length of crayons was encased in copper.

It was time to test her invention, but first she put the other items back into her knapsack and zipped it up. If her idea worked, she'd need to work quickly and there wouldn't be time to pack.

Summer held the tips of the crayons to the candle flame. Almost instantly the crayons caught fire, showering the area with more light than expected. The flame from each crayon was at least ten times brighter than the flames on the candle and tuna can. The sheer size of each crayon flame and the number gave her hope this new plan might work.

The bend in the pipe allowed her to hold the new torch at an angle to the snow, giving her better access and keeping most of her body away from the freezing water. As the snow melted, she used the can opener in her other hand to dig her way out, one inch at a time.

CHAPTER 13

Security Chief Krista Carr waited for the personnel transport truck to navigate the last corner and come to a stop in Summer's assigned Seeker grid, then she opened the door and shot out, landing both feet in the dirt.

Her men did the same, then gathered around her in silence, their eyes keen and attentive.

She also kept silent, using only hand signals to deploy her men in teams, aiming her fingers in the direction they were to follow.

They did as she commanded, taking off in sprints, leaving her alone with the truck and its subtle engine whine.

She leaned inside the vehicle and turned the ignition off. Every ounce of battery power was priceless, which was why she stowed the keys in her pocket—to thwart any unauthorized engine starts, especially now that the sun was asleep for the night. Headlights burned through more energy than a daytime rescue mission.

Krista walked to the front of the truck and stood with one boot on the bumper as she unfolded her area map and laid it across the hood. At least the moon was full, giving her some light to work with and avoiding the need to turn on her LED headlamp.

Krista ran her finger down the paper, bringing it to the southeast corner of Summer's assigned area. She studied the layout and contours of the grid. "Where the hell are you, Summer?"

There were several alleys to check, as well as a long string of industrial buildings that seemed to be squeezed in like pack rats, all of it dense and all of it laden with blind spots.

Ambushes could happen anywhere, even with Scabs and certainly with Frost's men, if they chose to cross the No-Go Zone. Regardless, it was going to be a long night.

Thirteen minutes later, one of her men doubled back and came to her position, stopping a foot away on her right. It was O'Neil, a curious but loyal man she handpicked for this assignment.

She didn't address him right away, letting the slender, dark haired man hang in silence to set the tone before she spoke, not because it was procedure. More so out of spite. Spite against the universe and her own fate. She didn't agree with this rescue mission and wanted everyone to know about it, even if she did so without words or a verbal protest.

"What do you have for me, O'Neil?"

His deep-toned voice was crisp when he said, "Team Two cleared both streets to the west. Moving on to the next block."

"What about Teams One and Three?"

"Haven't reported in yet, ma'am."

"Any Seeker Marks?"

"Negative. Team Two reports all doors are clear."

"What about secondary marks?"

"Windows are clear as well. If the target worked this area, she didn't mark her progress as required. No infinity signs anywhere."

"Well, there's a shock," Krista said, rolling her eyes. She had no idea if Summer had worked this area and forgotten to follow procedure with her marker chalk, or if she had skipped this section altogether. It was also possible the girl never made it here in the first place.

This is why Summer needed to be banished. Rules exist for a reason. They can save your life when followed or they can end it when they are ignored.

Now Summer was putting the lives of others at risk, looking for her skinny ass in the middle of the night and in an uncontrolled sector of town.

She brought her attention to O'Neil. "I want you to head over to Team One's position and find out what's going on. Then check on Three. Report back on the double."

The man didn't hesitate, turning in the dirt and sprinting with a tactical vest loaded for bear. He carried his assault rifle in a firing position as he moved, giving Krista hope that at least one of her team might make it out of here alive.

* * *

Summer jammed the can opener into the melting snow pack above her, expecting to hit more resistance, as had happened ever since she'd started the dig out.

When her hand poked through the snow in a sudden lurch, it scraped against something about a foot beyond the hole. She cried out in celebration and in pain as a fresh batch of air came rushing in.

She yanked her arm back and let the torch melt more of the snow around the opening until it was about a foot wide.

There was something running left to right across the opening. It might have been wood, or perhaps metal; she couldn't tell in the diminished light. However, it was round and she could reach it.

Her chest filled with a sudden rush of energy, allowing her to punch at the snow around the hole, making it wider on one side. The rapid-fire impacts stung her knuckles, but she didn't care, working faster than she ever thought possible.

A few strikes later, the hole was oblong on one side and shoulder width, allowing her to put down the torch, then bring both arms up and grab hold of the round object. She pulled herself up and out of her tomb, dragging her pack along by the straps she'd tied to her foot.

Once her legs were clear and the pack was too, she rolled away from the opening, spinning like a log. When she came to rest, she was on her back with her eyes peering up at the missing cannery floor above. Beyond that opening and another floor up was a gaping hole in the roof.

There were stars, but not as many as she expected, probably due to the full moon washing out a portion of the night sky. Regardless, freedom never looked so amazing.

Summer brought her hands together in front of her chest and mouthed the words, "Thank you."

Now all she had to do was figure out how to get out of the basement and up to the cannery's production floor.

She sat up and looked back at her would-be tomb—more specifically, at the pole she'd grabbed onto to pull herself free.

That's when she realized it wasn't a pole after all. It was the handle of push broom. She didn't remember seeing a broom in the production area before, yet there it was, exactly where she needed it, lying on top of the other stuff that had fallen through from above.

Talk about lucky. What were the odds?

That's when she saw them. Footprints. Two sets. One leading to the broom and one leading away.

Summer unhooked the straps of her pack around her foot, then got up and went to inspect the prints, checking the edges with her index finger. They were clean, perfect edges and soft to the touch.

Someone had just been there.

Her heartbeat shot up, adding pressure to her chest as she followed the tracks leading away from her. They took her under the edge of the hole in the production floor. That's where the tracks stopped.

She looked left, right, and behind, but she didn't see anyone. If someone was with her, she couldn't see them, reinforcing the notion that the someone was gone.

Whether they were still around or not, it didn't change the facts. Whoever it was had just helped her climb out by placing the broom handle above the hole.

Her mind went into analysis mode, working through the scene.

She'd been buried deep and unless someone had been tracking her and stayed close, they would not have known where she was under all that debris. Not unless they heard her scratching at the snow with the can opener or had seen the light from the crayon torch just beneath the surface. Either way, that's when they took action with the broom.

Given the sudden halt to the tracks, a rope must have been used from above. It was the only explanation, other than some kind of ghost had walked to this spot and then flown away.

A rope would allow a quick descent to place the broom, then a fast retreat. If she was right, then this person was a friend, not a foe, only helping for a moment.

They weren't looking to take her into custody or do her harm. Therefore, it wasn't any of Frost's men, that was for sure. Nor was it the Scabs. They would have stuck around for dinner.

Summer put her foot inside her helper's prints in the snow. They were at least six inches longer. They belonged to a man. A big man.

"The Nomad," she mumbled, wondering if he might still be around, hiding in the shadows somewhere, watching her.

She craned her neck up and cupped her hands around her mouth before adding volume to her words. "If you're still here, mister, thank you!"

She waited for an answer, but none came.

He must have taken off. That's why nobody knew who The Nomad was. He never stuck around after helping those in need.

She thought about it for a moment and realized his tactics made sense, assuming he wanted to remain anonymous. If that were true, he would never remain to chat with those he saved.

Too bad he didn't leave her his rope; then she could climb out in a snap. He must have figured she could do it on her own. Or perhaps he was needed elsewhere, heading out in a hurry to go help someone else.

Either way, she had to figure this part out on her own.

Summer went back to her pack. After a quick check of its contents, she slung it over her shoulders, then looked up.

The floor above was a good twenty feet away. Even if she scaled the highest point of the debris that had almost crushed her to death, she still wouldn't be able to reach it.

It was too bad, too, because there was a section of conveyor just beyond the edge of the missing floor. If she could get close, there would be plenty to grab, allowing her to pull herself out.

Her eyes went in search mode, but she didn't see anything she could use as a ladder. There was plenty of twisted metal and of course, snow and ice, plus some broken lumber, exposed wires, and other odds and ends. But nothing she could use to build a pyramid of boxes and climb out.

She opened her pack and took out the bundle of paracord. It measured roughly a hundred feet in length, but without being tied to something sturdy on the next floor up, it was basically useless without a grappling hook.

Some of the metal wreckage in front of her would work, but only if she had a blow torch or hacksaw. She'd need to cut off a section of conduit and bend it, or do the same with one of the metal support struts lying about.

The crayon torch she'd made might have helped, but she'd left it behind without thinking. And since there was no chance in hell she was going to push her luck and climb back down into that hole, she'd need to figure out a different plan.

That's when she remembered the caster wheel.

She snatched it from her pack and held it up for inspection. The weight was good and she could tie the paracord to its axle fork, just below the ball-bearing swivel. So that's what she did, using a few extra knots to make sure it would not come loose.

Now that the wheel was attached, she swung the rope in a series of vertical circles, like a cowboy preparing a rope trick. After the fifth revolution, she let the wheel fly, sending it straight up.

It clanked hard against one of the legs of a conveyor, making a horrible pinging sound, then bounced off. Gravity took over, sending it straight back at her, making her duck out of the way.

Summer picked up the wheel. "Come on, girl. You can do this."

She prepped the paracord again, swinging it the same as before. This time when she let it go, she aimed higher, setting the lariat free from her hand a split second sooner and with more force.

The wheel took flight, soaring above the edge of the conveyor with the paracord trailing behind it. A second later, it disappeared from view, clanking again when it hit something beyond her view.

Summer yanked on the rope.

It didn't budge.

That was the good news. The problem was, she didn't know how secure it was on the other end. She'd thrown it too far, landing out of sight. Now it was stuck and she couldn't bring it back for a better shot.

There was only one way out—straight up.

It was now or never.

She wrapped her hands around the cord and began to climb, praying the makeshift grappling hook would hold.

* * *

Franklin Horton gave his newly-acquired patrol the hand signal to move ahead, working in four sets of pairs along the south side of a partially demolished store called the Liquor Barn.

He could see inside the smashed windows from his position. Several snow drifts remained in pristine condition, protected from the sun's reach by the shadows. No obvious footprints.

The plan was to sweep each building, checking every inch for signs of their intended target. Unlike his predecessor, the late Slayer, Horton believed in caution before advancing.

Slow is steady and steady is fast.

Simon Frost had given Horton a clear set of objectives—take command of Slayer's unit and find the girl named Summer. Bring her back to him alive.

Horton didn't need Frost to lay out the penalty for failure, either. He already knew the answer, thanks to what he witnessed in Frost's office at the time of his promotion to team commander.

The blood and guts being cleaned up on the floor were all he needed to see. Well, that and the mangy dog chewing on a spiral of intestines, working a gory hunk of Slayer through its teeth and down its gullet.

"Team One, left flank. Two, you got right. Three, cover our six. Four, you're with me," Horton said in a whisper a few minutes later, after they had cleared the accessible parts of the liquor store. He waited for the members of his team to respond with a head nod, then advance outside.

They moved in concert and with purpose, turning a corner onto the next street with rifles, packs, climbing gear, and attitudes in tow. Just ahead was the old LaDean Cannery—the last place they'd found signs of the girl.

Even though Horton knew Summer had a head start, the cannery needed to be searched from top to bottom. All he needed to find was a footprint or a blood trail. Something to indicate which way she went.

Then they'd have her, assuming she was injured like the evidence had suggested on their previous mission.

CHAPTER 14

"Almost there," Summer told herself in a grunt, feeling the sting in her hands from the paracord. Her arms felt like limp noodles, almost ready to quit. But her heart wouldn't let them, convincing them to press on.

Two more yanks and a final leg push brought her to the opening in the bottom of the production floor. She took a deep breath, then grabbed hold of a bent angle bracket hanging from a floor-mounted support strut.

She assumed it used to secure some kind of equipment—equipment that was now buried in the mound of wreckage below. The bracket was the closest item within reach, allowing her to pull herself up and scoot out of the hole on her backside.

Summer pushed to her feet, then brought her eyes around and followed the paracord in search of the caster wheel. When she found it, she took a step back in a gasp, realizing it had caught itself on the very edge of a red-colored push knob on the front of a control station, somehow remaining there under the weight of her climb.

It only took a slight amount of sideways force to release the wheel, verifying that she'd gotten beyond lucky with the way that thing had held on.

A part of her half-expected to find the wheel wrapped around a sturdy machine and tied in a wrap-around knot—a parting gift from the Nomad. Since the wheel wasn't hanging on by much, that obviously wasn't the case.

Summer shook her head, realizing she just escaped certain death—again. Had she known how weakly the wheel was attached, she might have chickened out with the climb.

"Ignorance is the fuel for cowards," she said, channeling something that Security Chief Krista had once said. Summer didn't understand what that phrase meant until now. You'll never chicken out if you think you're safe.

Summer brushed off her clothes—not because she was covered in dirt or snow. It was more out of habit, allowing her mind to formulate the next step in her plan as she arched her back, taking a few moments to peer up through the open ceiling in the cannery.

The moonlight showering the room gave her a sense of awe as it washed over her face and caressed her body. Maybe it was because she was still alive, despite all that had happened today. Most who ventured into the Frozen World alone and encountered deadly scenarios failed to return. Yet here she was, still alive and breathing.

Technically, she didn't believe in the almighty. However, if she did, she would have been certain at that moment that he was there, watching over her. Just as the Nomad had done.

"Time to rock and roll, Summer," she muttered, pulling her focus from the night sky.

First up, stow the grappling hook she'd made, then figure out where to head to next.

She wound the cord around her arm, wrapping the entire length in a tight circle until the caster wheel landed in her palm.

Then she brought her pack around and fished out her Seeker Map before stuffing the wheel and cord inside.

Twenty steps later, she was on the far side of the room, standing in front of a stainless steel table at one end of the conveyor system. It was in front of a massive piece of equipment with a control arm and some kind of spring apparatus attached to a belt-driven pulley.

The flat surface may have been an infeed table. Or a sorting table. There was no way to know for sure. Not that it mattered. It looked to be large enough to hold her grid map, so she unfolded the paper and spread it out for a quick survey.

It took a minute to find the bridge she'd used to cross the No-Go Zone on her way to the bookstore. She figured she'd run about a mile into the territory owned by Simon Frost.

Granted, she was in a panic at the time, but she was certain it wasn't any farther than that. She'd passed a string of warehouses and an old skateboard park, which the map indicated was near a street named Valencia.

Summer figured Krista had probably sent out a search team by now, deploying them to her assigned grid, not far from the No-Go Zone. It was standard operating procedure when a Seeker was late for debriefing after a mission.

And she was late—very late. There'd be hell to pay when she got back, especially if the search team spotted her in or leaving Frost's territory. It was one thing to get lost on Edison's side of the No-Go

Zone, but it was an entirely different problem to trespass into Frost's section of town.

Summer needed to take a wide route across the No-Go Zone, just in case one of Krista's search teams was nearby. If she kept to the shadows where the moonlight couldn't reach, she'd see them before they saw her. At least, that was the theory.

If she was able to make it back to the silo before the others, she could sneak into the complex using the emergency air shaft, then hide in her bed in the storage closet. Nobody ever went in there, knowing it was her space and off limits to everyone but her.

All she'd have to do is claim that she'd gotten back hours earlier and gone to sleep, forgetting to check in upon her return. It wouldn't be the first time she'd used that excuse, nor the last. Besides, admitting to a small goof is better than getting caught making a large one. Small mistakes never got anyone tossed out of Nirvana, not with Edison's tendency to forgive most errors.

"Should work," she decided after running her little white lie through her head again. Her plan was sound, assuming she was careful on her way back to the silo.

Summer reached inside her sweatshirt to pull out the Infinity Chain and kiss it for luck, but her hand came up empty. Nothing but air inside.

"No! No! No!" she cried out as her hand went back in and swept left to right in a fury, searching the skin around her neck without success.

The chain wasn't there. She'd lost it. Somewhere.

A heavy pressure slammed into her chest. Edison would be pissed. He'd never forgive her. The breath in her lungs evaporated as she spun on her heels and scanned the area beneath her feet. No sign of the trinket.

Her mind flashed a series of events, each one a possible location where the chain had fallen off.

First, the trip over the pallets and painful face-plant that tore a hole into her cheek. Then the sudden fall through the floor when the roof collapsed, leaving her buried under the snow. The vision finished with her crawl under the debris and her dig out through the snow.

The keepsake could be anywhere.

She turned and stared at the hole in the cannery's floor, debating if she should retrace her steps to find it, starting with her crawl out from under the ice.

"Hold it right there!" a man's voice yelled from her left.

Summer flinched after turning a step.

"Don't you move, missy! Hands up where we can see them!" the same voice said.

Summer froze in her tracks, her eyes moving toward the voice as her arms went up.

The beat in her chest ran wild, seeing nine men with rifles pointed at her. They were Frost's men, none of them wearing sleeves, about twenty yards away, near the same entrance where she'd tied the dolly to the worktable.

An instant later, they began to spread out in pairs, working themselves around the equipment with their rifle sights trained on her. There were a few sections of the conveyor system standing between her and them, most on the other side of the gaping hole in the floor, giving her a few seconds to think.

A voice inside her mind yelled *RUN!*

Summer ducked for cover and took off, heading away from the patrol using a hunched-over running style, zigzagging her course.

She expected the Neanderthals to open fire, but they didn't. There were no commands from their leader, either, almost as if this encounter was planned in some way. All she heard was the clatter of their boots hitting the floor.

Her mind couldn't let go of the fact that Frost's men hadn't started shooting. Maybe they were out of ammo and couldn't shoot, or possibly they weren't allowed to shoot.

If either was true, she had the advantage. The threat of force only works when the risk is credible. If they weren't going to shoot, then she had nothing to fear, other than getting caught.

The wall section dead ahead didn't have a door—at least not that she could see. She turned right and kept low with her feet moving, searching the area ahead for an exit.

The equipment in this section of the cannery was different from the paraphernalia she'd been buried under from the main production floor. This section had huge machines with handles and doors along the farthest wall, stacked next to each other with almost no space in between.

Each one had an overhead vent, probably for some kind of heat-related finishing work, she guessed. Two of them reminded her of exhaust hoods over a stove; tapered at the highest point, but fat and wide near the bottom. The rest were thin with a curved end that fed into long stretches of rectangular sheet metal, much like the ductwork she'd seen in the silo.

Before her next step, her mind flashed a sudden thought, showing her a snapshot of her Seeker Map lying on the flat infeed table.

Damn it!

She'd left it behind.

Summer stopped her feet, turning her head in the direction she'd just come from. Maybe she could sneak past the men and snatch it, assuming they hadn't found it already.

It took another second to realize her idea was not only a mistake, it was most likely impossible. Even though Krista would be super pissed at her for losing the map, it wasn't worth getting herself killed in the process.

Summer resumed her trek, wondering if the Nomad might still be around and watching. If so, would he step in and help her? Something inside told her the answer was no. She'd never get that lucky twice.

Deep down she knew he was gone, off to save someone else. Or else he didn't want to tangle with Frost or his men. The Nomad carried a pair of swords, but they were useless against the range and power of assault rifles, according to Krista and constant preaching about weapons and ballistics.

Right then, another phrase came tearing into her mind—one that Krista had had drilled into her. *The only way to stop a bad guy with a gun is a good guy with a gun.*

Summer passed a yellow plastic tub with roller wheels. It was about three feet tall and twice the size of a bathtub in length and width. She could see inside as she moved past the container.

It was filled with gloves, most of them blue and torn in at least one spot. Finger holes were the most dominant defect. Plus there was also a smattering of masks mixed in—the same type she'd seen Liz Blackwell use in the infirmary.

There was a door ahead, just beyond a stack of empty storage units. Well, almost empty. The scattered remains of shredded boxes and torn paperwork sat on some of the shelves, almost like someone had detonated a grenade inside a box of old reports.

Three fifty-gallon drums hugged the wall between the door and the shelves. They were blue, like the gloves, and made of plastic. She wondered what was inside but didn't have the time to stop and pop their lids. If she ever got back this way, she needed to check them out. Perhaps they contained something worth scavenging.

She grabbed the door's lever-style handle and pushed it down. The latch released after a metallic click, letting her swing the door open and see outside. Freedom was only a step away.

Summer wasn't sure why, but she decided to glance back along her path. It was probably the pull of her Seeker Map. It was all by itself, wondering if she'd abandoned it.

At least there was no sign of the men yet. So far, so good; however, she knew they'd be there any second.

It was time to make a run for it.

CHAPTER 15

Franklin Horton waved Team Two forward on his left. Team Three was already in position, driving the target toward the far corner of the cannery to keep her hiding spots to a minimum.

Teams One and Four had remained behind to cover their unit's six in case the girl somehow managed to elude their pursuit and double back.

The adrenaline in his chest confirmed what his mind was thinking—somewhere ahead was a clever adversary. She'd already given them the slip once, and her ingenuity had cost Slayer his life.

Unlike Slayer, Horton wasn't about to underestimate this girl, not when his life was on the clock. Failure was not an option for any commander under Frost's rule, and there was zero chance this girl would cause the end of him.

Every cell in Horton's body told him she was close, hiding in the shadows, probably watching his every move. But the sheer amount of equipment and the poor lighting conditions forced him to advance with caution.

He wasn't sure if the girl had an ambush planned. It was possible, given the extensive amount of time she'd spent in this location after their last encounter. Ambushes can come at you from any angle, especially when you are not familiar with the sector being swept.

Horton worked his way around the hole in the floor and caught up to Team Three, nestling in next to the shortest of the two men, Sketch—all 5-foot 9 inches of him—a 39-year-old dark-skinned man who doodled when he was bored.

Sketch tilted his cover up with his free hand, revealing his receding hair line and buzz cut. The black man with a dimple in his chin gave Horton a folded piece of paper. "Found this, commander."

Horton opened the paper and scanned it. It was a map of some sort, with grid lines and numbers. The No-Go Zone was clearly marked.

"Important, sir?" another man asked him in a guarded whisper.

"Probably," Horton said, his eyes moving from the map to the redhaired man who ran with the nickname of Dice. His long, flaming red locks made him easy to identify and remember. So did his perfectly white teeth and athletic frame.

Dice was relentless when it came to his morning jogs, claiming he pounded out eight miles a day. However, since nobody else ever tagged along, that fact couldn't be verified.

Even so, Horton had no reason to doubt the 44-year-old, wondering if Dice jogged as often in his former life as a dealer in Las Vegas. Dice was in fabulous shape and was more than capable of defending himself.

Horton had seen it first-hand when they first encountered the Scabs as a unit, and Dice used lightning-fast Karate moves to take out a slew of the crazed cannibals.

The man's unique backstory was easy to remember because of the Karate Master that Dice had studied under—a feisty female Sensei who was also a world champion. Someone named Pam Poland that he'd first met at a trade show in Vegas back in the day.

Horton brought his attention down to the map, studying it for a few more seconds before folding it up and jamming it into his front pocket.

"Orders, sir?" Sketch asked, the index finger on his left hand resting on the trigger guard.

Horton didn't respond, his mind working through the facts.

His eyes swung up, peering through the opening in the ceiling, wishing the full moon was overhead for better light. Flashlights were out of the question. They'd give away their exact position. Active flashlights in tight quarters are how good men become dead men.

When his focus returned to Sketch, he pointed at the towering machine ahead and whispered, "Cover me. Going to higher ground."

"You got it, boss."

Horton kept low as he advanced to the apparatus, then slung his rifle over his shoulder.

One side of the machine fed horizontally into the conveyor system, allowing him to use the platform as a middle step. He worked his body up and grabbed the top ledge of the apparatus. The unit's cover was made of metal and didn't feel hollow, possibly sturdy enough for his weight.

He pulled himself up and swung his legs beyond the top edge, then brought his torso and head over. The surface bowed a bit at the middle, but held as he scooted forward.

A second later, his rifle was off his shoulder and nestled into a firing position. He flipped the lens cover up on his 3x42mm IR scope, then turned the unit on. Hopefully, the battery wouldn't run out of juice today like the last time he'd used their one and only night vision scope.

Doc had said earlier that it was fully charged, but one never really knew with that man. Sometimes Doc flat-out lied to avoid work he didn't deem critical or couldn't repair.

Horton brought his dominant eye to the enhanced multi-coated optics and peered inside. He could see the illuminated red duplex reticle, meaning both the battery and the device were functioning. He adjusted the incremental brightness setting for max exposure, adapting to the ambient light in the building. Once set, he began a scan, working left to right, looking for heat signatures.

His search came up empty. If the target was still in the building, she wasn't in his line of sight. He scanned for another minute, then hopped down and returned to Team Three.

"Let's move," he told Sketch and Dice, waving an advance signal at the others across the way. Team Two advanced in lock-step with Horton and Team Three, keeping their rifles pointed in the same direction as their eyes.

A line of industrial grade ovens with exhaust hoods above them was next, then a rolling tub of safety clothes—gloves mostly, plus a few protective masks.

Horton used his hip to nudge the container back, pushing it toward the wall to make more room for his team to pass. It was heavier than he expected, bringing a sudden thought into his mind.

He paused with his eyes locked on the tub, then put a closed fist up to stop his team's advance. A quick head nod in the direction of the container told his team what he wanted them to do.

Dice stepped forward, while Sketch provided cover. Dice brought his rifle up and stuck its barrel into the gloves, stirring the contents like soup, working from left to right. When Dice was done, he looked at Horton and shook his head, then removed his rifle from the container.

Horton rallied the squad with the signal to proceed ahead, back on their original course. That's when he spotted a door ahead. It was just beyond a stand of shelving units holding random hunks of cardboard and what looked like confetti paper.

By his calculations, the door was the most likely exit. If he was correct, it would explain why his night vision scan turned up zilch. The girl must have left the building. The question was, how big a head start did she have?

A sudden vision of Frost's Ka-Bar knife entering his gut flashed in his mind. There wasn't any pain, but plenty of blood. He held silent, vanquishing the scene from his mind, then pointed at the members of Team Two to take the lead.

They responded with a head nod before marching forward, taking a measured route with knees bent and eyes locked.

Teams One and Four closed ranks behind him, setting up interlocking fields of fire just as they'd been trained by Fletcher.

Horton was pleased to see his unit working with such precision. He figured the news of Slayer's demise had reinvigorated everyone to perform at optimum levels, exactly the way the former military man, Fletcher, had trained them.

Before the Scabs showed up, training was mostly what they'd done, other than lock down the border around Frost's camp and provide security for their monthly meets at the Trading Post. Well, that and party like fools once Doc built the old-fashioned wood-fired still.

As Teams Two and Three approached the door, three 50-gallon drums greeted them. They were positioned along the wall in a series—each of them blue, with a lid sitting on top. Horton caught the attention of Dice and Sketch with only his eyes, then directed them to check the contents.

The first to react was Sketch. He stepped forward to the first drum and put his hand on the edge of the plastic lid.

Once Dice was in position on his left with his rifle held high, Dice pried the cover loose and leaned forward with his eyes behind the sights and peered inside. He didn't fire. "Clear."

Sketch moved to the next container and removed its lid. This time the plastic drum rocked an inch or so, signaling it was most likely empty. A second later, Dice had checked its interior and cleared it as well.

Horton waited as the pair moved to drum number three and repeated the same process. This time, though, Sketch pried the lid loose and Dice scanned inside. Dice looked at Horton and shook his head.

"She's outside. Let's move," Horton said as Teams One and Four joined them from the rear, crowding in tight with gear and weapons.

Once again, the girl was a few steps ahead of him. A girl who was apparently better at this than Horton was—at least so far.

* * *

When Summer heard the door close and the handle rachet itself into place, she waited a while longer, listening for the sound of boots, equipment, or frustrated men.

All was quiet, so she unwrapped her feet from the overhead water pipe, being careful not to catch her clothes on the spray heads attached underneath the cavernous hood.

It was at that moment when she understood how a koala bear felt while hanging upside down under a tree branch—without all the fur and total cuteness, of course.

She kept a firm grip on the pipe as she lowered her legs, but in the process, the backpack she'd stowed on her belly fell. It skimmed the side of the stainless steel exhaust hood and slammed into the equipment below, making a pinging thud.

Summer brought her legs up in a lurch, keeping her eyes peeled at the equipment below. There was a chance the men chasing her had only pretended to leave the building. If so, they would appear below with rifles at the ready.

Ten seconds ticked by. Then thirty. And finally, a minute. She thought about waiting longer to be sure, but her stomach muscles were getting tired. She couldn't hang there all day. It was time to chance it.

She let her feet dangle, this time aiming them to the outside of the pack that had slipped free. She let go of the pipe and dropped out from underneath the hood, landing on the surface below.

Her eyes scanned the area in a flash—no sign of anyone. A smile crossed her lips. "Good thing men can't think three-dimensionally."

A wave of pride washed over her, filling her with hope. If she got really lucky, she just might make it back to the silo in one piece.

She scooted off the machine and plopped to the floor with her pack in hand, then slung it over her shoulder and took off.

From the sound of it, her decision not to hide in one of the plastic drums was the right choice. So was skipping the rolling tub filled with gloves. The men had checked both locations, identifying them as prime hiding spots.

Her plan was to retrace her path through the cannery and see if her map was still where she'd left it, then head out the same door she'd come in originally—the one by the mess of pallets that had torn her cheek open.

Who knows, maybe she'd even spot her necklace somewhere along the way.

CHAPTER 16

When Summer arrived back at the silo, the twinge in her gut told her that her troubles weren't over. In fact, the sensation gnawing away at her insides was screaming just the opposite—that her problems had just started.

She knew as well as anyone that word traveled fast in an eight-story coffin made of rebar and stink, meaning most everyone had to know she was late. Again. All the whispers. All the hatred. All the disapproval.

Even so, she was used to it—the gossip, that is. And her reputation. In a way, her unpopular image was what made her different. And different was good when your days were strung together with the same conversations with the same people who all do the same things day after day after day.

She flushed the negative thoughts as she finished her descent down the air shaft that fed the silo, stepping off the last rung of the ladder. The towering cement chute was also the emergency exit, though she doubted many in Nirvana knew it existed.

At least her long trek was officially over, bringing a pressure release across her chest the moment her knees found their way into the short tunnel that led into the back of control room through a hatch.

In truth, you're not really safe until you've made it home—all the way home—with both feet and your ass intact. Somehow, she had, despite everything that had happened in the past 24 hours.

Edison had placed trees, rocks, and bushes around the access point on the surface. He feared someone might use the air shaft as an entry point, like she had done many times, including today.

In fact, it was so well hidden that if Edison had not showed her its location ten years earlier, when he first brought her to the silo, she never would have found it on her own.

Back then, it was just the two of them after June died, right before Edison started recruiting others to join his new project.

Summer wondered if the Professor even remembered showing the access to her, given all the years that had passed. Likewise, she didn't think the others in the silo knew about the air shaft, its ladder, or where it led. But then again, she hadn't asked anyone, wanting to keep the secret a secret.

The passage allowed her to come and go undetected, or save a ton of time when she didn't want to deal with the hassles of a multi-step check-in process through a series of heavy, vault-like doors. Today was one of those days—she knew Krista would be standing behind the last blast door, wearing a scowl on her face.

The way Edison explained it to Summer, the US Air Force built the Titan II Missile Silo with redundancy in mind, including allowing the rotating two-man teams to escape the facility in case of a catastrophic event.

Apparently, such an event had happened back in the 1980s at the Damascus, Arkansas silo—an exact replica of the one Edison had purchased and refurbished as Nirvana.

If she remembered correctly, a careless maintenance worker dropped a five-pound socket wrench down the eight-story missile bay, tearing a hole in one of the liquid fuel tanks near the bottom. The rupture eventually led to a massive explosion several hours later, sending the silo bay doors airborne.

The air shaft was the entry point for the rescue crew during the Damascus crisis, at least until the complex blew up in spectacular fashion.

Summer couldn't remember how many people were killed, just that some had been. Death tends to make those in power rethink their plans. In this case, it led to the closing of all Titan II silos around the country, with the brass declaring the facilities archaic and obsolete, replacing them all with a new kind of missile, one that didn't use liquid fuel as the propellant.

When she ran it all through her head, she came to one conclusion about death versus destiny. If it weren't for a socket wrench accident, Nirvana never would have come to be. All those who lived in Edison's cement cave today would have died along with most of the planet after The Event, including her.

"Thank you, Mr. Mechanic," she mumbled, scooting her frame through the hatch that took her into the abandoned missile control room.

Edison told her the equipment in this area was technically classified as *computer* equipment, but the tubes, wires, knobs, and switches were ancient—from the electronic dark ages. She couldn't believe any of this junk ever worked, let alone could deliver such fire and fury clear around the world.

When she walked past the controller's chair, something caught her attention from the left, giving her pause. She turned and saw one of incandescent bulbs flashing on the console. It was a few inches below the red phone that hung vertically. Everything else in the room appeared to be dead, typical for this unofficial museum that Edison told her stood as a 'testament to never-ending government paranoia.'

Summer leaned in to take a closer look at the lettering under the light. It was faded, leaving only two letters remaining: a C and an S, but they were not close together. Could mean anything, she decided. Probably sparked to life by some random surge of electricity. Or perhaps, someone had been in this room recently, tinkering with the crap that hadn't worked in decades. Either way, it didn't mean squat to her. She needed to keep moving.

Once in the hallway, she passed two Nirvana members she didn't recognize. One was a heavy woman with a chest that hung down to her waistline; all of it moving like a bowl of Jell-O. The other was a tall, skinny man with no teeth. He had to walk hunched over to avoid his head clanking against the pipes overhead.

Summer made two more rights and a left before she found the storage closet she called home. She opened the door and went inside, putting her hand up for the pull chain she knew would be there.

A quick yank turned on the only light. She sidestepped her lumpy foam mattress on the floor and stood in front of the mirror hanging at an angle on the wall. One of its corners was cracked, but the rest of it was useable, even if it was only a few inches wide and twice as tall.

When she uncovered her hair, it sprang to life, sending out a web of tentacles like an octopus on amphetamines. Normally, she would take a few minutes to run a comb through her mop, but at the moment, she was too tired to care. What she needed was a good night's sleep and some food. Oh, and a good excuse as to why she was late.

Her eyes found their way down to the bandage across her cheek. It was full of blood. She was tempted to tear it off, but she didn't have a replacement.

As much as she hated her hair, walking around with an open gash on her face would be worse, especially in the humid, recycled air of the silo.

It seemed like there was always someone in Nirvana who was coughing up a lung or sneezing snot everywhere, especially the kids. They were walking petri dishes, touching everything with those germ-filled, busy little hands.

It was pretty obvious to her that viruses spread rapidly in air-tight quarters, a fact that Edison didn't seem to realize. Or maybe he did, but didn't care. About half of the time, he'd come back from a trip to the Trading Post with another family in tow, adding to the already crowded conditions.

Summer understood the man's desire to help those in need, but there had to be limits. Edison couldn't save the world—what was left of it anyway.

At least the handwritten sign on her door that said KEEP OUT was working. There were no signs of entry into her private space. Everything was where it was supposed to be, despite the lack of a lock on the door.

As Krista liked to say, everything was in a pile and there was a pile for everything. Not that Summer cared. Her mess was still her mess and that was all that mattered.

She kissed the tip of her finger before touching it lightly to the faded photograph stuck to the edge of the mirror. The tape holding it in place had lost some of its grip, but it was still doing its job, mostly, clinging to life like most everyone else on the planet.

Summer ran her finger around the outline of her older sister, Hope, who wore a fancy dress and even fancier makeup. Her outfit was all white with lace trimmings, a perfect complement to her blonde hair that was done up nicely, working its way into a twisted fray that rose eight inches above her head.

Hope stood next to their amazing brother Blaze, with Summer on the other side of him, all three locked arm-in-arm, looking the part of the happy siblings.

Little did Summer know at the time, but that would be the last time she saw her brother Blaze alive. An IED would take him out once he returned to active duty a short while later. No warning. No mercy. No chance to kiss him goodbye with a peck on the cheek. One day, he was just gone. Dead. Blown into a million pieces.

At least her nightmares about him crawling around in the dirt of Iraq looking for his legs had stopped. That haunting took years to fade, but it finally had.

Blaze was older than Hope, six years to be exact. He looked proud, standing in his polished lieutenant's uniform, his hair high and tight and waist trim.

Even after all this time, she missed her family more than anything else. More than chocolate. More than a warm bath in a private room. More than her own seat in the back of the library where the building's heating system worked to control the temperature.

Her long-lost family was an open wound, one she knew would probably never heal, no matter how many times she convinced herself to push past it and suck it up, like Krista always said to do.

The gash on her face was bad, but nothing compared to the pain in her chest. While one of them would never heal, the other would, but only if she took care of it before it got infected. That meant a trip to go see Liz in the infirmary and get a little TLC.

A quick turn of her heels and a fast walk took her from her room and down the hall. Her backpack was now over one shoulder instead of two as she worked her way past the mess hall and down the green corridor that connected the silo to the control pod.

The medical bay was a few minutes away. Hopefully, Liz would be there so Summer didn't have to go looking for her, increasing odds of a run-in with Krista along the way.

The first ladder was clear, allowing her to make quick work of the painted rungs to the next floor. Her feet hit the deck in a clank of galvanized metal. The catwalk was narrow, but she was able to work her way around the outside of the hydroponics bay, using the handrail to keep her balance.

A window on her right gave her a priority view of the plants, mirrors, and grow lights hanging inside what used to be the missile bay.

Edison's genius was on full display—the greenery was in full bloom. Summer wasn't a huge fan of vegetables, but they were growing on her.

A girl's gotta eat, even if it's nothing more than tasteless rabbit food. Yuck.

Two kids were up ahead—a boy and a girl—sitting on the floor near a ninety-degree corner in the hallway. Summer wasn't sure where their parents were, but at least they weren't crying. If she had to guess, neither of them was more than five years old.

"Have you seen my mommy?" the blond-haired girl asked when Summer arrived, her voice soft and adorable. The boy remained quiet, staring at Summer with his baby blues blinking rapidly.

The two looked related, though the boy had curly red hair, so maybe not. Summer bent down on one knee, feeling compelled to comfort the kids, especially at this hour of the night. "No honey, I haven't. Are you lost?"

"Mommy told us to wait here until she got back."

"How long ago was that?"

The girl shrugged.

"What's your name?" Summer asked her.

"Emily."

Summer looked at the boy. "And who might you be?"

"That's my brother Josh," the girl said, tugging at Summer's sleeve.

Summer ignored the yank. "I'm Summer," she said to the boy, hoping he might speak.

The boy giggled but didn't respond.

Emily yanked again on Summer's sleeve and spoke in her little girl's voice. "What happened to your face, Summer?"

Summer looked at her, not wanting to scare the child with any of the gory details. "Oh, nothing really. Just had a little accident, which is why I'm on my way to see the doctor right now."

"I don't like the doctor," the girl said. "It always hurts."

Summer scanned both intersecting hallways but didn't see anyone. She needed to get moving but didn't want to leave these two children alone.

Just then, a man appeared at the end of the hallway, far beyond the girl. Summer pointed, then asked Emily, "Is that your dad?"

"No. We don't have a daddy."

Summer's heart sank, knowing what these kids were going through. She didn't have a dad, either. Or a mom, for that matter. In fact, if it weren't for Edison and his wife June taking her in after her parents were killed, she would have spent her younger days in a foster home.

Life throws a ton of grief at everyone, but Summer felt like she'd had more heaped on her than most.

First some terrorist took out her older brother Blaze. That was bad enough, but then Hope ran off to college and disappeared, only days before a car accident that claimed the lives of her parents.

Sometimes she felt like the Universe had decided to focus on her and her alone, unloading on her life with more grief than any newly minted teenager should ever have to deal with.

Summer decided these kids needed a friend and someone to watch over them, just like Edison and June had done for her.

She took off her pack and unzipped the main pouch. Her hand went in and pulled out the crayons she managed to save after her ordeal in the basement of the cannery. She split them up, giving some to Emily and some to Josh.

"What are these?" Emily asked, sniffing the wax.

Obviously born after The Event, Summer reminded herself quietly. They'd missed out on all the cool stuff, like video games and cotton candy. "They're called crayons. You draw with them."

Emily grabbed her brother's arm and ran the crayon across his skin in a zigzag pattern. Nothing happened. The girl's face scrunched in frustration.

Summer couldn't help but laugh. "No silly, like this," she said, taking the girl's hand and making the letter X on the cement wall with the tip of the crayon.

"Oh, cool," Emily said as the man in hallway walked past, taking a left and vanishing a short minute later around another corner.

The boy started to draw on the wall but stopped as his eyes went wide. He pointed. "Mommy!"

Summer brought her eyes around in time to see a slender redhead closing fast with a shoebox in her left hand.

Summer got to her feet.

The woman arrived in a huff, never making eye contact with Summer.

"Here you go," the mother said, giving the box to Josh. She grabbed both kids by the hand and tugged. "Come on, it's bed time."

Summer watched Josh and Emily being towed away, wondering why the woman seemed so pissed. All Summer was doing was keeping the kids company. No harm in that.

A moment later, precious little Emily looked back over her shoulder and waved at Summer just before the family turned the corner and vanished. Just like Hope had done.

The gesture brought a tear to Summer's eye.

CHAPTER 17

Summer was about to knock on the door to the medical bay, when it opened on its own, bringing Doctor Liz Blackwell face to face with her.

"Hey Doc," Summer said, wondering what kind of reaction she'd get.

The doc's eyes locked onto the makeshift bandage on Summer's cheek. "What happened to your face?"

"Got into a fight."

"With who?" Liz asked, escorting Summer inside, leading her to the edge of an examination table.

"Not a who, Doc. A what. Tripped over some stupid pallets and landed on one. I came around this corner and boom. Never saw them until it was too late."

Summer put her pack on the floor before she spun and sat down. The paper down the middle of the table crinkled under her weight, sliding a few inches to the rear.

Liz peeled the bandage back with a gentle hand. "Is this why you're so late? Did you lose consciousness?"

"Uh, yeah. Lost consciousness. That's what happened. How did you know?"

"It's my job to know these things. Did you clean the wound before you dressed it? You had water with you, right?"

"Nah, there wasn't time. I was kind of being chased."

"Chased? I thought you said you tripped and fell. Then lost consciousness, which is why you're late."

Summer stuttered a bit, then answered in a hurried tone. "Well, they were chasing me, but I'd lost them for a bit before I fell. Don't think I was knocked out for very long. I was able to run inside this old cannery and hide in one of the machines. Had to wait until they left."

"Frost's men?"

Summer didn't want to admit her run-in with Frost's people, not when she was on their side of the No-Go Zone. A better version of the facts was needed—something that everyone would believe and never bother to check.

"No, some ugly Scabs. Took forever before they left. Thank God they're not too bright. It's easy to hide from them, if you know what you're doing. For a while there, though, I thought maybe they could smell me."

"Smell you or the blood?"

"Both, I guess. My next shower rotation isn't for a few more days."

"I'm just glad you're back safe and sound. I know the Professor is worried sick. You need to go see him when we're done here. I'm sure he wants to talk to you."

"I will. Promise."

"Looks like you're going to need some stitches. I'll keep them small so they don't scar. A pretty girl like you never wants that."

Summer appreciated the kind words, but the last thing she thought of herself was pretty. Plain was more accurate, if she had to judge herself.

Besides, worrying about your looks after the world ends is pointless. And dangerous. Pretty girls are bigger targets when you have a run-in with men like Frost. It's better to look scary or even repulsive, so they think twice about wanting to put their hands on you. "Thanks, but I really don't care about a scar. It'll make me look bad ass. Like Krista."

"Speaking of Krista, she's out there looking for you."

"For me? Really? Not one of her teams?"

"She went with them. She's not happy with you at the moment."

"So what else is new?" Summer quipped after a roll of her eyes. "I'm pretty sure she has it in for me."

Liz worked quickly to apply a cleaning agent to the gash with a cotton swab.

It stung like hell, but Summer didn't react.

Liz put down the gauze. "The Professor will fill you in on the rest, I'm sure."

"Rest of what?"

Liz didn't answer, her hands beginning work with a needle and thread. "Let me know if the pain gets to be too much."

"I'll be fine, Doc. Do what you need to do," Summer said, holding firm as more pain hit. Each stitch pulled at her skin, but she wasn't about to flinch. Not even a little. Only girly-girls flinched. And that she wasn't.

"That ought to do it. Good as new," Liz said when she was done a few minutes later. She applied a fresh bandage, pressing gently along the edges where it was sticky. "You need to keep this clean and dry.

In fact, I want you stop in every day so I can check for infection and apply some ointment. It'll help with the healing process."

"Cool. Thanks," Summer said, hopping off the table. She grabbed her pack and put it on the table. The zipper was still open from her encounter with the kids. She pulled out the glass picture frame and held it up. "This is for you. I found it when I was out."

Liz took the frame. "It's gorgeous."

Summer pointed at Liz's desk. "Figured you could use it for that photo of your dogs. I know how much you miss them."

Tears came to Liz's eyes, then a smile to her lips. She hugged Summer. "Thank you. I just hope you didn't put yourself at risk finding this for me."

"Wasn't really looking for it when I found it. But the second I saw it, I just knew I had to bring it back for you."

"Well, you didn't have to."

"I know, but I wanted to. You always take good care of me, so I wanted to let you know how much I appreciate all you do. For everyone around here."

Liz gave her another hug. "I love it. Thank you."

When the doctor let go, Summer asked, "So how mad is the Professor? You know, on a scale of one to ten."

Liz hesitated. "I'd say about a nine."

"Whoa, that's not good," Summer said in a matter-of-fact way.

"You've put him in a tough spot."

"I know. I screwed up. Again. But this time, it really couldn't be helped."

"Just tell him the truth and I'm sure it will be fine. Krista is the one you need to worry about. But like I said, the Professor will explain it all to you."

Summer kissed Liz on the cheek. "Thanks for the repairs, Doc."

"Anytime. Now don't forget, come see me every day until that heals."

"I will. Promise," Summer said as she turned and walked to the door.

Today hadn't exactly gone according to plan, but at least she didn't have to worry about running into Krista in the hallways—for a while at least. There were still plenty of things to do before that woman caught up to her. Important things.

After a short walk, Summer stood in front of the door to Alexander Morse's lab, her eyes face to face with his name stenciled on the placard, just below Nirvana's Infinity Logo.

Morse was Engineering Chief and in charge of both communications and technology, two areas of expertise the silo desperately needed.

Summer ran her fingers through her hair, trying to control some of the crazier strands, then gave up. She didn't know why she even bothered, but it seemed like the right thing to do before knocking three times. She couldn't wait to see the look on his face when he saw her gift.

"Come in. Door's open," Morse said, his deep tone filling her heart with glee. Some men's personality and body type matched their voice, but in Morse's case, they didn't. He sounded like a big, powerful man, but in reality, he was a total cupcake. A feeble grandfatherly type. The kind that smells like mothballs and too much humidity.

When she entered, she found the round-cheeked, gray-haired black man standing, with the aid of his walker, in front of one of his many grease boards that had been attached to the walls around his work area. Each board contained a combination of handwritten notes, diagrams, and calculations.

The board in front of Morse at the moment featured rows of mathematical equations, none of which Summer understood. He'd written them in red marker ink, unlike the other boards that contained blue ink.

The right-hand side of the red-inked board also held a column of numbers—nine to be exact—with three letters scribbled above them as a column header: E. O. D.

A single red line had been drawn underneath the bottom-most figure, then the number 35 had been written and circled three times. Must have been a total, she figured, even though it didn't match the summation of the numbers above it.

Across the room was a pair of worktables, one with a broken shortwave radio transmitter sitting on it. A spread of electronic parts she recognized sat in a cardboard box next to it.

The other table was a new addition and empty. One of its folding legs was bent at an odd angle, making her wonder how it was able to remain standing. Sort of like Morse and his walker. Broken and bent, but still functional. Mostly.

The rest of the lab was how she remembered from her last visit. Neat. Tidy. Everything in its place.

"Oh my God, you're back!" Morse said, turning his walker around in a flash of movement. It was missing a wheel on one of the legs, forcing the old man to move unevenly across the room. She worried he might topple over, given his age and health problems.

After he arrived, he gave her a powerful hug, squeezing her tight. "I thought something terrible had happened to you."

"Nah, just ran into a little bad luck, that's all."

"You can't keep scaring us like this."

"Wasn't my plan, but sometimes things happen out there. Like today when I—"

Morse let go and put his hands up, motioning in a hurry. "Wait. Don't tell me. I don't need to know. As long as you're back safe and sound, that's all that matters."

Summer twisted a lip and let sarcasm fuel her words. "Well, it's nice to know at least one person missed me."

Morse narrowed his eyes, his tone turning sharp. "I hope you know that's not the case. We all love you, Summer. We really do."

She blushed for a moment, then regained her self-control. "I appreciate that, Alex, but I doubt everyone cares like you do. Krista, for one. That bitch totally hates me."

"Trust me, we all get worried and we all care. Even Krista. It's part of being a real human being. When you're old like me, you'll understand. Everyone is your son or daughter. You can't help but want to protect them."

A smile energized her lips. Somehow Morse seemed to know exactly what to say to rid her mind of worry. Maybe it was his age. Maybe it was his disability. She didn't know. In truth, it didn't matter. He was a kind man and the silo needed more like him. Plus, he never stunk. Not in a bad way. Just those mothballs. A huge plus.

Summer took a step back to make room for her backpack to swing around without hitting him. Once it was on the floor, she bent down to fish around inside. "I've got something for you."

"Really? For me?" he answered, rubbing his hands together like a kid waiting for a present. The only way to describe his tone was *bouncy*—a stark contrast to his usual baritone, steady voice.

She held back a chuckle, enjoying his playful side. "Just a little something I picked up at the store while I was out. Finally found it after months and months of shopping. Boy, are my feet tired. Those malls are huuuuuge."

He laughed, wobbling on a pair of unstable knees, balancing between the legs of the walker. His hands were extended, palms up. "I'll bet."

"You have no idea," she quipped, as her fingers latched onto his gift.

Morse continued their charade. "And if I know you, I'd lay odds that you got a smoking deal on it, too. Probably used up all those coupons you've been saving."

"Oh yeah. A great deal. In fact, the best one ever. Just wish the lines at the checkout counter weren't so long all the time. Why is it that no matter when you go to store, a busload of old ladies and their blue hair always seem to beat you to the line and hold things up? It's a conspiracy, I tell you. Like they plan it or something, just to piss everyone else off."

Morse laughed again, his eyes still in anticipation mode. "Okay, so what did you bring me?"

Summer paused for a few beats, letting the tension build before she pulled out the caster wheel from her pack with a sweeping theatrical flair, holding it up like a magician at the end of his trick. "I'm guessing this might just help fix your walker."

He snatched it, his eyes bulging. "Where on Earth did you find it?"

"If I told you, I'd have to kill you," she said, laughing.

He tested the bearing, spinning the rubberized wheel around its axle.

Her giggle vanished before she added, "Hopefully, you can make it work. I know it's not exactly the right size, but—"

"Thank you. It'll work. Just need to thin down the pin to fit. Shouldn't take long," he answered, giving it back to her. "You hold on to it for me. I've got something important to show you."

She followed him past the empty worktable, taking the opportunity to put the wheel on its surface before they arrived at the equipment table next to it.

Morse moved his walker out of the way and sat down in the chair facing the radio. He shot a look at the shortwave transmitter, raising an eyebrow. Its microphone was missing, as usual.

Summer was slammed with a new thought. "Don't tell me you got it working!"

"Almost. Just a few more tweaks and it should be good to go," Morse said, flipping its power switch on. The device roared to life, its lights blinking, and cooling fan whirring.

"Should I get the microphone?" she asked, knowing he kept it stored in a drawer along the back wall.

"Not until I fix the transmitter and it's ready to go. Don't want to jinx it, now do we?"

"No, of course not."

"Patience is a virtue in all things we do."

She nodded in a matter-of-fact way. "Trust me, I remember."

"We'll plug it in when it's time. Not a moment before."

"Yep. Makes sense," she said, even though she didn't believe in the whole patience is a virtue thing. Not when Scabs are chasing you. Patience is the last thing you want.

He tapped an index finger on the box of parts sitting nearby. "By the way, your last score really helped."

"Awesome. I just grabbed that stuff. Wasn't sure if any of it would work."

"Well, it did. You have a great eye, my dear."

"Yeah, as long as I can get that stuff past the backpack Nazi. You never know with Krista. Sometimes she checks and sometimes she doesn't."

"I don't know if you've heard or not, but she's on the warpath."

"I heard," Summer said in a downtrodden voice, pointing at her cheek bandage. "Liz told me."

Morse nodded. "Did she also tell you that there was a Council Meeting while you were gone?"

"What kind of meeting?"

"Not the good kind."

"About me?"

"Yes, but Edison will have to fill you in. He let it be known that you are to report to his office the second you're back."

A twinge of pain hit her chest, making her struggle for air. A few breaths later, she asked, "Any chance you can talk to him for me? You know, smooth it over."

"Not this time, I'm afraid."

"That bad, huh?"

"Yep," he said, turning off the radio. "Even I can't fix certain things."

She blew out a long, slow breath, letting the air roll across her lips. "Great. This is gonna suck."

"Just be honest with him, regardless of what happened out there. Honesty is always the best policy."

She wanted to change the subject before Morse became even more disappointed in her. "So when do you think you'll make the first broadcast?"

"Soon, I hope. Gotta figure out a couple more things."

"Can I be here when you do?"

"I don't see why not," he said in a cautious voice.

Summer recognized his tentative tone and knew why. "I know. I know. You gotta clear it with the boss first."

Morse nodded. "He's never been real keen on letting others know we exist."

"What if Edison says no?" Summer asked.

"Then I'll probably fire it up anyway. We need to see who else might be out there," he said, glancing at the grease board with the calculations written in red.

"Now who's breaking the rules?"

"Sometimes, they need to be broken, for the greater good."

"Except when I do it," Summer quipped.

"Too often, my dear. Patience wears thin."

"I try really hard, but it seems like no matter what I do, it all goes haywire."

"I think you and I both know you could do better. Just space out the rule breaking a bit, then people won't get so upset."

Summer nodded, realizing Morse was correct, as usual. "I *have* been pushing it a bit lately. Especially with Krista. I just hate that she's always telling me what to do and how to think. She's always on my case."

"I understand. I'd push back, too. But you need to work it out with her before things get outta hand. Trust me on this."

"Okay, I will. Promise."

CHAPTER 18

Summer waved a quick goodbye to Morse and left his work area, closing the door behind her. Edison's office wasn't close, giving her a few minutes to formulate her summary of what had happened on today's Seeker Mission.

Morse suggested she tell the truth, giving her the whole "honesty is the best policy" speech—the same speech she'd heard a million times when she was little, back when she still had a family—a real family, not some adopted group of strangers who were packed together and living underground like a bunch of zombie gophers. She hated the books of hers that contained stories about zombies—decomposing a little bit each day, despite their best efforts. Almost like the Scabs, though they were real.

Summer figured Liz would want her to tell the truth to Edison, too, but the truth didn't paint a good picture of her recent activities. Maybe she could soften her mistakes, spinning them to become lesser failures in Edison's eyes.

The Professor was like an uncle to her and she couldn't bear to disappoint him. Not when he'd saved her from a horrible existence after her family vanished from her life.

She knew she couldn't please everyone all the time, but there are certain individuals in everyone's life that rank above the rest. They are the people that matter—the ones you can never disappoint. Not when you depend on them for your very survival.

Summer adjusted her backpack so the straps weren't cutting into her shoulder, wondering if the Professor was still awake at this hour. Liz and Morse had been, but that was no surprise. They were workaholics. So was the Professor, mostly, but he'd been known to crash early some nights, like old people do.

When Summer made the first corner, she came face-to-face with another person, bumping chests.

It was Security Chief Krista Carr.

"There you are!" Krista said, latching onto Summer's arm with a wicked two-hand grab. The powerful woman tugged hard, yanking Summer off her feet.

"Let go of me!" Summer screeched, but Krista kept her grip tight, dragging Summer down the hallway, her feet trailing behind in a skid.

Summer tried to break free, but the former Army soldier was too tall and too strong, the veins in her biceps bulging like twisted rope.

Krista continued down the corridor, her combat boots marching with purpose. "Do you have any idea what you've put us through, young lady? We've been out there looking for you all night. Do you know how dangerous that is?"

Summer was able to get her feet under her, though now she was stumbling forward in large steps instead of being dragged like a sack of flour. "Yeah. I'm sorry. Ran into some bad luck. Just look at my face."

"I don't want to hear any more excuses. We are *way* past that. The Council has ruled. Your skinny ass is mine now."

Summer thought about throwing a punch, but Krista was too well trained and outweighed her by at least sixty pounds. Maybe more. Probably wouldn't make a dent in that thick skull of hers anyway.

Summer decided to stop fighting, shedding her body of its resistance. "Where are you taking me?" she asked, hoping her arm wouldn't break as Krista pulled with even more force than before.

"To the brig. A little time in solitary will do you some good. Maybe you'll come to your senses and realize that the rules apply to everyone. That you can't just do whatever you want whenever you want. That every action has a consequence."

"I already know all that," Summer snapped, wincing in pain. "You're hurting me."

Krista seemed to ignore her plea, taking her to the wire mesh elevator that ran between floors. There were two male guards waiting, one of them inside the lift. The other was outside, standing at a slight angle, yielding enough space to allow entry into the elevator.

Summer felt a sharp jab hit her back, forcing her into the elevator in a forward lunge. Her shoulder crashed into the back of the cage, stunning her for a second.

When she turned, she saw the bronze-skinned woman slide a metal lever to the side, then press a green button, sneering at Summer with that penetrating look of hers.

Summer had been in trouble before. Lots of times. But this felt different. "I said I was sorry. I'll do better. I promise."

"When have I heard that before? No, this time you're going to spend some time behind bars. Like everyone else who breaks the rules. Edison is not going to save you, either. Neither are the rest of your cronies. Not after The Council gave me the authority to take action."

"Come on, Krista. It's me. You don't have to do this. Please."

"Oh yes, I do. We all play by the rules or we don't have a community. It's as simple as that."

"I demand to speak to the Professor at once!" Summer yelled.

Krista stood silent, waiting for the lift to arrive at the designated floor. When it did, she adjusted the headband covering her short-cropped hair, then pulled the manual safety door open.

Another guard stood outside. This man was twice the size of Krista, with a broad chest and a nasty scar across his forehead. It ran from one side to the other as if he'd been sliced open with a meat cleaver.

Summer couldn't help but stare at his disfigurement, even though her mind was reeling with thoughts of prison. Krista's version of it, anyway, with hours of lecturing first, then days of boredom to follow.

Krista ripped off Summer's pack, then looked at Scar Man. "Frisk her and put her in two, Wicks. I'll be there in two shakes."

"Hey that's mine!" Summer yelled, making a stab for the backpack.

Krista wheeled sideways, holding the pack out of Summer's reach. "Nothing goes inside the cell but you."

"What about a strip down, body cavity search?" Wicks said. "She could be hiding a weapon somewhere."

Summer shot her eyes to Krista. "No, no, no, you can't let him. Please. You can't."

Krista paused for a few moments, acting as if she were considering it. "Just put her inside, Wicks."

Wicks looked disappointed as he tugged at Summer with his long fingers wrapped around her elbow.

Summer fought back out of instinct, trying to wriggle free, but stopped when the sting of his backhand landed on her chin. The man's whack spun her head to the side, bringing a wave of dizziness with it.

Wicks held up a coiled fist, his eyes screaming at her to just give him a reason. He was ready to pummel her.

Summer put her free arm up and ducked to protect her face. "I surrender! I surrender!"

Wicks put his hand down.

Krista gave the pack to Wicks, then he started his trek with Summer in tow.

Thirty or so steps later, the two of them were in the jailhouse where a pair of metal cages sat along the wall, both with doors open.

Inside each was a foldup cot, a thin mattress, a pillow and a blanket, and last but not least, a five-gallon bucket with a board atop it. The board had a round hole in the center.

Wicks brought Summer to the second jail cell and ran a probing hand over her clothes, patting her down to check for threats. That much was expected. What she didn't anticipate was him lingering in places where no man should ever linger, not unless he was married to the prisoner.

When Wicks was done checking all her parts, he shoved her inside with force.

Summer lost her balance and fell chest first, almost smashing her head into the frame of the bed.

The door clanked behind her, then the sound of a lock being engaged found her ears.

Summer spun and sat up, locking eyes with Wicks.

The man said nothing as he took two steps back, then put the backpack on the table behind him, tossing it like it was empty.

"Hey, easy with that! There are breakables inside."

He didn't respond or seem to care, standing with feet frozen and his square chin jutting out. He folded his arms across his chest and became a statue.

"So what? You're just going to stand there and stare at me? Like some mindless robot? Really?"

The man never answered, his eyes burning a hole into her.

She shrugged. "Then, I guess it's true. All you security guys are brainwashed to do whatever Krista tells you, no matter what. Just because she tells you to do something does not mean you have to. You have a choice. You really do."

"It's called following orders. You should try it."

Summer stood up, snorting a quick breath. "Well, how about that? The meathead can speak."

Wicks bit his upper lip, looking even more pissed than before.

Summer could see she was getting to him, so she decided to keep pressing. Maybe she could get him to do something really stupid. He'd already assaulted her more than once, deserving some sort of payback. The man obviously had issues. Issues she might be able to exploit.

Sympathy is a great thing when you're in jail. She'd read all about it in her books. The bleeding hearts—the people who love to rescue a lost cause—even when the prisoner is guilty as hell. All a prisoner had to do was wrap their claims inside some perceived injustice and they'd garner plenty of support.

That's what she needed to do—ramp up the level of mistreatment. Then it would ring true on the heartstrings of the social justice warriors. Warriors named Edison and Blackwell.

Summer grabbed the bars on the door and pressed her face between them, giving him a clear shot. "Come on, I'm right here, Wicks. I know you muscle-bound freaks can't control yourselves. You just love to hit a defenseless woman."

Nothing but silence from Wicks.

She switched into her coy, lively voice. "It's just me and you. Nobody else around. I know you want it, Wicks. Come on, do it. We're all alone. Nobody's going to stop you."

Wicks adjusted his arms, tightening them across his chest.

"It's a free shot," she said, watching his face for a reaction. None came, so she continued, raising her attack to a new level. "Nobody would blame a man like you. A pervert who gropes young girls. Probably how you got that nasty scar, too—touching the wrong little girl at daycare or something, back in the day. Even with that tiny pecker between your legs."

He still didn't respond.

Summer laughed, feeling the need for another insult. "Somebody's got a serious lack of 'danglage' and I think that somebody is you."

Wicks held firm, his eyes losing their intensity. It was clear he wasn't going to take the bait.

"No? Okay, your loss. But you know as well as I do that it would have felt amazing to sink your knuckles into my face. Or your fingers into something else."

Summer stepped back and walked the cell from one end to the other, retracing her steps as her mind went into analysis mode. There was something she was missing with this cement head.

Everyone has buttons you can push to make them do whatever you want, even though they know better. However, so far, the cretin hadn't reacted like she expected.

Time to change tactics, she decided, continuing her thought process. She wasn't sure how long "two shakes" meant in Krista's mind, but there was probably still time to make something happen with Wicks.

If not, then when Krista arrived, she would check the backpack and find the Seeker Map was missing and discover the other stuff that was personal in nature. Two huge violations of the rules in Krista's book.

When Summer's eyes found their way to the edge of the bedframe that she'd almost landed on earlier, a new idea came roaring into her mind. Summer stopped pacing, turned to Wicks, and rubbed her chin, the pain from his slap still resonating.

"I hope you know Edison isn't going to like you hitting me like that. Or tossing me into this cell. It's probably going to cost you your job. Might even get you banished. Who knows? I've seen worse things happen for far less."

He shook his head, looking steadfast. A slight smile took over his mouth, almost as if he knew her change in tactics was coming.

Summer wasn't done. "You guys really need to think twice about roughing up a valued member of the team. Seekers like me keep this place alive. You included. It's not too late to let me out of here and save yourself. It's what I would recommend before Edison comes down on you. Hard."

Wicks kept his tongue silent.

Summer waited to see if he might change his mind. When he didn't, she let her heartbeat calm, then took a step back. She tossed her hands up, preparing to finish the scene she'd cooked up in her head.

The next step wasn't going to be pleasant, but she couldn't turn back now. Not with Krista due back any minute. "Don't say I didn't warn you. Even Krista won't be able to save you once Edison hears about what you did."

"Nice try, Summer. But we're not all as gullible as you think. I know what you're trying to do. It won't work."

Summer twisted a lip, figuring he might say something like that. "Oh, really now," she said, sauntering back to the front of the cell. "You mean like this?"

Summer pulled her head back and rammed it forward, smacking her forehead into the steel bar directly ahead.

The metal clanged as her skin gave way, allowing the bone of her skull to make impact. She stumbled back in a fog, landing on her butt in front of the cot.

A flood of red raced down her face, bringing rivers of warmth along with it. She put her hands up and let the blood run wild across her fingers, then smeared it on her cheeks, neck, and sweatshirt to amplify the effect.

She rolled over to her knees and leaned forward, letting the blood find its way onto the floor in front of the bed. The throb in her head was intense. So was the blood pouring out of the gash, but the dizziness was fading, allowing her to focus better.

She smeared blood across the front of the bedframe, then moved to the right and spun around to sit. She pressed a hand onto the wound, figuring she'd lost enough blood.

Wicks shook his head, looking confident. "You really think that's gonna work?"

Summer nodded, pointing a bloody finger at the door next to him. "Depends on who walks in next."

Wicks turned his head toward the entrance.

Right on cue, Krista burst through the door. When her eyes locked onto Summer, she stopped with her eyes wide and mouth agape. But that look vanished a second later, her feet never moving.

Wicks laughed, bringing his eyes back to Summer. "You lose, bitch."

Summer pointed again at the door, sending an ocean of tears to her eyes. She let her hand tremble.

Wicks spun his head in a flash. So did Krista.

Professor Edison strolled in, followed by Morse and his walker, its new wheel already in use. Morse was right. It didn't take long to fix.

"Oh my God," Edison snapped, running to the cell door. He looked back at Krista. "Open this door at once!"

Morse waited in the doorway as Krista fumbled with her keys before unlocking the door. She pulled it open, then stepped aside as Edison raced in, taking a knee at Summer's side.

The Professor placed his hand over hers, helping to apply pressure to the wound. "What did they do to you, child?"

Summer pointed at Wicks, then changed her tone, chattering her teeth and sniffling along with the words. "That awful man . . . he hit me, Professor . . .

Then threw me in here really hard." She swung her head to the side, leading his eyes to the blood smear on the frame. "I hit my head on the bed. It hurts, Professor. A lot."

"We need to get you to medical," Edison said, helping her to her feet. He led her out of the cell with one hand on her forehead and the other around her waist.

"You're not seriously buying this, are you, Professor?" Krista asked, her hands out to her side. "She obviously did that to herself. Look at her. You can see it in her eyes. She's lying again."

Edison stopped and stared at Krista, his face pinched and eyes tight. "Were you here? Did you witness it?"

"No," Krista stammered, shuffling her feet. "But that doesn't mean—"

"It started in the hall," Summer told Edison, interrupting Krista's response. "Ask her. She was there. He slapped me and then wanted to punch me in the face. I was so scared, Professor. I thought he was going to kill me."

Edison fired another question at Krista, his voice filled with even more determination than before. "Is this true? Did he assault her in the hallway?"

Krista's face turned sour. She obviously didn't want to answer, but duty must have forced her to speak the truth. "Yes, sir. He did. But again, that doesn't—"

"Plus he felt me up when we were alone," Summer said. "Touched my breasts and everything."

"I've heard enough," Edison said, whisking Summer ahead. "I want that man arrested!"

"But, sir—" Krista said.

"That's an order. Make it happen," Edison said, whisking Summer out of the jailhouse.

Morse followed, the wheels on his walker in fast mode.

Summer pointed at the door behind them. "Don't forget my pack, Professor. Krista stole it from me. It's on the table."

"I'll get it," Morse said to Edison, making a U-turn. "You get her to Liz."

CHAPTER 19

Krista leaned back in the mess hall chair with arms up and fingers locked behind her head. She kept her eyes shut and focused on her breathing, trying to rid her chest of the tightness squeezing at her ribcage.

The pain persisted, even after two minutes of meditation, so she opened her eyes in frustration. Her vision changed to an unfocused stare, while her mind sank deep into itself, trying to make sense of the events of the day.

The cement ceiling, with its interwoven steel beams and lack of paint, reminded her of how closed-in everyone felt in the silo, even after a retrofit by their founder, Edison. The same man who'd helicoptered in and rescued Summer from the brig, then had her second-in-command, Nathan Wicks, arrested for some trumped-up charge. Well, mostly trumped up.

Krista knew as well as anyone that nobody could escape the reality of life in this place. She knew from her years in the military that anytime an oligarchy has control, democracy suffers. Especially a fake oligarchy—one actually being run by a single man.

She'd tried to be the voice of reason as a member of The Council, but it seemed that nobody was listening. Not unless her intentions fit neatly within Edison's vision for Nirvana. Everything else was dismissed. Ignored. Swept away, if it didn't fit the narrative. It was exhausting.

The video player in her mind took control without warning, showing her a replay of the jumper who died after a leap down the silo bay.

Krista figured that person wouldn't be the last victim of Edison's inconsistent application of the law under the Nirvana Code of Conduct, not with tensions mounting.

Most who came to live in the silo struggled to cope. Some failed, feeling the cement tomb sucking the life out of them until they just wanted to scream. That's how she felt at the moment—like she was trapped in a never-ending play—one whose climax featured her in a straitjacket.

Krista quashed the pity party, flushing it from her mind. She wasn't going to be one of the losers—not because of Edison and his propensity to circumvent his own rules. And certainly not because of a charming, yet completely unreliable twenty-something-year-old girl named Summer Lane. A girl who could spin a lie faster than lightning races across the sky.

Rod Zimmer walked in, twisting his handlebar mustache with his fingers, the salt and pepper strands winding in a circle. "There you are. Been looking all over for you."

"Needed a break. This seemed like as good a place as any. Nobody ever comes in here at this time of night."

"I heard what happened," he said, taking a seat next to her at the table closest to the empty stand of coffee pots. Dusty pots that hadn't been used in years.

Krista smirked. "Can you believe it? Even after The Council ruled in my favor."

"Kind of pulled the rug out from under you."

Krista sat upright, snorting an angry breath as she pulled her arms from behind her head. It was all she could do not to pound a fist on the tabletop. "What good is my title of Security Chief if I don't have the responsibility to carry out my duties? That girl needs discipline."

"We've all known that for a while now. Eventually, Edison won't have a choice. He can't keep protecting her. Her lies will catch up to her."

"You'd think so, but she's pretty damn clever."

"And charming, when she wants to be."

"All part of being clever, Rod. Knowing how to manipulate any situation for support," Krista said, running through a series of memories in her mind, each one another defeat. "I'm pretty sure everyone thinks I hate that little rule breaker, but I really don't. I'm just trying to do my job and keep everyone safe, Summer included. But she keeps getting in the way, like she's doing it on purpose, just to piss me off."

"Maybe it's time to change tactics."

"What do you mean?"

"I mean let her hang herself a little."

"How exactly?"

"Well, it's pretty obvious that riding her ass hasn't accomplished anything. Maybe it's time to give in and befriend that little snot. Give her some rope to go out and do her own thing."

His words were not what Krista expected. "Do her own thing? Are you serious?"

"Deadly."

She huffed a fake laugh. "I don't see how turning a blind eye will accomplish anything."

"You know as well as I do that she can't help herself. The moment she thinks nobody is looking, she'll be off doing whatever she's really doing out there."

"If I did that, she'd probably get herself killed."

"And that's a bad thing?"

"Come on, Rod. I don't want the girl dead. I just want her to grow up and contribute like an adult. It's more than time. She's not a kid anymore."

"I'm not sure that's true."

"What do you mean?" Krista asked, leaning forward with her elbows on the table.

"Earlier you wanted her banished. Left out in the cold."

His statement was true, though maybe not entirely. Sometimes her anger took her places where she had no intention of going in the first place. Tempers can do that. Krista knew she wasn't immune. Yet the calmer side of her personality would usually take over if she gave it a chance to rise up when she needed it most. Like now.

"I know it seems that way, Rod, but I really don't want her banished. I was just setting the bar

high with The Council so we could negotiate
something in the middle. Something that would be
constructive for everyone. It's the art of the deal,
Rod. Never make your best offer first."

He took a moment before responding, his
head tilted to the left as if he were in deep in thought.
"Hmmm. Thought you hated her and wanted her
gone."

"You know me. I always have a plan. Even
when I don't know what it is yet."

"Not sure what that means, but okay," Rod
said, scooting his chair closer to hers. He looked
around the room, his eyes darting left and right
before he brought them back to Krista.

He lowered his voice, speaking just above a
whisper. "I'm thinking if you assigned someone to
accompany her, you could cover all the angles. But it
would have to be someone you trust."

Krista hesitated, letting Zimmer's words soak
into her thoughts. The man might be on to something.
She responded in a whisper as well. "Maybe someone
her age. Someone who can get close to her without
suspicion."

"Exactly. Summer doesn't have the training
you do. She'll never see it coming. Especially, if it's

someone her age. A nice-looking young man who might turn her head, if you know what I mean."

"I do," Krista said, letting her mind sift through the people she knew, searching for someone who might fit the task. "But she'll balk at the idea. Probably run to Edison like she always does. I can see it now, both of them quoting regulations about Seekers being sent out alone."

"What if you spun this as some kind of a training mission?"

"For her?"

"No, for the spy. I'm guessing that Edison would agree to a new Seeker Training Program. One that would develop new talent. We're going to need more Seekers with the recent explosion in population. Edison has to know that we need more resources than we have now. We can't keep growing like this. Not with limited food stores and a maxed-out hydroponics bay."

"Interesting idea. If I present it right, it might just get around The Council's mandate."

"Exactly. Plus, if Edison goes for it, you'll cover your ass, no matter how this plays out. It's time to start thinking about yourself, Krista. In the end, it'll be good for Nirvana. And maybe even for

Summer, depending on what happens. She might just grow up a little."

Krista nodded, feeling the pressure release in her chest. "I knew there was a reason I hung around you, Rod. You always think outside the box."

"That's why I'm in Supply. I climb in and out of boxes all day," he said, snickering.

"Well then, I'm glad it's you," Krista said, touching her hand on his forearm.

A long pause hung in the air before Zimmer spoke again, his face turning serious. "There's something else you should know."

"What's that?" she asked, pulling her hand back.

"Have you seen all the signs going up, with motivational quotes on them?"

Krista nodded, but didn't respond.

"Aren't you curious as to who's behind them and why?"

Krista knew the answer but chose not to reveal it to him. She wanted to hear Zimmer out without any influence from her end, potentially tainting whatever he was going to reveal. "Been a little busy, Rod. Only so many hours in the day."

"It's Edison. He's damn worried. Been scribbling them like crazy and having me put them up all over."

"Worried about what?"

"A mutiny, I'm guessing. Morale is at an all-time low. I'm sure you can feel it."

"As a matter of fact, I have. You can almost taste it. But then again, I thought it might have been my own stress. Got that meeting to cover at Heston's tomorrow and I haven't begun to tackle duty assignments. I'm so far behind."

"You can only do what you can do. Gotta prioritize."

Krista rolled her eyes. "Easy for you to say. You don't have all the Summer crap on your plate."

"It's a lot to deal with, I'll agree, but you'll figure it out. You always do."

Krista appreciated his confidence, but he never answered his own question. "A mutiny? Seriously?"

"It's a possibility. In fact, the more people we rescue, the higher the chance of a revolt. Just too many personalities in play."

"Plus we really don't know anything about these people. They could be criminals for all we know."

Zimmer narrowed his eyes. "Exactly. There's no telling how this will play out. Especially if food and supplies run low. Tensions build with every new body he brings in."

"And yet he keeps bringing them in."

"Insanity, brought to you by a man named Edison. I'm sure his great-great-grandfather Thomas would have a different take on all this."

"Cousin, not grandfather," Krista said, feeling the need to correct her friend.

"Same difference. You get my drift."

She did. "All they have to do is claim they need help and they're in. No way to check them out or verify their story. Boom, he just opens the door and gives them all a great big hug. It's nuts, Rod. Just nuts. Where are they all coming from?"

"That's the million-dollar question," Zimmer said, shaking his head. "Well, that and how did they survive all these years?"

Krista felt her kinship with Zimmer growing by the second. "I'm afraid we'll never know."

"In the end, does it really matter? They're alive and they're here."

"True. And now they're our problem."

"I think Heston is just glad to get rid of them. The last thing he wants is more and more people showing up without anything to trade. That crusty old cowboy knows Edison will take them in, without question. The only thing Heston cares about is keeping his business running smoothly," Zimmer said.

"Can't blame the guy. I would, too. Those people bring nothing to the table. I just don't get Edison and his insatiable need to help everyone. Talk about a major security risk. What if one of these new people brings in some kind of virus that gets loose? We can't deal with that. Might as well put a gun to our heads right now and end the suspense."

"That might be a little drastic."

"You know what I mean," Krista said.

"If we're right about Edison's fear of an uprising, then he's ripe for picking. Now is the time to ask for changes, especially if he's willing to try new things to save this place. You know what today is, right?" Zimmer asked, not giving her time to answer. "The anniversary of his wife's death."

"Yeah. Always a tough day for him. He loved her a lot."

"It means he's vulnerable. Now's the time."

"You might be right, but it's never easy to get him to change his mind. On anything. I know; I've tried. So have you."

"It won't always be that way, trust me."

"What does that mean?"

"It means, someday, you'll be running this place and we can change the rules. Like granting entry based on merit, not need."

"Me? Really?"

Zimmer nodded, looking determined to make his point. "Edison ain't gonna live forever. You're the only choice in my book."

"I'm not sure the others would agree."

"It won't be up to them. The Rules of Succession are clear. Edison gets to name his replacement. He has to know you are the one and only person qualified to take over for him."

"Then I suppose I should stop confronting him all the time."

"It wouldn't hurt," Zimmer said.

CHAPTER 20

Horton stumbled forward with his hands bound behind his back, feeling the energy fading from his body. He spat out a patch of blood to rid his mouth of the metallic taste, sending a tooth along with it.

The two men hauling him by his elbows used to be his friends and part of his squad: Dice and Sketch. Now they were on the other side of the equation. All it took was one failed mission to change their loyalty.

Horton peered through the moonlight at the path ahead, wondering how long he had to live, his ribs screaming at him in pain. It started with fists to the gut and ended with blows to his face, every punch taking him closer to death.

Each man in the execution team had to land a blow. It was all part of their ritual when purging the camp of a failure. No one was allowed to abstain, not unless they wanted to join the condemned.

Horton knew Frost got off on it and so did most of his men, taking their frustrations out on whoever was being eliminated.

Frost measured failure on a scale from one to ten, ruling the punishment based on his primal need to hurt something. Or someone, as in this case.

As bad as this was, it was still better than the ending Slayer had endured. A knife to the gut doesn't allow a man to prepare to meet his maker.

Horton appreciated these extra few minutes of misery, as twisted as that would sound to an outsider. When you're facing death, moments are precious. So are seconds, allowing you time to organize your thoughts and say a final prayer.

A minute later, they arrived at their destination—an old telephone pole near the abandoned skateboard park, its wooden surface pitted with decades of wear.

The pole was a symbol, he figured, standing alone in the Frozen World. It was how each man had come to Frost's camp—alone. And now that was how he would go out.

Horton had been this way only hours before in search of the frizzy-haired escape artist known as Summer Lane. One of Edison's group. A girl that was about to get another man killed.

He guessed there was poetic justice wrapped inside the events of the day, only his mind couldn't reconcile it. All he knew was that Summer was clever. Damn clever. More so than he was.

Dice and Sketch spun him around and cut the rope keeping his hands secure. A second later, they had his wrists on the other side of the pole, and soon after, once again bound in restraints. Only this time, it wasn't rope. It was bailing wire, cinched tightly, cutting into his skin.

Next, his feet were bound to the front of the pole with another stretch of wire, adding to the pressure of wood against his back.

He could feel the frigid night air wafting over his exposed skin like an invading virus, seeking out more of his wounds to penetrate.

At first, he expected to be stripped naked and left for Mother Nature to take her revenge. That would have fit Frost's mantra: humiliate then execute. A stark reminder of what happens when you failed the man.

But that was not what happened.

Frost left him some dignity in the form of clothes, including boots. Horton wasn't sure why. It didn't ring true. Neither did the windbreaker Frost carried in his hand.

Even so, the clothes weren't going to be enough against the subzero temperatures headed his way. Maybe Frost thought it would extend the torture with a false sense of hope. That ruse would fit the man better, wanting to ramp up the cruelty.

Frost bent down and put the windbreaker on the ground, laying it out as if he was getting ready to fold it like a handmaiden would do for her master. His hands worked methodically, eliminating each crease in the material, then he covered the corners with rocks.

Fletcher moved a few steps away from Frost and tossed a pile of oil-stained rags to the ground. They were from the maintenance shop—old and grungy, all of them needing a thorough wash.

One of Fletcher's men stepped forward with a gas can and poured fuel on the three-foot-high pile of rags, dousing them until they were soaked. It was gallons of fuel they couldn't spare, not with the refinery on the fritz. Yet Frost didn't seem to care. In fact, he looked as if he was enjoying himself, his face covered in a full-on grin.

Frost took a strike-anywhere match from his pocket and lit it with a scratch of his thumbnail. It burst into a flame as he held it in the air, making eye contact with each of his men.

Horton got the impression the gesture was a precursor to some kind of medieval ceremony, almost as if this entire process had been rehearsed to perfection.

Frost flipped his wrist and sent the match end over end, leaving his fingers in a high, sweeping arc. Right then, time seemed to slow down, ticking by one frame at a time.

Horton watched the match spiral in flight before it landed on the pile—dead center—as if his boss had done it a thousand times. The material erupted into flames, sending a fireball billowing into the sky.

The flash from the sudden ignition lit up the area, making Horton flinch. "Give me another chance," he said with blood dripping from his lip.

"You know the rules, Horton. Failure is never an option," Frost answered, waving at his loyal dog to approach Horton.

Sergeant Barkley came forward in a measured strut, his front shoulders low and snout leading the way. The fur on the dog's back stood at attention as he sniffed Horton's feet, then wandered around to the back side of the pole to continue with his heels.

Horton wasn't about to give up. There still a chance, he convinced himself after spitting out another patch of blood. "We almost had her, sir. At least we recovered the map. Doesn't that count for something?"

Frost's grin vanished, his face turning sour. "That's why we're here instead of back at HQ. Otherwise, we'd be scraping your sorry ass off my floor with a sponge. If you can make it out of here alive, then you're free to be on your way."

The rest of the men erupted in a community laugh. Each of them must have realized the odds were slim.

Horton knew it, too. There was zero chance he could free himself and stay alive without food, water, or a heavy parka. That's why Frost had put the windbreaker just out of reach—to torment him.

This was just another inventive execution cooked up by the man they called *boss*, all in an attempt to give the condemned a glimmer of hope. Hope in the form of light clothes and a temporary fire for warmth. None of it would matter. Death was coming for him, snaking closer with each tick of the clock.

When Horton's eyes found their way to the burning material, the intensity of the flames brought a new thought to his mind—the Scabs. That's why

Frost wasted the gas. Not to taunt him with warmth. It was to bring them in.

Horton's vocal cords took over, firing before he could stop them. "I'll find her, boss. I swear to God. I will find that bitch, no matter what I gotta do. You have my word."

Frost never responded, his eyes still watching the mutt standing behind Horton's legs, panting like a freight train.

Horton wasn't about to stop his plea. "I know her tactics now. I'll be able to anticipate her next move. You need me, boss. Nobody else here knows her like I do. Let me prove it to you. I beg you. I can do this."

Frost put his hand out toward Fletcher, who was standing next to him.

Fletcher gave him a folding knife with a three-inch blade.

Frost deployed the blade with a pull of his fingers, then slid its metallic handle gently into Horton's mouth. "Here, you might need this. If nothing else, it'll shut that pie hole of yours until we leave."

Frost looked around the area, his eyes stopping at four points on an imaginary circle. "I figure you have twenty minutes, tops. If the cold doesn't end you, our hungry friends out there will."

Horton's heart sank as he watched Frost and his men turn to walk away. Then Frost stopped his feet and turned back to face him.

Wait, check that. Frost's attention was on Sergeant Barkley.

"Okay boy, get some!" the man said in a commanding voice.

The dog opened its mouth and sank its teeth into the side of Horton's ankle, twisting its head from side to side, as if it was in a tug of war with a play toy.

Horton screamed, sending the knife from his lips, as a hunk of skin was torn from his body. The pain raced up his leg and landed in his throat, making his next breath a short, powerful one.

Frost whistled a sharp note. "Come on, boy. Let's go!"

Sergeant Barkley let go of Horton's leg, running off in a darting leap to catch up to its owner.

Horton looked down past his heaving chest to see blood everywhere, most of it pooling next to a chunk of skin lying in the dirt. He figured the scent of blood would attract the Scabs like sharks to fish chum in the water.

The fire that Frost had set would burn for a while, using the gas and oily rags for its longevity. The heat would give him a temporary reprieve from the nighttime freeze that would soon descend on the area. The flames would also bring the Scabs in like a homing beacon.

It was the perfect execution plan. If he weren't the victim, he might have appreciated the elegance of it all, topped off by a dog bite and tissue tear to elevate the bait for the Scabs.

He peered off into the distance, his eyes struggling to detect movement. The Scabs must have seen it by now. His situation would soon turn ugly.

Scab ugly, with teeth shredding tissue.

CHAPTER 21

Alexander Morse adjusted Summer's pack across his back before he took another step with the revamped walker. He could now travel with more speed thanks to the girl he'd known for years. It took a bit of jury rigging, but he was able to modify the replacement wheel with the help of his trusty angle grinder and a working caliper.

He smiled, thinking of the moment Summer had given him the wheel, acting like a proud parent who'd just brought a treat home for one of her little ones in the nest. Morse wasn't sure why that analogy seemed to fit, but it did, even though he was four times her senior.

Summer wasn't the most consistent personality he'd met in his life, but she was a pleasant young lady. Her heart was always in it to win it, as they used to say on his block before The Event, sinking her teeth into whatever came next. Unfortunately, she had a tendency to veer off track, her attention easily swayed.

The caster wheel wasn't the first item Summer had brought back for him, but it was the most useful—other than perhaps the spare parts for the vintage shortwave radio transceiver he'd been working on in secret. Only a few more repairs and it should be working.

He wasn't sure how Edison would react to his desire to open communications with it, but he planned to sell the idea with the help of the EOD calculations. The number 35 should force Edison to listen. Hopefully it would be enough. A long-range broadcast was critical, or else they'd have to resort to drastic action.

The door to the medical unit was only ten yards away, but Morse wished it was a thousand miles. He'd spent far too much time in there with Liz in recent months, a fact that only Doc Blackwell knew. He wasn't a fan of secrets in general, but sometimes you had to make an exception.

News always flew around Nirvana at light speed, especially bad news, but not because the walls were thin. In fact, just the opposite. They were susceptible to one thing—gossip. You can't test for it. You can't plan for it. You can't stop it. It's part of human nature.

Morse didn't blame any of his fellow members. They needed something to help pass the time. Regrettably, spreading rumors was easy, allowing them slip out of their mundane existence for a spell.

As bad as gossip was for morale, secrets were far worse. Gossip could be ignored, but secrets withered trust. More so in a community run by unelected officials.

He knew his secret had to come out—eventually. But not now. Not today. There were too many other items burning a hole in his to-do list. His bombshell could wait a while longer.

The door to the infirmary opened before Morse arrived, catching him off guard when it almost smashed into the legs of his walker.

Edison stuck his head out, then his body, making eye contact. "I figured you should be close." He stepped sideways, keeping the door open with one hand.

Morse slipped through. "Thanks for the help."

"Look at you!" Summer said from the examination table, her eyes wide. Liz was with her, tending to the gash on her forehead, trimming a stitch with scissors.

"Someone order a pizza?" Morse asked, winking at Summer when he arrived. He took the pack off and put it on the table next to Summer.

"Thank you! I thought for sure Krista was going to steal all my stuff," Summer said, grabbing her pack and unzipping the main pouch. Her hand went inside and stayed there, just as Edison arrived from his doorman duty.

"My pleasure," Morse said, shifting his weight to his strongest leg. "Figured it was time I return the favor and brought you something for a change."

"I hope it's pepperoni with extra cheese," Summer said, taking a moment to peer at everyone in the room. Edison smiled, while Liz chuckled.

"So tell me, what did I miss?" Morse asked, wondering if Edison and Summer had cleared the air about her most recent Seeker Mission. There was much to talk about.

"Just a little needlework," Liz answered, pushing the words through her lips as if they were an afterthought. She must have thought Morse's question was meant for her.

"Looks like our girl will be fine," Edison said, pointing to the bandage on Summer's cheek.

"For the second time today, apparently. Luckily, we have the best damn doctor on the planet."

"Or the only one," Liz added, sounding trite.

"Getting to be a habit," Morse said, looking at Summer, wondering if she had finally come clean with Edison.

Summer shrugged but didn't respond.

Morse assumed that meant she hadn't explained her activities to the boss.

"Need to run a few tests," Liz said, her eyes focused on the patient. "You might have a slight concussion."

Summer pinched her lips and shook her head before responding. "I'm fine, Doc. I've smashed my head a lot worse than this."

Liz applied a bandage to her forehead. "Still, I want to be sure." She turned and walked to the wash sink, tossing a handful of blood-stained wipes into a metal container on the floor. She tore off her surgical gloves in a snap of latex and threw them in the bin as well.

"Do you two need a minute?" Morse asked Summer, then looked at Edison. He planned to take Liz to the hallway with him, if the answer was yes.

"Nah, we're good," Summer replied, giving Morse the slightest of head shakes.

"Professor?" Morse asked, wondering if he'd had his talk with the girl.

"It can wait, Alex," Edison said. "Let's get her back on her feet first."

Morse bit his tongue, holding back his displeasure at both. The last thing the silo needed was more secrets, even if they were only temporary ones. Secrets had a tendency to multiply, like unattended weeds after a rainstorm, smothering Nirvana's future with them.

Summer pulled her hand out of the pack and held up a wad of bubble wrap. "I found this for you, Professor. I hope you like it."

Edison took the gift and unwrapped it. Inside was a piece of stained glass. He held it up to the light beaming down from overhead. "Where on Earth did you find this?"

Summer smiled, showing a mouthful of teeth. "That's one of June's, right?"

Edison ran his trembling thumb over the center, tracing the contour of the Infinity Symbol. "Yes. In fact, she made it for me the Christmas before she, uh, passed. I thought it had been lost forever." He turned to sit down in the chair next to the bed, his eyes filling with tears.

Morse locked eyes with Summer.

She seemed pleased with herself, apparently spinning the meeting to avoid answering any questions.

He flared his eyebrows at her, but she didn't seem to notice.

Edison's voice cracked when he said, "Thank you, Summer. I can't tell you how much this means to me. Especially today."

"That's one of the reasons I was late. I wanted to get you something special, on account of what today is."

Edison choked back the emotion, then said, "Even though it was years ago, I still remember it like it was yesterday, June lying in my arms with those big, beautiful eyes looking up at me. I'll never forget that last moment we shared together. She was in such pain, but she still found a way to make it not about her."

"She was an amazing lady. I miss her so much," Summer said, crying along with him. "What happened was so unfair. She deserved better."

Even though Morse had joined Nirvana after June died, he could still picture the scene of her death in his head. Edison had told him the story on more than one occasion—usually on or around the anniversary of her death, like today.

June had been gunned down at the convenience store, trying to stop law enforcement from shooting a man who'd just robbed the place at gunpoint. At the time, some of the newspapers called June reckless; others labeled her a brave champion of the oppressed.

Morse wasn't sure what to think. He could see both sides of the argument. However, one thing was clear, stepping between two armed camps was more than dangerous. It was deadly. Not only did June lose her life, so did the criminal and two of the police officers before the gun battle was over. In truth, nobody won.

Morse put a hand on Edison's shoulder, squeezing it twice.

Edison looked up with tears flowing, sending Morse a 'thank you' look.

"It's important to remember why she sacrificed herself," Liz said. "For the good of the community. We all must rise to the occasion when trouble strikes, even if it means putting ourselves at grave risk."

"A noble act, indeed," Morse added, finally taking a side in the matter.

Liz changed her tone from one of compassion to more take-charge. "I think it's time for everyone to get some sleep. Nirvana has a big day tomorrow."

"Sounds like a good idea," Edison answered, bringing his eyes to Summer. "Can you stop by my office in the morning? We need to have a little chat."

"Uh, sure."

"I'll walk you back, Professor," Morse said, waiting for his teary-eyed friend to stand.

* * *

Doctor Ben Lipton shot a momentary look at the door to his lab in Frost's compound, as he continued stuffing his customized pack with the essentials he'd need. Essentials that included clothes, bottles of water, and a few hand tools.

A pistol was below all of that, one he'd liberated from the armory when nobody was looking. It was a .45 caliber semi-auto. Black, of course. The only color Frost's men would carry.

He took a toothbrush from his pocket and tossed it in as well. The instant it came to rest inside, the door flew open with a swoosh. It smashed against the adjacent wall, driving the knob into the plaster. In walked two men, arm in arm, like old Army buddies, their heads leaning side-to-side on their thick necks.

Lipton slammed his pack shut, then spun around in front of it to conceal his activities. He wished just once that someone would knock. But they never did, elevating his hatred for this place to somewhere a hundred miles beyond the stratosphere.

The men stumbled inside, taking off-balance steps, bouncing off each other with mile-wide grins. One of them burped, sounding like he was purposely trying to extend its resonance.

The belch came from Sketch, the man who loved to doodle. "Hey Doc, this shit, it the bomb," he slurred, holding up a pint of colorless moonshine. Some of it sloshed out of the glass, splashing the front of his sleeveless shirt.

Lipton was thankful this would be the last of the relentless pop-ins. "I'm glad you like it. But I need you both to run along now. Genius at work here."

The other man, Dice, responded, his words a slurred mess of syllables and hiccups. "You really need to chill-lax, Doc. Come join us. Fletcher said that's an order."

"Oh, did he now?" Lipton answered, raising an eyebrow. He knew the men's heads were spinning, meaning their focus wasn't primed at the moment. Yet he didn't dare take a step away from his pack. Even blockheads like these two might figure out what was happening.

Sketch let go of his pal's shoulder, took a long, uncoordinated step toward the corner of the room, bent over, and heaved a stream of vomit at the floor.

"I love the smell of puke in the morning," Dice said, laughing at his friend from behind.

Another round rose up from Sketch's stomach and soiled even more of the floor. He remained bent over for a few more seconds, then he stood upright in a lean and wiped his mouth on his arm.

Sketch spun and teetered on his legs, raising the glass in a makeshift toast before taking another swig of the booze. When he returned to his teammate, his walk could only be described as belonging to a seasick, one-legged pirate.

They wrapped arms again, spinning themselves around unexpectedly, almost toppling over.

Lipton took advantage, moving forward to cross the room and put his hands on their backs. He nudged them in the direction of the entrance.

Dice swung his head around, his eyes glazed over. "You should come with us, Doc. It's going to be biblical tomorrow."

"No thanks. I think I'll pass. I have other, more pressing plans," Lipton said, escorting them outside. He slammed the door shut and took a step back, wishing he had a lock on the knob.

Seconds ticked by, then a minute as he waited for a second round of belch and vomit to return. When he was certain the men were gone, his eyes found their way to the brown chunks lying in the corner.

Normally, he'd call maintenance to remove the mess, then raise an issue with Frost about both the intrusion and the disgusting bile deposit, but there wasn't time. Nor would it serve his immediate purpose.

Lipton returned to his backpack and finished his packing by stowing three of his most valuable notebooks inside. Each one contained revolutionary plans, written in code of course, none of which he thought he should ever attempt to build. Not around Frost or any of his men. No, what he had in mind needed a different type of leader and support group. One that didn't shoot first and ask questions later.

When you work for a gang of lunkheads who can barely form a sentence, it's essential that you keep your best ideas to yourself. More so when those ideas are experimental in nature and the man in charge is Simon Frost. Failure was never an option with him, even when the project was futuristic and not guaranteed of success. As a result, Lipton had adopted the motto of *under-promise and over-deliver.*

He figured his survival came down to three things: slow walking projects, stonewalling the results, and covering his mistakes with layers of technical mumbo jumbo. Words they'd never understand. Meanings that would obfuscate the truth. In layman's terms, it was all about coverups and spin.

It's how he kept himself safe from a brutal end. Well, that and playing the out-of-control, insolent scientist they all hated but couldn't live without. The latter of which was clearly a sliding scale, depending on the success of the latest project.

Right then, the walls began to shake with music blaring. The ruckus down the hall was now in full swing, with Frost and his men joining together in a lungs-deep rendition of their favorite song, *We Are the Champions*, by Queen. A curious choice indeed.

Lipton could hear the slurred words and tuneless notes. If he didn't know better, he'd think he was in a college dorm, listening to room full of testosterone-filled meat sacks celebrating another round of final exams they'd just passed. Assuming any of these cretins could read.

When the music stopped, the chants began, filling his ears with a mix of bass and baritone. No topic was off-limits once the inebriation escalated, especially when it involved a man-to-man challenge over some twisted feat of strength.

He never understood any of it. Instead of trying to improve their lot in life with some late-night reading, they preferred to wash it all away with a few gallons of hooch. And puke, for that matter. It was all about hangovers and killing brain cells, not that they had any to spare.

In retrospect, maybe his idea to fabricate an old-fashioned still wasn't a good one, not when alcohol had a propensity to turn violent men into something even worse. Men like Frost's have very few filters to begin with. When you add booze to the mix, those filters disappear altogether.

However, there were times when the 190-proof swill provided him with a modicum of peace and quiet—after they all passed out, of course. But more importantly, he'd pick up some useful crosstalk occasionally, like recently, though he needed to decipher the drunk-speak to find the true meaning behind the words.

Their drunken overshares had provided Lipton with news about the recent failures of Horton's team and some new treaty violations, meaning Frost and Fletcher would be hyper-focused on Dr. Edison at the Trading Post in the morning. Once their heads cleared.

That meeting and its timing gave him a singular opportunity, one he'd been waiting for ever since the refinery first came online—a refinery that had given Frost the upper hand in all things caveman.

It didn't take a rocket scientist to see this moment coming from a long distance off. Anytime a dullard gets their mitts on technology that provides them with a clear tactical advantage, it becomes an overwhelming addiction.

And like most addictions, Lipton knew they'd become dependent on that advantage—a point-of-no-return kind of dependency. And now that same reliance had morphed into a threat.

For Lipton, it had become a deadly threat since he couldn't repair the homemade fuel processing plant. Not after it nearly burned to the ground due to his attempt to up the output, as demanded by Frost.

Lipton had spun the failure as something else, calling the needed repairs "upgrades." Of course, Frost didn't catch on. He was too busy planning his next expansion of fuel-consuming activities. War-like activities to spread his reign of control over a nearly dead city and break some long-standing traditions in the process.

Lipton smiled. His plan was set. His pack was ready. Nobody was aware. Now he just needed to get his feet moving, before the entire situation turned against him.

CHAPTER 22

Horton whipped his head to the side when he heard a rustling crunch behind him. He wanted to spin around, but couldn't, not with the wooden pole pressing into his back and his hands and feet lashed into place.

He was alone, bleeding, and at the mercy of whomever or whatever came along. Plus, his vision was blurry, thanks to the cold, the beating, and the blood he'd lost. He knew this moment was a foregone conclusion, ever since Frost had set the pile of rags on fire, setting the flames free into the night sky.

Horton heard two more crunches, then a growl. Maybe it was an animal. A coyote, perhaps. They seemed to be the only creatures able to sustain themselves within the city limits, except for the Scabs.

The nose-less humans weren't animals in the classic sense, but some might be able to argue that point, if their cannibalistic actions were taken into account. Then again, others might say that the Scabs were an afront to animals everywhere, eating their own in some twisted sense of moral superiority.

In truth, Horton believed that everyone has a right to survive, whether human, animal, or something in-between. With that said, eating your own kind had to be a red line in the sand. One you never crossed.

The vision in his eyes finally cleared as more sounds came to his ears. The noise was closer this time, sounding like pebbles being ground into the asphalt.

The growl had been replaced with heavy breathing, bolstered by the occasional grunt, much like a gorilla would make.

A shadow came out from his left, taking position in front of him in the moonlight. He expected to see a four-legged animal or possibly a gang of hungry Scabs. But that's not what his eyes reported.

It was a scraggly-haired girl. Small in size. About fifteen years old. Maybe twenty. Maybe twelve. No way to know for sure.

The blonde was naked with long, curly, dirty hair covering her privates. The rest of her was a blanket of scars. Knife cuts, if he had to guess, plus a litany of bruises and other blemishes.

The tip of her nose was missing. That meant only one thing—frostbite, like the others. A Scab.

This was the first time he'd seen a female version of the meat eaters. All the others had been males and they all had clothes, tattered as they were.

He wasn't sure why a female Scab would be running alone or be naked out here at night—or in the daytime, for that matter. She had to be freezing but wasn't showing any signs. He figured her adrenaline was keeping her warm.

She took a step closer, her nose-less face in the air like a wild dog on high alert.

"Easy now. Let's not do anything rash," Horton said, keeping a close watch on her jagged teeth. It looked like she'd been chewing on a box of nails, honing the edges for months.

He didn't know if Scabs could sniff without a nose, if that's what she was doing. If she was, then it must still be possible with only a nasal cavity intact, though he couldn't hear any sniffs. Perhaps she had evolved, or it was a special trait, limited to only the female version of the cannibals.

She circled around his back, sending a shower of choppy breaths across his shoulders. She was close—too close, able to take a bite out of him in a snap.

When she finished her circle, she stood in front of him once again, her eyelids held thinner than before, as if she were considering her options. Or she was curious; Horton couldn't tell which.

He wondered if she could communicate. She was old enough to have been around since before The Event. Maybe she still understood English. "What's your name?"

She grunted in response, her eyes now wide.

"My name's Horton. I could really use your help," he said, looking down at his feet, hoping she'd notice Frost's blade in the dirt. "Do you think you could use that knife to cut the wires behind me?"

Her head tilted to the side, looking confused, her grunts continuing, though faster now. She looked left and then right in momentary flashes, alternating between the two, reminding him of a chipmunk keeping watch for predators.

The girl's excitement was clear, yet he didn't know if it was a bad thing or not. His gut was screaming at him that it was, but his gut had been wrong before. Mostly with that girl named Summer.

Horton waited until she locked eyes with him again. "I swear to God; I'm not going to hurt you. I just need your help."

She peered down at the knife.

"Yes. The knife. Go ahead. Pick it up."

She bent down and grabbed the lump of skin left behind by Sergeant Barkley and jammed it into her mouth, chewing with grunts mixed in.

Horton sucked in a short burst of air, then gulped. Shit! She'd just acquired a taste for him, literally.

Before he could decide what to do next, she grabbed the knife and straightened up, bringing the tip of the blade to the center of his chest. There was pressure, but it didn't break the skin.

"Please. Don't do this. I'm a friend. I can help you."

She blinked, but that was her only response.

"Like I said, I'm not going to hurt you. In fact, if you help me, I'll help you. With food, clothes, shelter—whatever."

She never moved, only staring at him like a hawk, no longer the frightened chipmunk. Even her eyes had stopped blinking like machine guns.

"I swear. I'll help with whatever you need. You have my word."

She pulled the knife back after a long second.

Horton took that to mean she understood and agreed. But then again, it was just a guess. A hopeful, desperate guess. "Now go behind me and cut the wires around my hands."

She craned her head back and held it for a beat, then hunched and turned at an angle, her eyes darting from one side to the other.

Her new position gave him a slanted look at her back. It was covered in scars, much like her front, only these looked like whip marks. Hundreds of them.

A moment later, she shuffled her feet to the left, then repeated the same hold, hunch, and spin maneuver.

Horton turned his head in the same direction as her. "Someone out there?"

She whipped her head around and grunted twice, sending him an intense look.

Horton took that gesture to mean *shut the hell up!*

She scurried to the other side of him, checking the area with her multi-step process. A minute went by before she moved again, this time turning to face him.

"Are they gone?"

She grunted once, then moved behind him.

He felt the cold metal blade pressing against his wrists as she started to pry at the bailing wire. She applied heavy force, sending a jolt of pain into his hands just before the wire snapped free.

Horton brought his arms around to the front and rubbed his wrists to dispel the pain. There was an indentation in the skin, but he didn't see any blood.

She came around in front, taking a stance two feet away.

He held his hand out. "Can you give me the knife?"

She didn't move.

"I won't hurt you. I promise. I just need to cut the wire from my feet, then I'll give it back to you."

She huffed, sounding more like a dog than a girl.

He repeated his words.

She paused, then gave him the knife.

He bent down and made quick work of the wire, freeing his feet. He fell to the ground, tumbling forward on his knees, surprised by his lack of energy.

She took a step back, keeping the distance between them the same.

He flipped the knife around in his hand to grip the blade, then held the handle up, closer to her. "Here, this is yours."

She took it but kept the weapon down at her side, not in a defensive posture.

Horton got the impression she was confused. Or needed confirmation. "Like I said, I'm a man of my word. You helped me and now I will help you. That's how I roll."

His kneeling position gave him a different view of the scars on her belly. They were thick like the others, but directly under them were stretch marks. Lots of them. Stretch marks meant only one thing—she'd had a baby. Maybe more than one.

She turned to the side and waved at him to follow.

The pain in his ankle from the dog bite was intense, but he was able to stand, peering at the path ahead.

He took the windbreaker from the ground and held it out for her. "You need to wear this. It's too cold out here."

She tilted her head again, but didn't grunt this time. He took it to mean she was studying him.

He shook the coat. "It's okay. Trust me. It'll keep you warm."

She put out an arm.

Horton slipped the covering on her, then helped her wrap the garment around her back and shoulders.

She grunted twice, looking thankful.

"You're welcome," he said, holding out an arm, pointing at the path ahead. "Lead the way, my friend."

He walked behind the girl, admiring her ability to instantly trust him. One minute he thought he was dead. Now he had an ally. At least it appeared so.

Perhaps living in the wild had heightened her senses, including the ability to sense friend versus foe. She'd obviously been through hell but still found a way to make a connection with a total stranger.

He wasn't sure he would have done the same if the roles had been reversed. Either way, he couldn't believe his good fortune at the end of a very long day. Albeit an odd twist of fate.

He'd been beaten, eaten, and needed medical attention.

She'd been whipped, stabbed, and needed more clothes.

And a bath.

So did he.

A match made in heaven.

CHAPTER 23

"Good, you're still up," Krista said, walking into Edison's office.

The old man was at his desk, shuffling through some paperwork. He looked up. "Yes, but I wish it wasn't the case. Hard to sleep with that meet tomorrow."

"And all the Summer crap."

"That too."

"Which is why I'm here, Professor. Got a minute?"

"Sure. Shoot," he said, putting the paperwork down on his desk, then sitting back in his chair.

Krista planted her weary ass in one of the empty seats in front of his desk, feeling the need to backstep a bit. It was imperative for the founder to be on her side. She knew from experience that offering an apology to start was a great way to accomplish that goal. Plus, it was the right thing to do. "About before—I'm sorry I got so upset. Sometimes my temper gets the better of me. Been on edge lately."

"We all are, my dear. It happens. Don't worry about it. You're just trying to do your job. I know your heart is in the right place."

"Thanks, Professor. Appreciate that. And that business with Wicks . . . that never should've happened. That was my fault. I know he has a tendency to take things a bit too far. I should've never put him in that position."

"Still, he must take responsibility for his actions. Those were his choices, not yours. Assaulting a woman is never an option."

"No, it's not. That's why I put him on lockdown, per your orders. I'm sure The Council will take it from there, like they always do. Rules are rules."

"So what's this about?"

"I have an idea I want to pitch to you. It has to do with Summer and her missions."

"What kind of idea?"

"One that will help all of us, including her."

"I'm all ears."

"It's become clear to me that riding her all the time has had the opposite effect."

"Which is typical with a young person."

"Especially one who's independent."

Edison flared an eyebrow. "She is that. And a free-thinker."

"Summer pushes back every time I try to get her to do something."

"Again, typical."

"I think it's time to switch gears and deploy a completely different tactic. One that will not only help keep her safe, but allow us to keep a better eye on her. For everyone's sake."

"How do you suggest we do that?"

"We start a new Seeker Training Program."

"Okay, you've got my attention."

"If we find a young person, like her, and assign him to her, he can keep an eye on her and provide backup in case she gets into trouble."

"What about The Council's mandate?"

"If we spin this as only a temporary program, one designed to help bolster our Seeker staff, they just might go for it. Plus it will only apply to her, not to our other Seekers. Let's face it, we're going to need more Seekers anyway with the increase in numbers around here. Zimmer told me we're getting low on supplies. Critically low."

"Makes sense. Kill two birds with one stone type thing. Plus, this trainee can feed you information when he gets back."

"Well, there is that, but additional intel is just a bonus. The most important aspect here is to keep her safe and on task, which ultimately keeps everyone else safe in the process."

"She'll hate the idea."

"No doubt. But I'm hoping she'll take to it, eventually, once she learns that it's only temporary. I'm sure you can get her to see why this is important. For the greater good. She listens to you."

"I suppose I might be able to. Maybe if we put her in charge of this new program, she'll want to help. Like you, her heart is in the right place. All she needs is a little push and I think she'll start taking her role a little more seriously."

"That would be nice. For all of us."

"Do you have someone in mind?"

"Yes. There is one young man. He seems eager to contribute. Been hanging around my guys during mess hall, trying to ingratiate himself."

"Do you think she'll connect with him? That'll be important for this to work."

"I think so."

"But can he keep her on task?"

"Not sure yet. But my gut tells me yes."

"You'll need to watch over them to make sure this doesn't go sideways. Without them knowing, of course. If Summer feels you hovering, she'll revolt."

"I can keep my distance. In fact, I might even use one of my guys as a go-between."

"Like a handler."

"Exactly. Another degree of separation. Effective leaders do that."

Edison nodded. "They do. It's important to empower the people below you. It's how loyalty is cultivated. They must become vested in the success of the project. And to do that, they must be given more responsibility."

"Exactly," Krista said, figuring the man was talking about Summer, not just the new trainee.

Edison let out a short laugh after the tension in his face disappeared. "It's kind of funny you bring this to me now. I've been noodling on our morale problem for a while. More specifically, I've been trying to figure out how to reach Summer. She's had it rough over the years and I'm afraid I've been coddling her too much. Maybe if we give her more responsibility, as we are discussing, she'll grow into the young woman I know she can be. There's a lot there; we just have to get her to see it. And believe in herself."

"We can only hope, sir."

* * *

Horton winced from the ankle pain as he stepped over a smattering of bricks along the road. They were part of a toppled wall that used to belong to an old transmission shop. He couldn't make out the lettering on the red and blue sign hanging sideways on the building. It had been washed out from a decade of weather abuse.

The Scab girl ahead of him had suffered her share of abuse as well—years of it if he had to guess, her body a roadmap of the damned. So many scars. So many cuts. So much pain.

If she could only talk, he was sure her story would make a compelling science fiction novel, *The Last Scab Girl*, or something along those lines.

Horton wasn't doing much better than her, with one eye blurry and the other one swollen. Every inch of his face seemed to hurt, having taken so many punches that he'd lost count.

Then there were his ribs. Each one a bruised mess. A few may have been cracked, meaning every breath was a chore to take in and release.

His ankle had stopped bleeding about a mile ago, but the open wound was taking on the cold directly. Every step stung like a red-hot poker, but he'd been able to push through it.

He'd decided from the start to let the Scab Girl take the lead on this trek to wherever they were headed. She seemed to know where she was going, her route specific and calculated, using that strange stop, hunch, and hold maneuver as she went, as if her senses were in charge.

Thus far they'd been zigzagging mostly through a residential area of city, passing neighborhood after neighborhood, stopping occasionally to take shelter in a burned-out building or some other makeshift cave.

She seemed to prefer abandoned strip malls for some reason, taking refuge inside various commercial establishments that girls her age would have never visited back in the day.

First it was a pawn shop with bars on its windows, but no glass. Then it was a tool repair shop—lawnmowers mostly, based on the remnants of engines and other equipment inside.

The last had been a spy shop, the kind that jealous husbands would frequent when they needed to eavesdrop on their slutty wives.

None of those establishments were of much use anymore. Back then, the world was filled with drama, everyone busy with their tech-filled lives, ignoring each other on the street as if they were the only person still alive on the planet. Little did they know that reality would soon come to pass.

The only clothing that Scab Girl had on was the windbreaker Frost had left for him, yet she didn't appear to be as cold as Horton was, despite his pants, boots, socks, and a muscle shirt.

It must have been just like Doc Lipton said, *Life finds a way.*

She'd evolved, somehow, appearing to have developed a resistance to the cold. It didn't make sense, but neither did the world in general.

Perhaps it was a mental thing, her choosing to ignore the gusts of wind sending chills across her skin. There hadn't been any snow flurries for a while, but they'd return soon enough, he figured.

The Earth had started its recovery, though it was a slow process. At least the sun had broken through the endless freeze, giving the planet a chance to come back to life after the volcanic ash covered the globe.

There were plenty of rumors floating around a decade ago about who caused it and why. Now the culprits were probably dead, along with most everyone else, so the reason behind it mattered not.

One thing was for sure, ninety-one volcanos don't go off by accident. Not all of them at the same time. Someone wanted to end the world. Yet Horton couldn't help but wonder if the perpetrators thought anyone would survive. The chances were slim, so they had to assume their actions would bring about an extinction-level event.

He figured history would judge the guilty long after he was gone. It wasn't up to him to decide. He was busy with the here and now, feeling the sense of renewal everywhere.

Every week or two more survivors would arrive. Hungry survivors. Many of them finding their way to town, hoping to find a new life at the Trading Post. The girl in front of him was one of those hopefuls, except for the Trading Post part.

"Hey, where are we going?" he asked her, following her path through the debris.

She turned her head and peered back, giving him a penetrating stare. Her eyes told him to be quiet.

"All right, all right," he said in a whisper, unable to stop his tongue. "Just wanted to know, that's all."

Maybe it was his nervousness turning him into a chatty Cathy. It wasn't every day you found yourself wandering around the middle of the night, wounded and weak, following the lead of a naked cannibal who'd been tortured and didn't speak.

He wondered if he should give her a name. Her blonde, frizzy hair reminded him of pictures he'd seen of his grandmother when she was in her twenties.

Grandma's hair was the same as Scab Girl's, stretching down to her waist as it fanned out, almost as if she'd spent hours crimping it with a curling iron, then rubbed the strands across a balloon for static.

His grandmother's name was Helena. Maybe he should call Scab Girl the same name; then they wouldn't feel like such strangers. It's harder to trust someone when you don't know their name. If he gave her one, perhaps it would calm the tension in his chest.

Horton increased his pace until he could grab her by the arm. "Hey, stop for a minute. I need to rest."

She spun around, flaring her jagged teeth before pulling away in a grunt, snapping her arm free.

He held his hands up. "Sorry, but you need slow down, Helena. I'm not operating at a hundred percent here."

Her eyes pinched after a head tilt. The name obviously caught her by surprise.

"That's right. I'm going to call you Helena, after my grandmother. I'm tired of saying *hey* all the time."

He took a seat on a short retaining wall to rest his injured leg. His arms felt like limp noodles. So did the rest of his body. He needed sleep. And food. Water wouldn't hurt either.

The brick fence was part of someone's landscaping, though everything was dead in the area. The house behind him used to have a southwestern style tile roof, most of them broken or missing now.

There wasn't a chimney along its roofline like the other houses on the block. He figured that meant its former residents were the first to perish once the world turned perpetually cold.

The rest of the home was in rough shape as well, its windows smashed and the front door hanging open. The doorknob was missing, as if someone had kicked open the door, leaving only a hole in the wood.

He imagined a happy family living there back in the day, with their 2.5 kids frolicking across what he assumed was a lush front yard. His vision changed to show him an SUV. It was shiny and new, an all-black, four-door monster, with chrome wheels and some of those little white stickers on the back window—the kind that depicted a happy family holding hands. They had a dog named Max, he decided, choosing an all-white German Shepherd for their pet.

"Do you know where you're going?" he asked, after catching his breath.

She grunted twice.

"Does two mean yes?"

Two more guttural sounds came from her throat.

"How many for no?"

She didn't answer.

"Does nothing mean no? Or does one?"

Two more grunts.

"How much farther?"

She turned and pointed in the same direction they'd been traveling, jutting her arm forward in a repetitive shove.

"Yeah, I know that's where we're going. But how much longer? I'm about done here."

She turned her head away, taking a frozen stance like she had before—hunched over and on high alert.

A moment later, a stick cracked.

Horton whipped his head around in the direction of the sound.

So did Helena.

"Hold it right there, you two," a man said in a muffled voice. He was holding a pistol and dressed in black from head to toe, with goggles covering his eyes and a mask over his nose and mouth.

CHAPTER 24

When Horton saw the gun in the masked man's hand aimed at Helena, he got up from the wall and ran in front of the girl with his arms out to the side. "Wait! Don't shoot. She's with me."

Helena pushed through his arms, then bent forward, her mouth open, snarling with her razor teeth showing.

Horton grabbed her by the elbows and yanked her back, moving her behind him once again.

"Stay!" he told her with an index finger pointing up. "Let me handle this."

He turned his attention to the man with the gun. "What do you want? We don't have anything to steal."

"Horton? Is that you?" the gunman asked.

Horton didn't recognize the voice.

The assailant pulled the mask from his face, then the goggles. "It's me, Doc Lipton."

"Doc? What the hell are you doing here?"

"I could ask you the same thing."

"How the hell did you find me?"

"The cretins were up all night partying. It amazes me what drunks will reveal when their brains are mush with a little help from a gallon of 190 proof."

Horton nodded. "Loose lips sink ships."

Doc smiled, looking proud of himself. Then his face turned serious again. "Who's the Scab?"

"A friend who rescued me from my little dust-up with Frost."

Lipton laughed, his face twisting into a smirk. "Well, how about that. Beaten to the punch by a Scab Girl. An ugly one at that."

Helena growled at him, showing more teeth than before.

Horton needed to calm the situation before someone else had skin torn from his body. "Her name is Helena and you might want to check the attitude, Doc. She's not deaf. She understands what you're saying."

"Helena? You gave it a name?"

"Had to call her something."

"Next thing you know, you'll be taking it out on a date. You know, flowers, dinner, and then a little bumping of uglies. Scab uglies, to be precise." Doc pointed at Horton's swollen eye, then at Helena. "Did it do that?"

"No. Frost did." Horton turned the side of his leg toward Doc to give him a direct view of the open wound on his ankle. "Compliments of Sergeant Barkley."

"Damn, that had to hurt. That's why Frost barely feeds that fur-covered mongrel. Speaking of which, when's the last time your new friend got its fill? Shouldn't you be worried? A starving animal is hard to anticipate."

Horton was tired of the man's rhetoric, choosing to ignore his last set of questions. "Does Frost know you're here?"

"Of course not. He'd carve me up like a two-hundred and fifty-pound catfish, then feed my old bones to that flea-infested mutt of his."

"That's what I thought."

"I'm here because I need your help."

"Why?"

"Birds of a feather, my friend."

"Come again?"

"We both have something in common."

"What? Frost?"

"Precisely. It was only a matter of time before he figured out I couldn't repair the refinery. And I'm sure you know how that would have ended."

Horton did. "Failure is never an option."

Doc nodded, lowering the gun in the process. "Seemed like the proper time to take my leave of him, and his band of merry men." He took his backpack off and put it on the ground.

"Tell me you have food and water in there, Doc," Horton said, his eyes glued on the pack.

Doc pulled the zipper open and took out a water bottle. He tossed it end over end.

Horton snagged it with two hands, twisted the cap off, and downed half of it. Then he gave the bottle to Helena.

She put the opening next to the hole in her face where her nose used to be for a three count, then moved it to her lips and guzzled the water down her throat. When she was done, she grunted while holding the bottle up and shaking it.

"I think that's more than plenty," Doc said. "The rest is for us humans."

"You need to quit saying things like that. She is human."

"In your eyes, perhaps," Doc said, pulling out more items from his pack. Once again, he tossed them to Horton, one at a time, keeping his distance.

First, it was a spare windbreaker. It matched the one Frost had left by the telephone pole as a cruel joke.

Horton put it on, then zipped up the front.

Helena needed to do the same thing, but she only snarled in response when he motioned with his hands for her to do what he'd just done. She preferred to keep the front open for some reason. That was fine by him. He wasn't about to argue with a flesh-eating machine.

Next, Doc gave him a blanket. It was Army Green and only half-sized, but more than enough for Helena's five-foot frame.

Horton gave it to her, then motioned with his arms to wrap it around her shoulders or her waist. She did the latter, working the cloth around her midsection, then she held the front closed with her fingers.

"Stretch marks?" Doc said in a sharp tone. "Tell me I didn't just see that, Horton."

"You did, but don't get all squirrely about it."

"You know what that means, right?"

"I do. But you need to stay calm, Doc. She can sense changes in mood."

"Mood? Is that what you're worried about? They're multiplying, Horton. Or can't you see that? And what about all those other scars?"

"None of that is my concern. Or yours either," Horton answered, his eyes flaring to catch the man's attention. He changed his tone to one of controlled conviction, hoping Doc would catch his drift. "Right now, we need to keep things calm. We are a team. Teams work together. Teams don't pry into each other's past."

Doc's eyebrows pinched, his lips holding tight.

Horton could feel the tension building.

Helena would surely sense it as well.

He needed to break the silence and focus everyone's attention elsewhere. "What else you got in that pack?"

Doc pulled three ammo magazines from a side pouch, but chose to hold them in his hand while he yanked out the next item: his black fedora. He put it on his head, tilting it to the side, looking like one of the Rat Pack from long ago. "No reason not to wear this now," he mumbled. "The secret's out."

He looked at Helena and pointed at his hat. "This is what real people wear. It's called style."

Helena narrowed her eyes as Doc continued, "You also might want to think about a comb. And a bath. I can smell you from here."

"Jesus, Doc. Why are you such an asshole all the time? She's not one you should antagonize."

"Well, if it's human like you say, then it ought to be able to take a little ribbing now and then. And a little constructive criticism. If not, then maybe I'm right about it being something less."

There was no moderation with this man. Horton knew he was wasting his breath trying to get through. Doc was never going to change. "Don't say I didn't warn you."

Doc held up the gun. "I'm not worried in the least."

Horton wondered who'd win that battle. A Scab Girl with animal-like reflexes and years of living in the wild, or a pudgy old man who could barely hold the pistol still in his hand.

He figured it was a toss-up on paper. But if he was putting money on it, he'd take Helena. Either way, it was a fight he didn't want to see. "If that's all you have in that pack, then we need to get moving."

Helena grabbed Horton's arm and squeezed.

He brought his head around to see what she wanted.

Helena was in her hunched over stance, torso leaning forward, her face tilted up and frozen.

"Do we have company?" Horton asked in a whisper.

"What's wrong?" Doc asked, also in a whisper.

Horton held up a hand to keep the man quiet.

Helena tugged at Horton to run, using enough force to make him stumble.

Horton looked back as they sprinted toward the house behind them, the one with no chimney. "Come on, Doc. You don't want to stay there."

Doc followed as Helena led them into the house. They crouched below the front window with Helena on the left, Horton in the middle, and Lipton on the right.

Helena took a piece of burned wood on the floor and smeared its black soot over her face, neck, and chest. Then she dropped the blanket and finished with her legs, feet, and butt.

Right then Horton understood why she wanted the garments left open. For easy access. She'd done this before.

Helena grunted at Horton to do the same.

Horton grabbed two hunks of charcoal and gave one of them to Doc. "She wants us to mask our scent."

"Why?"

"Someone's coming. Time to strip, Doc," Horton said, tearing off his clothes. Once naked, Horton smeared the soot across the front of his skin.

Helena helped him finish the back of his legs, neck, and shoulders.

Horton did the same for her, smearing the mess across her back after she shed the windbreaker.

Both of them were now covered from head to toe in black.

When Horton brought his attention back to Doc, he saw that the man hadn't moved, other than the position of the gun in his hand. It was aimed over the window ledge.

"What are you doing?" Horton asked.

"I'm not getting naked for anyone. Certainly not for some random Scab. Sorry, but this is where I draw the line."

"What the hell is wrong with you? Can't you see she's trying to keep us safe?"

"How do we know that thing isn't maneuvering us into some kind of trap?"

"For what purpose?"

"To steal our possessions and leave us out here to freeze."

"That doesn't make any sense. Why would she do that after rescuing me?"

"It's what I would do, if I were it."

Horton snagged the gun away from Doc with a flash of his hand. He turned the weapon around and pointed the barrel at him. "Clothes off. Now. That's an order. I'm not going to ask again."

CHAPTER 25

Doctor Ben Lipton kept his privates covered with both hands while Scab Girl smeared charcoal across his naked body. It was humiliating, feeling her hands touching him everywhere. Pressing. Rubbing. Probing. Covering him in black.

He stood there, helpless, like a turkey being basted before Thanksgiving dinner. He really didn't have a choice. Not with two rows of shark teeth and a gun aimed at him.

"Do you mind?" Lipton said, shooting a look at Horton's weapon. "I've already agreed. Besides, it'll go faster with two."

"You're okay with that?"

"Just get this over with, already."

Horton froze for a moment, his eyes tight. Then he put the gun down and joined Helena with her work.

This wasn't what Lipton had in mind when he left Frost's compound. It never occurred to him to factor in the possibility of a Scab Girl during the design of his plan. He obviously missed something in both his initial assessment and his ongoing reconnaissance. Otherwise, the only other explanation for this failure to anticipate was that he wasn't as smart as he thought he was—a first in the annals of all things Lipton.

"Lift your arms," Horton said, loading his fingers with more of the soot.

Lipton obliged him, letting go of his privates and putting his hands over his head. He now understood the meaning of the old movie title "Free Willy."

He continued his analysis in silence, hoping the mental exercise would keep his mind off the embarrassment. And the sensation of four hands, rubbing.

The last thing he wanted was for a cannibal to see an erection right in front of her teeth. Who knew how she'd react to such a thing?

He let the castration thoughts fade, returning to his self-analysis.

There was a chance Frost had deceived him somehow. Whether on purpose or otherwise, he wasn't sure. Perhaps he'd underestimated Frost and his men, assuming their lack of a collective IQ had removed the possibility of subterfuge.

Lipton figured any scientist in his position would have agreed with his assessment: Frost was a dumbass. Not exactly a scientific term, but it fit. More so when Frost would give in to the driving need to kill something—anything—leaving a wake of entrails. Those primal urges were both frightening and easy to anticipate. With that said, knowing the wrath was coming had never once helped any of Frost's victims.

Rage always wins. It's simply too violent, too swift and too indeterminate.

"Turn around so we can do the back," Horton said, applying pressure with a set of fingers on Lipton's kidney.

He had been careful during his spying, planning every move while eavesdropping on the conversations between the drunks. It's never easy snooping on those who'd kill you in a heartbeat.

Lipton assumed that Frost's men thought of him as a special kind of prude: part asshole, part genius. A man oblivious to all things fun. One who would never stoop to their level and partake in a quest to defile himself during another one of their endless drunken gatherings.

Yet, they couldn't have been more wrong. He'd purposely kept his true self hidden from their prying eyes. They were always watching him. Always judging. Never taking a moment off.

The truth was, he'd been known to hit the bottle before The Event changed the world. He knew firsthand that theoretical physicists can party with the best of them. More so after they learned their government grant had been renewed with no strings attached.

He missed the old days when you were paid for nothing. You never had to produce anything, as long as there was a glimmer of hope in your research. That was the key to keep the cash flowing from the government trough. A glimmer. Just sprinkle in a modicum of results in your progress reports and the higher-ups were happy.

But that was then.

This was now.

"Almost done," Horton said, smearing more of the black on Lipton.

Lipton was sure there was never a mention of female Scabs. Only males. Helena must have been an exception. She was rare. Possibly valuable. Others of her kind would most certainly be looking for her, assuming they were the ones responsible for the scars across her skin.

He wondered if Frost and Fletcher knew female Scabs existed. There'd been no mention of it in the crosstalk Lipton had picked up. Then again, it was possible his boss had his own secrets, beyond the ones Lipton had already discovered without Frost's knowledge.

Lipton had more he needed to relay to Horton, but not with this Helena person at his side—the same person, albeit a loose classification, who was rubbing black across the backs of his inner thighs, approaching Lipton's version of the No-Go Zone.

Helena's hands continued on, skipping the one area of his body no one else's touch should ever penetrate.

Lipton studied Horton as his hands worked the black. Horton was clearly compromised, unable to see the threat next to him, literally and figuratively.

It meant Lipton would have to keep his plan quiet until the right moment came along. A moment when the female Scab was no longer inside Horton's circle of trust.

Lipton was certain she'd turn on Horton, eventually. Animals do that. More specifically, wild animals. Once she did, that's when Lipton would make his move and read Horton in.

Helena grunted three times, smacking Horton on the shoulder in the process.

Horton looked at her. "What?"

She pointed outside the window and to the right, just beyond a string of parked cars. Each was gray with heavy rust spots across their hoods, no doubt due to the freezing temperatures the past decade. Well, that and the acidic nature of volcanic ash.

Whether it was mafic ash or felsic ash, it was all categorized by its silica content. Lipton had read all the papers. Sampled his own deposits. Crunched all the numbers. Salts, acids, and sulphuric acid are never kind to man or machine.

He'd also detected trace amounts of radioactivity after The Event first ravaged the planet, though those readings were no longer present. He wasn't sure if the radiation was part of the cause or simply an aftereffect. No way to know without more data.

Helena pulled Horton down, then did the same with Lipton, all three of them peeking over the ledge of the windowsill, its glass missing.

A second later, a gang of at least twenty Scabs moved into the neighborhood—all men, of course—each carrying some kind of hand weapon. Knives mostly, but a few held garden tools and pipes.

He watched them spread out like a swarm of bees in search of pollen—blonde, female pollen, he figured, with endless scars, like Helena, and a face that could stop a clock.

Lipton grabbed Horton by the neck, pulling him close to whisper into his ear. "I told you she would set us up."

Horton pointed. "Look, Doc. What do you see?"

"Hunger, obviously."

"No, you idiot. Look. Don't assume. They don't know where we are; otherwise they'd be making a dash straight for our position."

"They could simply be avoiding a direct path on purpose. You can't know what they're thinking."

"So now you're calling them clever? Like they have intelligence? Which is it, Doc? Are they animal or human? Can't be both."

Lipton didn't have a response.

Horton didn't wait for one. "If she wanted us dead, she never would have led us in here or had us mask our scent. Trust me, she's on our side. You just need to accept it and put your prejudices aside for once. Not everyone is hiding something."

Right then, Lipton noticed a change outside. The Scabs had altered their course, heading directly toward their position inside the house. He motioned to the window. "I'd say that confirms my suspicion. Maybe you should let the grownups do the thinking from now on, Einstein."

Horton whipped his head around, his eyes glancing at the course correction outside first, then he aimed them at Helena. "Did you do this?"

She didn't respond, her eyes fixed on the activity outside.

Lipton smacked Horton on the shoulder to get his attention. "What do we do now?" he asked, letting his eyes drop to the weapon in Horton's hand. "There aren't enough bullets in that gun. Not unless you shoot one of those infamous magic bullets from the Kennedy Assassination and take them all out at once."

"We run. That's what we do. There's got to be a back way out of this place. Come on, follow me."

Horton went to stand, but Helena pulled him down. She pointed out the window.

When Lipton followed her finger, he saw a shadow blur into the foreground from the right. It was a man covered in a wrap of clothes, like a winterized toga that was open down the front, with what looked like body armor underneath.

His face was covered with a hoodie and his hands were fast, damn fast, as he wielded two curved swords, moving them in an over-under circular pattern, his hands gripping their leather-wrapped handles.

He slipped into the center of the hunger gang with the grace and speed of a fearless Ninja. The Scabs spread out and circled him, showing an excess of jagged teeth.

The man kept moving his swords, waiting and watching, as if he were baiting them to make the first move.

Then it started.

They came at him.

First in singles, then in pairs, each of them snarling with a weapon in hand.

He unfurled his swords in seemingly all directions at once, slicing at the threats coming his way, never remaining in the same spot for more than a heartbeat or two. Only once could Lipton see the curve of the man's blades as they minced skin and bone, blurring together faster than bullets could fly.

Reaction was impossible for the Scabs in such close quarters, their numbers working against them.

They were too close, allowing the man to use his extended reach, cutting through several of them with one swipe, his balance like that of a feral cat.

Three of the Scabs held back, looking dumbfounded, as their brethren met their demise with the speed of the wind.

Limbs were separated from bodies.

Trunks were opened up, spilling intestines into a growing pool of tissue and muck.

Arteries were severed, releasing their life-giving blood in geyser-like sprays, pulsating with each frantic heart-pump.

A few heads were liberated, too, no longer attached to the bondage of their frostbitten bodies.

Lipton couldn't help but picture the underside of a lawnmower, its blades whirling with power, carving up and spitting out anything that came within its reach.

The carnage intensified as the unidentified man continued his onslaught with the precision of an orchestra conductor, working through the hunger gang in a blur of precision.

If Lipton hadn't seen it with his own eyes, he would have thought he was watching a Hollywood movie, one that had been choreographed to shock and awe in a spray of red.

The last three of the Scabs rushed the man in unison, forming a skirmish line of teeth.

The swordsman took a long step forward to catch the trio midstride with a double swipe high on their bodies. Their eyes flared wide as their necks gaped open, spraying blood in a wide arc.

As quickly as he'd started, the man froze in place, holding his weapons in their follow-through position as he gazed at their gasping throats.

It took a ridiculously long time for the final three Scabs to topple over, their collective life-force running out in spurts. Each cannibal seemed content to accept its fate as gravity pulled their twitching corpses onto the pile of the cannibal slaughterhouse.

The swordsman released his pose, then stood in a defensive posture for a short minute, his eyes scanning the perimeter.

The prey had become the predator, searching for more victims.

There were none.

Just as an assembly line powers down after a productive day of work, he pulled his swords in and sheathed them in one fluid motion, tilting them at the ready for his next battle.

A gust of wind raked across Lipton's face as he watched the strange warrior stand in victory. He couldn't stop the words on his tongue from setting themselves free. "Holy shit! Who the hell is that?"

Horton didn't hesitate. "The Nomad."

"Where the hell did he come from?"

"Nobody knows."

"I take it he's some kind of vigilante?"

"That's the rumor. Though he didn't save me."

Helena bolted to her feet, then scaled the windowsill and slid through the opening.

"Wait!" Horton said, making a grab for her, his hands coming up empty.

Helena tore across the front yard and into the street, taking a direct route to the Nomad.

Lipton thought she was going to attack the man who'd just taken out her clan, but that was not what happened.

Helena's feet came to a stop, then she dropped to her knees in front of the stranger.

"What the hell is she doing?" Lipton asked, not believing what he was seeing.

"Looks like she's praying."

"What? Like he's a god?"

"Apparently," Horton said, as Lipton watched Helena grab the back of the Nomad's hand and pull it close to her face. She kissed it before holding it to her forehead, bowing in reverence, as if she were some kind of wild peasant.

Nomad pulled his hand free from her grasp, leaving her begging for his touch with a stab of filthy hands and fingers.

She cried out, sounding as though she couldn't decide on whether to grunt or snarl.

The Nomad continued to fend her off, taking a step back. He brought his head around and shot a look at Lipton's position, holding it for a few beats.

The man's face was obscured by the goggles and mask, but Lipton sensed he was looking directly at him.

The stare-down lasted another few moments before the Nomad turned and used a fast step to head away from Helena, his ankle-length cloak flapping in the breeze.

Helena got up and ran after the Nomad, once again trying to latch onto him.

"Shit, she's going with him," Horton said.

The Nomad whirled around and used a straight arm aimed at her chest to stop her, pressing her back to her knees.

"Apparently not," Lipton said.

Nomad held up his index finger and stared at her for a few beats before turning away and resuming his trek.

This time Helena didn't get up and run after him. Instead, she leaned forward in slow motion and fell face-first to the dirt, then rolled to her side and wrapped her arms around her stomach, writhing on the ground in a rocking motion.

"You don't see that every day," Lipton quipped.

"Something's wrong," Horton answered as he pressed to his feet in a grumble, then took an awkward step toward the window.

Lipton grabbed him with both hands, pulling him hard to the ground. "You can't go out there. It's not safe."

"Let me go, Doc. I have to help her."

"No. You don't. Leave her be," Lipton answered, watching the Nomad pick up speed, sprinting in a full gallop before disappearing from view between a pair of houses.

"Can't blame the guy," Lipton said. "I sure wouldn't want her following me like a lost puppy."

Helena remained in the dirt with her arms reaching out for the masked man for another minute before she stopped, got to her feet, and headed back toward them.

Lipton watched her head drop, her hair falling forward to cover up her face. "Looks like you have yourself a new pet, Horton. Just like you wanted. Gonna have to feed it, though. Failure is never an option with a meat eater like her."

Horton didn't respond, his gaze locked on Helena as if he were in a state of shock. Or disbelief.

Lipton released his hands from Horton, then wrapped his arms around his shivering body. "Now that that's over with, what do you say we get dressed? I've got a serious case of shrinkage happening here."

CHAPTER 26

Early the next morning, Stan Greco, AKA "Dice", put his hands under the faucet and let a trickle of water wash over his skin. The water pressure was still low, same as the day before, forcing him to cup his hands together to gather enough water to splash his face.

Doc Lipton still hadn't fixed the plumbing issue. Typical. Dice would need to remind him. Again typical. Only this time, Dice needed to finish waking up first, before he walked to Doc's lab.

Dice always slept like a rock. Last night was no different, except for the passing out part. His mind was running in super slow motion. He could hear his thoughts echoing in the empty space that was his head, sounding muffled and distant, as if he was underwater.

"Ugh, I never should have had those last three shots," he said, thinking of Doc's legendary moonshine. Talk about a real ass kicker. At least he didn't have a pounding headache. He'd had his share of those, both recently and long ago—before The Event.

He was ten years younger back then and able to party with a table full of local girls after his late-night shift at the Bellagio in Vegas. He could drink and screw for hours, then get up the next day and do it all over again.

His high-paying job of dealing cards was a great way to meet chicks. So was tending the craps table, everyone leaning over and needing his assistance. The scenery was everywhere, usually clad in a skimpy dress with plenty of cleavage, unlike the complete sausage fest that was Frost's compound.

When Dice studied his reflection in the mirror, the face staring back told the whole story. The thin slits for eyelids. The bloodshot eyes behind them. The bruises on his neck. All of it was a dead giveaway for a man without a purpose—a true purpose, other than doing Fletcher's bidding off the books.

"Come on, you pussy. Shake it off," he mumbled in a gruff tone, splashing his face with more water.

What he needed was a reboot. And some coffee. Gallons of it. Yet, the camp had none. Coffee was extinct, just like the rest of the planet.

Doc Lipton could make just about anything, but he couldn't grow coffee beans out of thin air. Nor could he synthesize caffeine. Two items that would be worth their weight in gold, if they still existed.

Maybe Dr. Edison across the No-Go Zone had solved the problem. Some type of new invention. Rumor had it Edison was at least as gifted as Lipton at making something out of nothing.

Even though Dice knew the odds of that were nil, it still didn't stop him from dreaming about it—a giant, hot, steaming cup of joe. Something to warm the body on a frigid morning.

He closed his eyes and let his mind sink into his memories, flashing back to his days in the casino.

Every morning he'd stop at Starbucks before clocking in for his shift. It was next to the high-end jewelry store and only a few steps from the security door that led into the inner depths of the hotel.

He missed the tantalizing aroma, the texture, and the instant energy. The Danish they served wasn't bad either, providing a much-needed sugar boost in the morning.

Dice swung his focus to the right, checking the condition of the bar of soap next to the sink. The homemade soap was a dirty, crusty white, with half of its original size missing. Its diminished state and layers of filth were expected, since more than two dozen men used this same bathroom. But the black hair wasn't.

He rolled his eyes. "You gotta be kidding me."

The thick, curly strand was about four inches long and looked to be stuck to the bar as if someone had embedded it there on purpose. It wasn't one of his, that's for sure, his flaming red hair a good five times longer.

The hair could have been from someone's head or possibly somewhere else on a man's body, conjuring a visual that he didn't want in his mind.

The mental image sparked a wave of nausea, making him bend over the sink just in case his system hurled some of the hooch back to its sender.

If he puked, he wouldn't have been the only one. There were plenty of chunks on the floor in the head, only inches from the toilet. He imagined more than one of his fellow campers had been on their knees the night before, praying to the porcelain gods.

He'd seen it all before; however, last night's celebration was off the hook. The strangulation tests were new, invented by a few of the deviants and ex-military types, all of them itching for a fight. Exactly the kind of men Frost loved.

Perhaps it had something to do with all the new weapons they'd been building. The fabrication teams had been working doubles to get them done before today's scheduled meet with Edison's group.

Dice figured the elderly professor and his sidekick Krista Carr had ordered a huge shipment of arms, but nobody knew for sure. Frost kept the details of each meet a secret.

The urge to vomit vanished a few moments later, allowing Dice to straighten up. It was then that he realized hangovers, hurling, and hair seemed to go together, a wicked combination that would make a billy goat sick.

Dice rubbed his hands together after deciding that friction should replace the need for a lather. There was no chance he was touching the bar of soap. Or the lid on the shitter, for that matter.

He planned to take a leak outside during his morning run. The cold weather would sting, but sometimes a man must make hard choices. More so in a shared bathroom where the disgusting always meets the nasty.

The world may have ended with The Event, but that didn't mean a little consideration for your fellow man wasn't still warranted. He didn't understand why his friends couldn't clean up after themselves. It only took a few seconds to do.

The yellow hand towel looked fresh, so he used it to dry his face and hands, then brought his fingers up to tighten the wrap he used to keep his ponytail in place.

It was time to go wake up Fletcher, a daily chore he despised. Even so, he'd never complain to the man dubbed by Frost as second-in-command. Every man in the compound had his duties. Duties that must be carried out without fail.

When Dice turned around, he found Fletcher standing in the hallway, just beyond the entrance, his face covered in a grimace. Probably from a headache, Dice figured.

Fletcher was known to partake a little too much, just like the rest of the men, usually announcing that his hangover was officially at DEFCON 1.

The chiseled black man didn't wait for Dice to speak first, rubbing his bald head with his enormous right hand. "You seen Doc?"

"No. But he needs to fix the damn water. Out again."

"Yeah, tell me about it. Got up to piss a little while ago and couldn't flush. So I went to his bunk to remind him, you know, gentle like, but he wasn't there."

"What about his lab?"

Fletcher shook his head, his lips turning silent.

"Where the hell is he?" Dice asked.

"He's AWOL."

"You sure?"

"Just checked his desk. His notebooks are missing. So's his favorite hat."

"The fedora?"

"He never goes outside without it."

"Shit. Frost will go ballistic," Dice said. "We have to find him."

"There isn't time. I need everyone to cover the meet this morning. That's priority one. We'll find Doc later. That lump won't get far on his own."

"I can skip my run, if you need me to. I'm sure I can track him down."

"No, I need you to go. They're expecting you," Fletcher said, handing him a folded piece of paper.

Its corners were torn at an angle and tucked under themselves, just like Fletcher did every day. It was his version of a safety seal, not that it was secure by any stretch. Anyone could open it, though Dice never did.

His job was simple: keep his eyes open and mouth shut. Arrive exactly when and where he was told, and never look at contents of the notes sent back and forth. "Where's the meet today?"

"Drop Seven. Usual time. They'll give you something to bring back. Keep it secure. Eyes only."

"Not a problem, chief," Dice answered, running a quick calculation in his mind. Drop Seven was the closest rendezvous point, meaning he could get there and back before the teams headed to the Trading Post. "Should be back in plenty of time."

Fletcher put a hand on Dice's shoulder. "I always know I can count on you. Always."

"Just doing my job, boss."

CHAPTER 27

"Hey ya, Summer," a nice-looking young man said in a friendly tone as he approached her in the opposite direction along the outer ring of the silo bay. She didn't recognize the stocky guy who wore blue coveralls and a t-shirt, but he seemed to know her.

"What's up?" Summer said, faking it with a half-smile, hoping it would appear legit. Her plan was to cruise past him, but he slowed to block her path. She brought her feet to an abrupt halt, almost running into him.

He stood close—way too close—the top of his head only an inch taller than hers. What he lacked in height, he made up for in weight. It was muscular weight, not flab, his biceps in clear view.

His blonde hair was an amazing shade of gold, the middle of it pushed up into a twisted swirl down the middle—like a rooster—offsetting his porcelain white skin.

His eyes peered into hers, as if he knew something she didn't. "You got a minute?"

"Well, uh, can't. Meeting someone," Summer answered, her tone unsteady.

She took a step back, looking past him, her heartbeat racing as a tingle rose up across her body. It came out of nowhere. So did the tremble in her hands. She stuffed them into her pockets, praying he didn't notice.

His eyes turned toward the observation window on his right, giving her the impression he was trying to appear cool, almost detached.

So this is what it feels like, she thought to herself, memorizing every nuance of the boy's face before following his eyes to the side.

A vegetable rack hung inside the former missile bay. It was loaded with overflowing greens, though a few of them looked black, almost dead, as if someone had taken a blow torch to them. She hadn't seen that before and wondered if someone had neglected the plants in that particular rack.

The six-foot-long tray was suspended by wires running top to bottom, with a mirror installed next to it, directing sunlight deeper into the hydroponics chamber.

"You don't remember me, do you?" the guy said, bringing his attention back to her.

Summer shrugged, unable to stop from staring at him. "Should I?" She wondered how long this chat would take. She didn't want to be rude, especially since he was very cute, but she was already late for a meeting with Edison.

A girl's gotta prioritize over glamorize, she thought to herself, even though she didn't want to leave.

"We met a couple of weeks ago. I was the guy who smashed your leg when I was sweeping the deck on six."

She didn't recall anyone hitting her with a broom. Especially a blonde guy with the face of Thor. Must have been a mix-up. But then again, there was his total cuteness and her not wanting to be rude thing, so she wasn't about to correct his goof. "Oh yeah. Now I remember."

He put his hand out. "My name's Nick Simms. But you can call me Simmer. Everyone else does."

She grabbed his hand and shook it, appreciating the whole Summer and Simmer thing.

Was the rhyming name thing kindred spirits or some random fluke? "Sorry, Nick. My mind was somewhere else. I'm usually really good with faces."

He let go of her hand, his eyes focused on her cheek. "Speaking of faces, what happened?"

Her hand went up to the bandages, checking that they hadn't come loose. "Just some bad luck." She wanted to say more, but that's all that came out of her mouth.

His face tensed as his soulful eyes grew cold, moving their focus to her forehead. "Did someone hurt you? Just tell me who it was and I'll go have a little chat with him. Man-to-man, if you know what I mean."

His unexpected gallantry brought warmth to her heart, even though if he tangled with Wicks, this kid would get crushed. "It wasn't anyone in particular. Just an accident while I was out on a mission. Mostly."

His intensity cooled. "Stitches?"

She nodded.

"How many?"

"Not sure. Wasn't really paying attention when Liz patched me up."

"Hurt, I'll bet."

"Some, but I'm used to it," she answered, deciding that she didn't want to sound like a helpless girly-girl, even though that's what she wished she looked like at the moment—a pretty, totally together girl who knew what to say and how to act. It's hard to reel in a fish when you don't have any bait.

"No doubt," he answered, his eyes indicating he was most likely probing her for weakness.

She had plenty of that. More so right now. There's nothing quite as embarrassing as meeting someone new and interesting with your face all torn up, as if you just lost an argument with an angry hedge trimmer.

Her mind took her deep into her memories, replaying a scene from her childhood. Her dad had just finished cutting the lawn, then fired up the noisy machine, sending puffs of blue smoke out from its engine.

She could still hear its high-pitched pinging as her dad trimmed the foliage around their house. Branches flew and her ears twanged, but she always followed him around the yard regardless. Not so much like a lost puppy, just a young girl who idolized her father.

That same annoying whine was the sound that her heart was making at the moment, screaming at her to say something to Simmer and not just stand there like a total spaz.

The pause in their conversation continued, stretching from a few seconds into a long minute.

She shuffled her feet.

He did the same, his hands in his pockets.

Summer finally regained control of her logic, leaning to the side to glance past him. She wondered how pissed Edison was going to be with her tardiness.

She wanted to stay and chat, but she needed to go. She wasn't sure what to do. Too many choices. Not enough time.

He seemed to sense her dismay. "Well, maybe later then?"

"For what?"

"You know, hang out. When you have a break in your schedule."

"Okay, sure. Maybe later."

"Cool. Catch you then," he said, resuming his trek.

She turned to catch his backside, wondering why a boy like Simmer was suddenly interested in her. The baggy coveralls weren't doing him any favors, but that was life in this place.

Endless cold. No privacy. And nobody ever looked their best.

At least this guy didn't stink. Plus, his smile seemed genuine. Then there was his nickname: Simmer. It fit perfectly. As in hot. This guy was all that and more. Plus, the whole one letter off thing between their names. Gotta love life's little coincidences.

Summer had no idea what he meant by "hanging out," but it intrigued her. She was certain it was more than just the wayward daydreams of a girl who was used to being alone.

It reminded Summer of her recent encounter with Krista. Both meetings were more than they appeared on the surface. If she had to categorize them, they were both more than chance but less than destiny. Something in between.

Her face blushed as thoughts of Simmer danced in her head, keeping her heartbeat thumping harder than normal.

Just then, her mind flashed a scene of her hands running wild in his beautiful hair, the soft strands twisting around her fingers in a gentle embrace.

Most of the young men in Nirvana kept their hair military short, but this boy had chosen a look that was bound to capture someone's attention. And that someone was her.

Other than Avery, nobody cute or age appropriate had ever looked her way twice. At least not in a romantic way, assuming she was reading the situation correctly.

She figured she'd remained a virgin because of her out of control hair. Or her plain looks. Or her complete lack of makeup or anything feminine. Or the whole End of the World thing.

The Event hadn't left her with many choices, unless she wanted to entertain the idea of one of the older guys running around the silo.

She shuddered, thinking about the endless string of middle-aged man bodies she'd seen waiting in the shower line. Some wore a towel. Others didn't. Body hair, man boobs, and sagging wrinkles everywhere.

None of it pleasant.

Well, that was not entirely accurate. There were a few of Krista's military guys. At least they took care of themselves. Mostly.

Though their shower rotations were on a different day than hers, so she really never got a good look at them. Without a shirt, that is. Or in a towel. Unless, of course, she accidentally wandered down that hallway at precisely the right time, looking shocked, even though that was a total lie.

And now there was Simmer. She was sure she hadn't seen him before. All of a sudden, she bumped into him. Weird.

Either way, she never paid much attention to the romantic side of things. Until now.

Maybe it was time to entertain new ideas— those that come with certain aspects that can change a girl's perspective. About her looks. Her life. Her future. Her insides. Everything.

Unfortunately, Avery wasn't around long enough to find out what those feelings might have been.

Maybe Simmer would be, now that those same feelings seemed to be back. She could feel them starting to germinate, ready to break through the soil covering her heart.

She smiled, then resumed her walk to Edison's.

Her run-in with Simmer had flushed her body of the anxiety, leaving her ready to take on the challenge of explaining her recent actions to the boss of Nirvana. There were facts and events Edison needed to know. Things he needed to understand.

Now that her heart was in the right place, maybe Edison's would be, too. She liked her chances, knowing that luck runs in streaks, both good and bad. Maybe hers had just turned. Simmer was the start.

She wasn't sure what to call her instant mood adjustment. Perhaps it was some form of cosmic rebalancing event. Or maybe a personality reboot.

In the end, the term didn't matter, but the chance meeting with a boy and his golden hair did.

CHAPTER 28

When Summer made it to Edison's door, she stood for a moment and adjusted her clothes. Edison wouldn't care what she looked like, but she did— maybe for the first time ever. Was it because of her recent encounter with the boy or was it because of her guilt? A good question, one that she wasn't prepared to answer. Not yet anyway.

Regardless, there was only so much she could do with the drabness surrounding her, but she decided it couldn't hurt to try.

Pride might have been one of the seven deadly sins, but laziness was worse. So was self-loathing, she decided, her mind charging into an area of her psyche she'd had never let it venture before.

Her mind flashed another image of Nick Simms and his adorable face.

She couldn't help but let another smile take over her lips. Smiles were hard to come by the last decade in the silo, but maybe that was all about to change.

She knocked three times, feeling a surge of energy across her body. Perhaps today wouldn't suck as bad as all the others that came before.

"Come in."

Summer turned the knob and sauntered in, feeling like she could conquer the world.

Edison pointed to a chair in front of his desk, his face stern, without a hint of emotion. "Have a seat. We need to talk," he said in a terse voice.

The redness in the old man's face was just as noticeable as the pinch of his eyebrows—a combination Summer had never seen before.

Whoever this man was, he wasn't the one Summer knew and loved. This was someone else, an imposter, and he was pissed, his downturned, beard-covered lips twitching.

Her worry returned with the force of a tsunami. A thousand words lined up on her tongue, but she wasn't sure which would be the appropriate response.

She decided to go with ignorance until she knew more. "Is something wrong, Professor?"

"I think you already know the answer to that, young lady."

She did, but the problem was, he could be upset about a number of things. She hadn't exactly been forthcoming since she'd returned from her Seeker Mission, nor had she followed many of the rules while she was out.

So many failures.

So much bad luck.

Where does a girl start?

She decided to begin at the end, focusing on the most recent. "Uh, well, I'm guessing this is about what happened with Krista and her pervert friend, Wicks."

"Maybe you should try again," Edison said, his forehead creased across the middle. "This time, try a little honesty. With yourself and with me."

Perhaps Edison knew about her self-inflicted head injury. There was only one way to find out.

She pointed a finger to her forehead.

Edison shook his head.

She moved her finger to the bandage on her cheek.

Edison folded his arms but didn't respond, his face turning an even darker shade of red.

Summer wasn't sure if that was a yes or a no. Could be either. All she knew was that it looked like his head was about to explode.

"I'm waiting," Edison said, his teeth clenched.

She shrugged. "I'm sorry, Professor. I don't understand. What did I do? I know I was really late, again, but—"

He didn't let her finish her sentence. "The necklace, Summer. Where is it?"

Her hand went to the collar of her sweatshirt before she could stop it. The lump in her throat doubled in size. "You know about that?"

"When were you going to tell me?"

Summer's mind tore through the events of the previous day, looking for answers. One came roaring to the top of the list: Liz. She must have noticed it was missing when she tended to her wounds.

Liz ratted me out?

Summer forced a fleshy bulge of mucus down her gullet, wishing she had a glass of water. She wasn't sure her lips would work properly, not with a long overdue confession peeking over the horizon. "My plan was to tell you this morning, but then I walked in here and you looked like you were already mad about something. I was scared. I wasn't sure what to do."

"When did you lose it?"

"Yesterday. One minute it was there and then it was gone."

"How did you lose it?"

"Not sure exactly. Could have been a couple of places."

"Give me your best guess."

"My best guess?"

"Yes, as if your life is on the line and you only have one chance to find it."

Summer hesitated, thinking it through. "Probably when I tripped over some pallets."

"I see," he said, uncoiling his arms before leaning forward on his desk. "How does that happen, exactly?"

Was he being sarcastic or genuinely interested? She wasn't sure. "I ran around a corner and there they were, all over the place, like the wind scattered them or something. Didn't see 'em until it was too late. I got up and never noticed it was missing. Just bad luck, Professor. Could have happened to anybody."

"I would think that necklace was important enough for to you to check that it was still around your neck. I guess not."

"It is important to me. In fact, I cried when I realized it was gone. It's all I have to remind me of June. I was crushed, Professor. You have to believe me."

"Why didn't you go back and look for it?"

"Couldn't. By the time I realized it was gone, it was too late. Plus, the pallets weren't the only place I could have lost it."

"Where else?"

"Might have been when I fell through the floor of this old building and was buried under a bunch of snow and other stuff. Had to dig myself out. I almost died in there, Professor. Like I keep telling everybody, there was a lot of bad luck yesterday. That's why I was late."

He nodded in a methodical manner, his upper lip tucked under. It took a few seconds before he spoke again. "Someone was chasing you, weren't they?"

She took a second, then gave him a head nod, sensing that he already knew the answer.

"Who?" he asked.

"Uh—"

"The truth this time," Edison said.

She wanted to tell him everything, but she couldn't. She had to pick and choose some of the facts, avoiding the stuff about her breaking the treaty and crossing the No-Go Zone. He would never forgive her for that. "Frost's men."

"Liz told me it was Scabs. So which is it?"

"Frost's men."

"Why did you tell Liz it was the Scabs?"

She shrugged. "I don't know. I just did."

He flared his eyebrows, the redness in his cheeks still burning. "Why do you do that? You don't have to lie. Not to us."

She wanted to crawl away and hide in her room, where nobody would ever find her. "Not sure. I just get this feeling inside and I can't stop it."

"Which is it? You can't stop the lie or the feeling?"

"Both, I guess. It's like they're the same thing."

"I just don't understand, Summer. Why do you continue to do this? Are you scared? Is that why you always lie?"

"No, it's not that. It's more like a storm inside me. It's full of fire and it hurts until I let it out. I'm not sure how else to describe it. But it makes me say things that aren't true."

"It's called guilt. Trust me, we all have it. None of us are immune. When that happens, the first instinct is self-preservation. That's why we lie, Summer. Everyone does."

She nodded her head yes. His explanation made sense. Mostly.

"But lying isn't the answer. You need to give people a chance. Not everyone will judge you like you think. Can you do that? Can you please just give me a chance to understand?"

"Okay, I'll try."

"So . . . tell me exactly what happened yesterday," Edison asked, his words barbed with intensity. "The truth, Summer. Nothing but."

Summer cleared her throat, waiting for a groundswell of courage to find her before she spoke. "Well, first the Scabs cornered me, then Frost's men came along and killed them just in the nick of time. We talked for a bit, then they let me go. A little later, more of Frost's men cornered me, but I got away on my own this time. At least until I ran into those damn pallets. That's when I cut my cheek. I got up and ran inside the nearest building before they caught up to me. Then the floor collapsed when they started yanking on the door to get in. I think I was knocked out for a while when I hit the bottom. When I woke up, it was dark outside and they were gone."

Edison nodded, taking time before he responded. "Let me make sure I have this straight. Frost's men saved you from the Scabs? For no particular reason?"

"Yes, Professor. They showed up out of nowhere, just in time to kill the Scabs. Blood was everywhere. I was so scared. I just wanted to go home."

"And then they let you go, only to corner you again?"

"Well, Fletcher did. Let me go, I mean. In fact, he offered me a gun so I could stay safe. The others wanted to sell me for ammo or something. It was intense. But Fletcher wasn't around the second time, when I ran into them."

"Where was this? Our side or theirs?"

"Which time?"

"Both."

Her heart skipped a beat, knowing another lie was coming. Well, sort of. She decided to answer his question about the first encounter, then it wasn't a flat-out lie. "Ours."

"That means Frost's men broke the treaty."

"Yep. But for a good reason, I think. They must have been tracking the hunger gang. That's why they showed up when they did. Lucky for me. Otherwise, the Scabs were going to kill me. I wouldn't be too mad at them, Professor. They saved my life. Sometimes, you have to make exceptions, right? Isn't that what you always say?"

Edison's eyes glanced to the side and down, at his wife's picture, then came back again. "Why didn't you report this the second you got back?"

"I was going to, but first I needed to get stitched up by Liz. Then Krista arrested me and threw me in jail. What else could I do? It all happened so fast. Plus, I was totally exhausted. I wasn't thinking straight."

"You tell someone. That's what you do. It's not a hard concept, Summer. These secrets of yours can't continue."

Summer thought of her lost Seeker Map and the store she loved to visit, Infinite Reads, wondering if she should tell him about both. Her can of secrets was so full it was bursting at the seams.

Yet, if she did, she worried she might not be able to stop, feeling the need to tell Edison everything. Then he'd hate her for sure. "I know, Professor. I'm *soooo* sorry. I really am."

"If there's anything else I should know, now's the time, Summer. Right now, this very instant."

"Well, uh . . ." she said, stuttering to buy time for her mind to make a decision. It took another thirty seconds to find her nerve. "Well, there is something."

She touched a finger to the bandage on her forehead. "This didn't happen exactly the way I told you."

"So, another lie," Edison said with a twisted scowl, looking as though he was about to swallow his face. "It just never ends with you, does it?"

So much for him not judging her. "I'm sorry, but things get complicated."

"How am I supposed to believe anything you say?"

"I don't know. Sometimes the truth just sucks, so I avoid it. I'm not sure what else to say. I'm not all perfect like you, Professor."

"Trust me, I'm not perfect. Far from it."

"You are to me. You always seem to know exactly what to say or what to do, way ahead of everyone else. Like when you built this place. It's like you can see the future or something. Otherwise, we'd all be dead."

Edison smirked, looking embarrassed. "Sometimes people make moves and just get lucky, Summer. Or they get advice from a friend. Either way, it's never about seeing the future. It's about trust, knowledge, and playing the odds."

"Well, just so you know, Wicks *did* slap me in the hall, then felt me up just like I said. Plus, he shoved me into the cell and I did fall head-first at the cot. But I didn't cut my head open right then."

"How then?"

"On the front bars."

"Did he do it?"

"No, I did it to myself. On purpose like."

"Why on Earth would you do that?"

"To get him into trouble. I needed everyone to believe me about the other stuff he did and I thought if I was bleeding, you would. You and Liz, I mean. I was already in jail, plus nobody was around but Krista when Wicks slapped me and wanted to punch my face in. She never takes my side in anything, so I had to do something to make sure. Plus, Wicks and I were alone when he touched me like a total pervert. I know what I did was wrong, but I panicked. Please don't be mad at me. Please."

Edison shook his head, his eyes dropping to his desk. They were aimed in the direction of June's photo again. He looked as lost as Summer felt, possibly looking for his wife's guidance.

Summer couldn't keep her lips silent. "I'm sorry I didn't tell you the truth. I was so scared, I just reacted. It was dumb, I know."

"And wrong."

"Yes, and wrong."

"You should know by now that we would have believed you either way."

Summer nodded, unable to find the words to answer him. Nothing sounded right in her head.

Edison exhaled, taking a long time to let the air out, as if he was deciding what to do with her. "I hope you know I had that man arrested based on your claims. A man who now faces serious charges. This isn't a game, Summer."

"No, it's not, but he deserved it for the other stuff he did. He can't go around hitting and feeling up girls whenever he wants. That's not right."

"Except now you're not a credible victim. There's no telling how The Council will react once they learn about you hurting yourself and then lying about it. We both know how Krista is going to vote."

"Do you really have to tell them? Maybe it can just be our little secret."

"Of course I have to tell them. The truth is paramount around here."

Summer put her head in her hands. She'd messed up big time. He must certainly hate her by now.

Edison's tone sharpened when he said, "By the way, there was a Council Meeting while you were out."

Summer looked up, releasing her hands from her face. "I heard. Liz told me."

"Krista wants you banished."

"So what else is new? She always wants me banished." Summer said, letting a beat pass before she continued. "I take it The Council said no."

"Correct. Otherwise, we wouldn't be having this conversation."

That's one piece of good luck at least, she thought to herself.

"The vote was damn close, though. You know I can't keep protecting you like this. I'm so disappointed in you, Summer. It breaks my heart. It really does."

She started to weep, unable to hold back the tears. "I'm sorry. I try really hard, but sometimes bad luck just happens."

"It's not about luck. It's about growing up and taking responsibility for your actions. This is Nirvana, not Summer's Vacation where she can do whatever she wants whenever she wants. It's time for the old Summer to end and a new one to take her place. No more lies. None. Do you hear me?"

She nodded with her head hanging low, the tears filling her cheeks. "Please, don't be mad at me. I can't deal with that. You're my only friend."

"I don't think that's the case. You have lots of friends; you just can't keep taking advantage of them."

She wasn't sure what to say. Between the lightheadedness swirling in her mind and the pain in her heart, she couldn't focus her logic. It was a jumbled mess.

Edison's tone turned harsh. "This was the last straw, young lady."

"You're not going to kick me out, are you?"

"No. But that day is coming unless you change. And I mean right now."

She nodded, wiping the tears on her face.

Edison continued after a pause, changing his tone to one of compassion. "Look, I know you've had it rough. It wasn't easy growing up in a place like this, especially after what happened to your family."

"No, it wasn't. But I hope you know I owe you and June everything. I love you both so much."

"Of course I know. And I love you, too. So did June. That's why we took you in. But that's all history now. It's not just about you and me anymore. There are others who depend on us. Whole families, in fact. We have to think about the bigger picture."

"No, you're right Professor. I'm such a total screwup. I'm sorry. I'll do better, I promise."

Edison shook his head. "It's good to hear you admit it, but in the end, without real change, those are just words, my dear. Words we've all heard a hundred times before."

"But they *are* true. I said I was sorry."

He didn't seem to care. "It's become abundantly clear to me that protecting you all these years hasn't helped you find yourself like I'd hoped. In fact, I think I've become your enabler. That was my mistake. You're old enough now to start taking responsibility. So there will be changes. Immediately."

"What kind of changes?" she asked, praying he wasn't going to take her Seeker status away. She needed those visits to her safehouse, where she could relax in privacy and read. It was the only thing keeping her from going insane.

"Krista pitched an idea last night about a new training program. And I agreed. We're going to assign a partner to you. Someone you can get up to speed as a Seeker."

"What?"

"We think it's best if you have a wingman for a while."

"You mean a spy."

"No, a training partner."

"Doesn't that violate the rules, Professor?"

"It's only temporary so I'm sure The Council will make an exception. We need someone to help keep you focused and provide a little backup."

"That's a spy in my book. Or you're trying to replace me."

"It's not like that at all."

"Yes, it is. I know Krista doesn't trust me, and now you don't either."

"It's not about trust, Summer. It's about safety. Everyone's safety. Everyone matters and everyone must follow the rules. No more leeway. You hear me?"

Summer sniffed but didn't say anything. She knew his words were true, even if she didn't want to admit it.

"Look, I'm not going to be around forever," Edison said, his words sharp and to the point.

"What does that mean? Are you sick?"

"No, I'm just old. Things happen. You need to stand on your own two feet. It's time, Summer. It really is. I hope that someday you'll want to take over for me and continue what June and I started here."

Her tears resumed, dripping into her lap. She didn't know what to say.

Edison continued, using his fatherly voice. "I know there's so much more to you just waiting to break out. You have greatness inside. I just don't know how to help you see it."

"Maybe I don't want to see it. That's a lot of pressure to deal with."

"You can handle it. I know you can."

"That's easy for you to say. But I'm not like you."

"Yes, you are. You're smart, you're capable, and you have a great big heart. Everyone knows that. Those are big components of what makes a great leader. You just need to apply yourself and stop being so selfish all the time."

Her tears stopped. She pointed at the door. "I'm sure everyone out there thinks it's easy being a Seeker, but it's not. Between Frost's men and those Scabs, people are always trying to hurt me. You can't expect someone to make perfect decisions every time. Sometimes a girl just has to react or run. Usually, there's no other choice."

"That's why you need backup."

"Don't I get a say in any of this?"

"Not anymore. The decision has been made. Changes are coming. For your own good as well as Nirvana's."

"Who's the spy?" Summer asked, thinking it was going to be another asshole like Wicks. Some behemoth who wouldn't be able to keep his hands off her.

"A young man by the name of Simms. And for the last time, he's not a spy."

A flash of golden blonde hair filled her mind. "Nick? Seriously?"

"I take it you know him?"

"Uh, well, sort of. Think I bumped into him once or twice," she answered, realizing Simmer stopped her in the hallway as a precursor to being assigned as her trainee.

What had started out as a possible romantic interest turned out to be nothing more than a ruse. A ruse that just drove a dagger of reality into her chest, slicing off a hunk of her heart in the process. She should have known she'd never get that lucky. Not with a boy as hot as Simmer. She'd let her guard down and gotten stung.

What was she thinking?

Edison sat back in his chair with a grimace on his face.

Summer got the impression that his spine was hurting by the way he moved. Or he'd just farted. Old people do that and never seem to claim it.

"I'm glad you're already familiar with him because he's the one you're going to train. However, before then, I need you to start taking your role as Seeker a lot more seriously. It's time to learn what's at stake and why, firsthand. To that end, you will be accompanying me and Krista today so you can get a taste of how serious this all is."

"To the Trading Post?"

"Yes. We have a scheduled meeting with Frost and his crew this morning. It's serious business with serious men."

Summer's heart sank. Someone in Frost's camp was bound to recognize her. Plus, they had her Seeker Map and might tell Edison they found it on their side of the No-Go Zone.

If that fact came out, she was history.

Edison would never take her side again, on anything.

CHAPTER 29

Rod Zimmer waited for Security Chief Krista Carr to finish addressing her men regarding how to cover the Trading Post meet. Their load-out was complete, every man wearing winter camos, helmets, goggles, boots, and tactical vests stuffed with magazines. Each held an assault rifle close to their chests, slung into place with a shoulder strap.

"I need everyone focused today," she said to the soldiers standing before her. She walked the line, landing a closed fist on each of their chest rigs, getting a "Yes Ma'am" in return as part of their pre-deployment process.

She stopped her pacing at the far end of the men, focusing on the group assembled there. "Remember the rules, Team One. No concealed weapons at the inspection point. Oh, and don't antagonize those damn dogs. Not like last time. That's an order."

The men in Team One answered in the affirmative, their tone sharp and jaws stiff.

Zimmer had seen this all before. Krista believed in tradition, just like she believed in the rules. Prepping her men was no different. There were steps to follow. Words to say. Adrenaline to spike.

Her ritual wasn't only to foster good luck. It was about channeling the warrior mindset. If a soldier wasn't in the proper headspace, he'd find himself on the losing end of a battle.

Focus, pride, and drive were all part of the equation, each one a close cousin to failure. Every man counted on the solider next to him, and all of them relied on her to lead the charge.

Krista resumed her walk, pacing the line, while addressing her men. "We don't know what we'll face out there, so keep your shit wired tight. We run this by the numbers. No mistakes, gentlemen. That's how casualties happen. Our one and only goal is to make sure everyone returns safely. And I mean everybody. The cargo is secondary. We can replace it, but not the Professor or anyone else on his team. Or ours. Am I making myself clear?"

The squad responded with another round of "Yes Ma'am," each man sounding even more determined than a moment ago.

"All right, let's roll out. Finish your preparations. We leave in ten. Team One, you're on point. Take the lead vehicle. Report anything you see. Two, you're with me. We cover the emissary vehicle. Three, you're on cargo, while Four, you've got our six. Nobody opens fire without my say-so. Understood?"

Once again, the squad answered with a resounding yes, signaling their allegiance to the proud leader. The men scampered off under the watchful eyes of Krista, leaving Zimmer alone with her a few seconds later.

Zimmer let a dozen seconds of silence pass by before he spoke, allowing her headspace to clear. He knew her well enough to know she needed time to transition from commander to friend. "How did it go with Edison last night? Did he agree?"

Krista nodded. "Actually, he did, which I honestly didn't expect. In fact, it wasn't as difficult as I thought. I got the impression he may have already been thinking the same thing. Not sure, though."

"Then there is hope."

"I think your idea to change tactics and pitch our spy as only a temporary trainee is what did the trick. Thanks for the suggestion, by the way."

"Anytime. You know I've got your back."

"I hope my men feel the same way."

"Why, is there a problem?"

"Not sure, but something's off. I can feel it in my bones."

"With the men or the mission?"

"Both. I've got a bad feeling about today. Especially with my number two missing. Wicks always seems to know what I want before I know what I want, right before the shit hits the fan. That connection is hard to replace."

"I guess Edison didn't agree to release him?"

"I never asked."

"Why not? We both know Summer lied."

"Not about everything. Wicks did cross the line and I never should've let that happen."

Zimmer understood where she was coming from. It was how she was wired. "The rules are the rules."

"Roger that."

"I'm sure he'll face the consequences admirably."

"That he will. Count on it. But it still won't make the knot in my stomach go away."

"I'm sure it's nothing," Zimmer said. "You've covered these meets countless times before and never a scratch."

"I hope you're right," Krista said, shaking Zimmer's hand with a powerful grasp.

Zimmer squeezed hers in kind. "But keep your head down, just in case. Nirvana can't function without its most valuable asset."

"Appreciate it, buddy," she said, releasing her grip. She turned and walked away, taking the same path as her squad.

"Godspeed," Zimmer said, wondering if she'd take his advice. Especially today.

* * *

Sketch finished working the only barrel of fuel into Frost's biggest transport, scooting it next to the other cargo. Normally, he'd load at least six fifty-gallon drums, but since the refinery was out, he assumed that drum was all they could spare.

He wasn't sure if Edison was aware of the supply shortage, but it wasn't his place to question. His job was to load the cargo and keep his mouth shut. Yet it didn't stop him from pondering the facts. No law against that.

If Edison didn't know about the refinery, then it would explain the extra containers stacked about. Frost needed something else to trade besides fuel.

Each carton was cold to the touch. He assumed snow was keeping their contents refrigerated, but that was the extent of his knowledge.

Yet he wasn't surprised. Not in the least. Everyone in camp knew that Frost kept the details of the exchange to himself. Even his second-in-command wasn't told. Fletcher never seemed to mind; at least, he never gave any indication of that being the case.

Sketch hopped down from the back of the truck, his feet landing on the concrete in a plop.

After he straightened up, his eyes locked on to those of Simon Frost as the towering man walked through the loading area. Sergeant Barkley was two steps behind, with his chain collar clinking, as was Fletcher.

Sketch took in a breath and held it while the dog sniffed at his leg during the leadership team's collective flyby, but the mangy dog didn't show any teeth.

He let his breath out ten seconds later when the mutt continued on, feeling fortunate. That's when a hand landed on his shoulder from behind, making him flinch.

"That mongrel had you worried there for a moment, didn't he?" Dice asked.

"You got that right, brother. All I could think about was what that dog did to Horton's leg. Thought I was next."

"They can sense things. You weren't a threat."

"Neither was Horton, that poor son of a bitch. I hope he didn't suffer too long out there."

"Depends on how he went out. Hopefully the cold got him, not the Scabs. That's no way for a warrior to die. Not like that."

Sketch shook his head, seeing a visual of Horton in his head. It was all about snarls, teeth, and body parts coming apart in a blood-filled rage.

He knew that eventually he'd fuck up somewhere along the way and find himself labeled a failure. "Sometimes I wonder if we're backing the wrong horse."

"Me too. But we had to choose a side. It was either Frost and his guns or Edison and his green beans. Not much of a choice, if you ask me."

"No, it wasn't."

"We made the right call, Sketch. Nobody can survive out there alone. Not anymore. In the end, it's always best to be on the side with the superior numbers and firepower. At that we are, my friend. It's not even close."

"Yeah, you're right. Edison's *love thy neighbor* bullshit would have driven me crazy."

"And then some. That kumbaya crap is for pussies."

Sketch smiled, remembering an old phrase from his drill sergeant in the Army. "Moderation is for cowards."

Dice didn't hesitate with his response, the two of them sharing this same camaraderie many times in the past. "Anything worth doing is worth overdoing."

Sketch smiled in appreciation of his friend's loyalty. "I just don't get why Frost lets those assholes dictate terms like they do. It seems like Edison always gets his way."

"It's all part of the treaty. You weren't here before we struck that deal. Both sides took a ton of casualties in the early days. Neither side would have survived if we hadn't come up with a way to co-exist. Our ranks were fixed in number back then. Not like they are now with new bodies showing up after the thaw started."

"Still, it seems like Frost has a soft spot for Edison."

"Or maybe it's Fletcher who takes it easy on the professor," Dice said. "We aren't part of those command decisions."

"Probably a good thing. If we knew what was really going on, it might be even harder to sleep at night."

"That's what the booze is for," Dice said, laughing. "But seriously, if it weren't for the treaty, the Trading Post never would have been created."

"Who picked Heston to run it?"

"Edison. He knew the old rancher would be impartial and fair. Without it, both sides would have never made it this far. We need that safe space. It helps keep the peace."

"Just seems out of character for Frost, that's all."

"It is, but he can't just invade Edison's side of the No-Go Zone."

"Why not? We'd crush them."

"Well, first of all, we don't know where Edison's camp is."

"Shouldn't be too hard to find. All we need to do is follow them after one of these meets."

"Again, that's not allowed in the treaty," Dice said. "Even if it was, Frost is smart enough not to do it. We need them as much as they need us."

"Free and fair trade."

"Exactly. They need our fuel and we need their tech and their greens. Can't eat that fucking mystery meat all the time. Gotta have some veggies once in a while. Plus, we need some of their manpower occasionally. Doc can't do it all by himself."

"Don't you mean womanpower?"

Dice snickered, looking amused. "Shaw was an exception and you saw how that turned out. I'm pretty sure that'll be the last female Frost accepts in trade."

"At least for work duty," Sketch added in his most sarcastic voice.

"No doubt."

"She was a handful, that's for sure. I kept trying to warn her. But she just didn't listen."

"Typical," Dice said.

Sketch wondered if there would ever come a time when Edison would trade some of the hotter women for a little personal time, one-on-one like. Moonshine helped calm the troops but a nice piece of ass would accomplish so much more. He could only hope.

Dice tugged at Sketch's arm. "Come on. We've got work to do."

CHAPTER 30

"Don't come back, Paulo," Heston scolded the drifter they had under arrest. The man had wandered into the Trading Post the previous night with clothes a tattered mess and covered in layers of dirt. His face wasn't any cleaner, his black hair long and stringy.

Heston grabbed Paulo under the chin with a firm hand, yanking it up to make sure his pale, weary eyes were focused. They were set deep in his face, beyond the wrinkled skin sagging in clumps. "We're not running a God damn homeless shelter. This is your only warning."

A quick hand gesture sent Heston's men into action. They whisked the vagrant away, pulling Paulo by the arms, his feet dragging in the muck, taking the cloud of stench with him.

Heston stood in his cowboy boots, his weight pressing down on one leg more than the other, wondering how many more of these people he'd have to kick out. They seemed to be multiplying, each looking for handouts. More so the past few weeks, bringing them out from wherever they'd been hiding.

His men led Paulo past the aging John Deere backhoe and the barrels of extra diesel fuel, through the maze of chain link fencing, then hauled him out of the main gate.

They tossed the vagrant forward, his chest, face, and arms spilling to the ground. The guards in the tower kept their rifles trained on Paulo, just in case the dirt rat turned around and attacked.

"I don't know where they're all coming from, but this stops now," Heston said to one of the men standing with him. It was Aaron Fox, a tireless worker in his forties who used to work magic with horses. The kind of magic involving whispering. "I can't believe I ever used to care for these people."

"Desperate times make desperate people," Fox said, his tone thick with a Texas accent.

Heston agreed with his foreman, but didn't respond, his heart a cold slab of granite. It used to bleed for these beggars. All they wanted was food and a spare blanket. Now his insides were ice, barely raising his pulse rate when another one had to be evicted. Or executed.

Fox tilted his wide-brimmed, black cowboy hat up with a tip of his finger, his eyes forever hidden behind sunglasses. Somehow the stocky man had kept the same pair intact for ten years—a testament to his unwavering tenacity. "You know, we might burn a lot of ammo, but we could save a ton of time and headaches if we just lined them up and shot 'em."

Heston appreciated the man's loyalty and his frankness. "I wish I could, but that goes against my agreement with Edison. He still holds the charter to this place."

"Just thought I'd offer. You know I'm here for whatever you need, boss."

Heston slapped his long-time friend on the back. The man had been at his side since day one of the Trading Post. "And it's much appreciated, Fox. But we'll have to come up with another solution for all these rodents."

"I hear ya. My barn was full of them back in the day. Like the rest of us, the horses didn't much care for them. Usually when I was in the middle of shoeing," Fox said, his hands rough like leather gloves. They carried years of calluses and scars, the kind that only a lifelong cowboy carries as a badge of honor. "Broke a few ribs that way."

"I'm surprised you didn't fabricate something in that blacksmith shop of yours. Some kind of trap. Take them all out at once. Efficient like."

"That's what the feral cats were for. When they did their jobs. Damn things had a mind of their own sometimes."

Michael Dean, the other man standing with them, finally spoke up. He was a preacher's son with a broad chest, just on the other side of 30. "Repair teams are just about done with the fence line, boss. We'll have her buttoned up in no time."

"Make sure they check it twice. These vagrants are getting in somewhere and it can't continue. Not today."

"Consider it done," Dean said, his prominent chin and dark eyes setting him apart from the other men, not just in looks, but in intimidation level. Few men had shoulders his size, regardless of age or former occupation. "Anything else, boss?"

Heston pointed to the hill above, where a trio of lifeless bodies, two men and a woman, hung from ropes by their necks. All three had been sentenced to death the day before. Each wore a white cardboard sign with handwritten black lettering that read: *Zero Tolerance for Thieves.* "Time to cut 'em loose. I'm sure everyone got the message by now."

"Feed 'em to the dogs?" Dean asked.

Heston nodded. "We waste nothing."

"I'll take care of it personally," Dean said, turning and walking away.

Heston didn't doubt Dean's last statement. The young man was an order-following machine. Never once did Heston have to issue an order twice with him, a welcome reprieve from some of the others.

Dean took off his white cowboy hat and ran a hand through his slicked-back hair, just like Heston had seen him do a thousand times before. The kid's black hair didn't contain a peppering of gray like Fox's, but Heston figured it wouldn't be long before it appeared.

Dean put his hat back on, fiddling with its fit until it was just so.

The fussiness didn't surprise Heston. Every cowboy has his traditions. And superstitions. Dean's were centered around his all-white hat. He spent more time cleaning his than anyone else in the crew. The kid kept it spotless, only taking it off to sleep or adjust his locks, like he'd just done. Dean preferred the sides of the hat curved up and the front angled down to match the back.

It's said that no two fingerprints are exactly the same. Cowboy hats are much the same, each one distinctively personal. None more so than Dean's.

"I'm sure the dogs will appreciate the extra meal," Fox said in a matter-of-fact way.

"And Dean the work."

"We all need a stress outlet, boss."

Heston couldn't agree more. "I'm sure he misses the old days."

"He probably does. But not me. I got tired of those late-night calls from the Sheriff pretty damn quick. I had better things to do on a Friday night than drive into town and mop up yet another bar fight."

"At least he never lost."

"Nah, too stubborn to ever go down. He liked the pain too much."

"Or back down. No matter how big the other guy was."

"That's part of his problem. Well, that and his temper."

Heston's eyes locked onto the corpses on the hill. "Someone has to do it. I'm sure you'll agree, we all appreciate his unique skills."

Fox nodded. "The right man for the right job."

Heston turned his attention to Fox. "I want everything ready to go in an hour. Let's move the backhoe and the extra fuel to the back, out of Frost's sight. No reason to rub it in."

"Still can't believe he agreed to let it go."

"Leverage, my friend. It's all about leverage. Even with an asshole like him."

"That it is, boss."

"I want extra guards posted at every station, too. We maintain the peace at all costs, understood?"

"Yes, sir."

"Let's get it done," Heston said in his firmest voice, the hairs on his neck standing at attention. Each month when Frost and Edison met, tensions would spike, for him and the rest of his men. Today would be no different.

Heston changed course and walked to the area known as Trader's Row. It was front and center, only fifty yards inside the switchback fences that guarded the main entrance.

Don Faster stood next to the first makeshift booth, waiting for Heston with a clipboard and pencil in hand. His wire-rimmed glasses were off level, like always, matching the unevenness of his bald spot. It looked like he'd been run over by a bailing machine, slicing off what little hair he had across the crown.

"I'm ready when you are," he said when Heston arrived.

"What's the count?"

"Thirty-seven," the thin-nosed former accountant said after glancing down at the top sheet for a beat. "Everyone is paid up. We went through an hour ago."

"Excellent," Heston said. Some of his men thought the ten percent fee levied on the traders should have been higher. But he knew that too steep a tax would drive more of the traders into the grave.

He needed them to be there every day, conducting business. Otherwise, he wouldn't get his cut. He had mouths to feed and ammo to acquire. Fuel, too. None of that would happen if Trader's Row turned into a ghost town because of too high a tax.

The booths down the center weren't normal setups, each with an improvised covering like a tarp or a blanket, and some kind of table for displaying their wares. A few of the traders used crates. Others deployed boxes. One even used an upside-down wash tub. Cast iron of course, its four legs acting as corner markers.

Faster led Heston to the first booth, where an elderly man and woman sat behind an old card table. It was gray in color and blended well with their fraying hairstyles, the wind just starting to pick up. They traded potatoes—something self-replicating and easy to cultivate in limited space. Every one of them was white and small. Yet each was of value, nonetheless.

The next booth displayed an impressive array of hand-forged knives, plus a few packs of cigarettes. The blades were rusty and the packs looked ancient. Even so, someone would come along today that needed what the purveyors had to sell, and would pay dearly for it.

Heston continued to walk the line like a general inspecting the troops, checking each trader's merchandise, shuffling forward a yard at a time, his eyes sweeping their inventory.

All of the traders had the same goal in mind: give and get on an equal basis. Worthless fiat script had been outlawed since the governments who'd backed the IOUs had long since vanished.

Paper bills were now nothing more than a poor man's toilet paper, if you didn't mind a nasty case of green-colored swamp ass, courtesy of Lincoln or Washington.

The next booth was staffed by an underweight man with dirty coveralls, flannel shirt, torn jacket, and lanky suspenders. He wore a straw hat that had been latched down to his head with a leather belt. He might have looked a thousand years old, but his three daughters didn't. Each was blonde and a real head turner. The oldest was maybe sixteen. There was no sign of a mother.

Heston had seen this same farmer and his kin there almost every day the past month, trying to move their swatch of goods. The middle-aged man had a little bit of everything: bandages, bar soap, gauze, scissors, salt, hard candy, a handful of drywall screws, powdered toothpaste, and even rat poison.

His odd collection of inventory wasn't what brought the buyers around. It was his daughters. Each one was available for an hour or two, depending on what you had in trade. The girls commanded a high price. No doubt they were what was keeping the family alive.

Heston had sampled each of the lovelies, rotating through them on the days when the farmer couldn't pay his fee. The youngest of the three was the most skilled, which seemed odd given the norms of society. Then again, society had vanished a long time ago, leaving what was left of humanity to reinvent the rules. And the standards.

Gold, silver, fur, and ammo were the preferred forms of money. Jewelry too. Either way, only fair exchange was allowed, including the peddling of flesh. Men, women, girls, or boys. Heston didn't give a shit. It was all legal. Just the way it had to be. It was simple to enforce and easy to police. In the end, it didn't matter what the traders sold, as long as commerce was done in a conflict-free manner. Oh, and he got his cut.

The rules were simple.

All deals were final.

No refunds.

No exchanges.

Just the way he envisioned it when he agreed to take over after Edison came to him with a proposition.

Handshake deals ruled the business of the day. Break them and your neck was on the line. Literally. No reprieve. No appeals. No second chances.

His way of running things might have sounded harsh to the glut of snowflakes that used to rule public opinion before The Event. Now those same bleeding-heart mouthpieces were nothing more than frozen Scab food, having perished first, their all-consuming focus on social causes keeping them from preparing for the obvious: the end of days. They'd been consumed by the minutiae, leaving them brainwashed and vulnerable. And now dead.

Heston stopped his trek, his eyes glued to the space between the next two stands. He held out a hand, palm up, to Faster, who promptly gave him a yellow measuring tape, ten feet in length. Craftsman was the brand, according to the label.

He uncoiled the ribbon of metal inside, checking the distance with the numeral markings. When the results were in, he raised his arm and backhanded the old woman tending the booth, sending her tumbling onto her backside. "You know the rules, Martha. Twenty-four inches. No more. No less. Understood?"

She nodded with tears on her face, her hand rubbing her cheek.

"Good. Otherwise, you'll find yourself outside the fence. Permanently."

CHAPTER 31

When the Nirvana convoy arrived at the Trading Post, Summer opened the rear passenger door and stepped out of the lead vehicle. She went to the door in front of her and opened it.

Edison swung his legs around and plopped them on the ground. She helped the old man out of the truck and to his feet, his face smothered in a grimace. Since she didn't smell any old man napalm, it meant his back was still bothering him, like before in his office.

Krista slid out of the driver's seat as two squads of her men descended on her position.

Summer knew from their conversations on the drive over that they were from Team One and Team Three.

Krista slammed the door and huddled with her men.

Summer couldn't hear what they were discussing as she helped Edison to the front of the truck. Summer swung her eyes to the right and scanned the fence line ahead, taking a read on the scene.

There were two elevated guard towers on either side of the main entrance. Each of them was staffed with tall cowboys carrying rifles across their chests.

A flat six-foot-long table was positioned in front of the fence line. Three guards stood behind it, each wearing Western gear like the others she could see. None of them had rifles, though their stainless steel revolvers were clearly in view, nestled in leather holsters on their hips.

The area between the table and the front of the fence was protected by two dogs—black and brown German Shepherds—pacing back and forth on leashes held by their respective handlers.

Beyond the guard dogs was a set of parallel fences, zigzagging left and right a number of times, much like a first-grader's maze. She assumed they were designed that way to funnel new arrivals into a narrow, single-file formation as a security precaution.

Summer thought the dogs looked hungry. Certainly agitated, their mouths agape and ears angled back. They reminded her of the Scab gang who tried to eat her before Fletcher showed up, except the dogs had their noses intact.

Just what she needed. More teeth. More hunger. More drooling.

Her stomach began to ache, as she felt the guards in the towers watching her. Did they know who she was? If not, then her first-time presence at this monthly meet might raise a stink with Heston or his men. She wasn't sure if Edison had to clear her attendance first, or if he could bring anyone he wanted.

Krista joined Summer and Edison at the front of the truck after her men dispersed. Team Three went back to their assigned duty station, while the others fanned out in a wide pattern, taking the lead toward the entrance.

The cargo truck remained parked behind the lead vehicle, its bumper nearly touching the vehicle in front. The chase vehicle was stationed behind the cargo transport that held the balance of Krista's men.

Summer figured Teams Two and Three would be brought forward later, when the meeting with Frost was over. Probably for some kind of inventory check. Or exchange. Maybe that's what the dogs were for? To look for explosives or something along those lines.

"I should probably just wait here, Professor," Summer said, the knot in her stomach tripling in size.

"No, you're joining us inside."

"But keep your eyes open and mouth shut," Krista added, her words tense. "You might just learn something."

"Shouldn't I have a gun or something?"

"Not a chance," Krista said after a huff, her tone fierce as she walked ahead, trailing her men by a few steps.

"That was a bit harsh," Summer said to Edison, leaning in close to his ear.

"I wouldn't worry about it. Heston won't allow any of us to carry past the inspection point," Edison said, shuffling his feet forward. "So it's a moot point. Just make sure they don't find anything concealed. If you have something on you, declare it and give it to them. You don't want to break their rules."

"I take it that would be bad?"

"Trust me. These men are not to be trifled with. Or underestimated."

"I thought you had some say here?"

"Not since we put them in charge. They are an independent oversight group with one job: keep the peace."

"What about Frost and his men?"

"Same rules apply."

Summer was pleased to hear that fact. If Frost brought that creepy Slayer guy or the other men who wanted a piece of her, they couldn't do squat while she was under Heston's protection.

Maybe today might not turn out as bad as she thought. Summer let go of the professor's arm long enough to move her hoodie into place across the top of her head, pulling the sides forward as far as they would go. She figured there was no reason to let them get a close-up view, in case she needed to make a run for it later.

When Team One made it to the inspection table, the men gave up their weapons and received colored ribbons in return, each a different color, length, and width.

"Ribbons? Seriously?" Summer asked Krista, standing a few inches in front of her.

"Claim checks," Krista said before moving forward to the table. She gave up her rifle, sidearm, and knife, tying a foot-long ribbon around her wrist. It was pink and about an inch wide.

"Seems kinda silly."

"You might want to keep those comments to yourself," Krista answered, her eyes watching the weapons she'd just given up.

The cowboys tied matching ribbons to the rifle, pistol, and knife they'd confiscated, identifying her as the owner of the items. Nobody said a word as the weapons were passed down the line and stored in a shoulder-high safe, its door protected by a gold-colored twist handle.

"All right, step forward. One at a time," the middle guy said. Like the others, he wore a cowboy hat, heavy jacket, handlebar mustache, and faded cloth pants. Blue in color. Trim fit. Pockets with rivets at the corners.

The skin of the cowboy in charge looked old, like Edison's, only his eyes were brighter and he stood with the posture of someone much younger.

Summer figured their guard duty had something to do with the premature aging of their skin, forever standing outside in the near freezing temperatures. "Does this place stay open at night?" she asked Krista.

Krista shook her head but didn't answer.

Summer peered at Edison, who was waddling next to her in line, hoping to glean an answer from him.

Edison shook his head as well.

Did that mean no, it didn't stay open at night? Or did it mean to shut the hell up, like Krista had snapped earlier? Summer wasn't sure. Either way, she decided to clamp her lips shut.

Team One began to walk past the snarling dogs one by one, each man unarmed, with his head on a swivel, angling his knees away from the four-legged chomp-fest. It was hilarious to watch grown men, who could probably wipe out an entire village of Scabs in ten minutes, react the way they did.

Krista's turn was next.

She took two deliberate steps forward. One of the dogs lunged at her, launching its open mouth. Its teeth came together in a snap, just missing the fingers on the hand closest to the beast—the same arm that had the ribbon tied to it.

Krista increased her pace, scooting past the animals in a dodging sidestep maneuver.

"Dogs know assholes when they see them," Summer mumbled, keeping her voice just above a whisper.

The guards frisked each member of Krista's team before clearing them for entry, sending them single file into the switchback fence system. The men looked helpless, a stark departure from their normal projection of unending strength.

Summer helped Edison to the table, the professor wincing again as he moved.

"Anything to declare?" the lead cowboy asked the professor, his face rigid like granite.

"Nothing but old bones and wrinkles," Edison said, his tone cheery. He put a hand on his lower spine. "And I emphasize the word *old*. The roads around here aren't doing my back any good."

Summer could have added to the conversation but choose to keep her mouth out of it. The professor might have been comfortable with all of this after years of monthly meets, but she wasn't.

The cowboy looked at her. "What about you? Any weapons or contraband? I need to hear a declaration."

So much for staying quiet. "No, sir. Just my girl parts and these godawful clothes."

He waved at them to move. "All right, continue."

Edison turned to Summer as they walked. "See? Nothing to worry about. We are just one big happy family."

She didn't respond as they approached the dogs. Both animals were now sitting on their hind ends, panting, their eyes still fixated and ears tucked back.

Edison walked past them without incident. They probably knew his scent, she decided, or sensed the old man wasn't a threat. Either way, he made it look like the process was no big deal.

The dog on the left stood on all fours as Summer came within striking distance. She sucked in a gulp of air and held it, forcing her insides to remain calm. They were just the opposite, but the oversized puppy didn't need to know about it. Or sense it.

The Shepherd came a step closer.

Summer didn't change her pace, continuing as if nothing was wrong.

Slow is steady and steady is fast, she reminded herself, remembering a military saying she'd heard Krista use before. She wasn't sure why her mind sent that flash at her. Perhaps when you're fighting panic mode, it opens your brain up for random thoughts.

A moment later, the animal's ears plopped up, no longer angled back like a dart. Its tail began to wag. Not in an all-out manner. More like a gentle sway.

Summer let out the breath in her lungs, feeling the tension in her chest release. She let her hand drift forward an inch or two.

The dog sniffed her fingers, but he didn't bite. When the cold of his snout touched her hand, she could feel the wetness across her skin.

Summer got the impression she was supposed to pet him. She wanted to but wasn't sure of the rules. The cowboys probably wouldn't like some stranger touching their animal.

She sauntered past the dog, keeping her hand steady, sending her most pleasant thoughts at the four-legged garbage disposal. She was just as big an asshole as Krista, but maybe the dogs couldn't detect it. Not unless she changed her aura or made a sudden move they didn't expect.

Edison looked back at her for a moment and said, "You okay back there?"

Summer turned her head and peered at the dogs, their eyes still trained on her. "Yep. Mostly."

"One more step to go," Edison said. "Just let them do their thing."

Summer closed the distance to the professor, remembering she needed to escort him. She'd gotten distracted, leaving him exposed with his stiff bones and aching back.

The remaining guard ran his hands over Edison for a minute before waving him forward. Then he turned his attention to Summer. She put her arms out to her side, giving him total access.

His touch brought back memories of Wicks feeling her up in the jailhouse. However, the cowboy's hands didn't linger or fondle, simply doing their job and moving on like a pro.

"Serious men with serious business," she mumbled to herself, increasing her pace to support the professor. It wasn't easy helping him through the narrow path of fencing. She felt like a mouse trapped in an endless maze. A maze with guns pointed at her. Edison didn't seem fazed at all, shuffling his feet a step at a time.

After they cleared the last section and were free of the confinement, Krista and her men met them with curious eyes. "Everyone okay?"

Summer remained at Edison's side, clutching his elbow. "Damn, that was intense."

"It can be for a first-timer," Edison answered.

"Do they know I'm part of this meeting?"

"No. And they don't need to. In fact, I probably won't even introduce you by name. I'll just tell them you're my new assistant."

"Heston won't care?"

Krista answered instead of the professor. "It's really not up to Heston, now is it?"

Edison put a hand on Krista's wrist, as if he were calling back one of the German Shepherds from attack mode. Then he shifted his focus to Summer.

"If he does, I'll smooth it over. Nothing to be concerned about."

"Okay, so you do have a say—"

"Sure, if you want to call it that. Heston knows his place. So do Frost and his men. As long as everyone stays calm, we'll get our business done today and be on our way."

"Do you think they're here already?" Summer asked, her eyes scanning the area for Frost.

"We'll know shortly. Just stay calm and listen once we're inside. There's an art to this that I want you to learn."

Dead ahead was a stand of booths on either side of the main walkway. Summer held onto Edison as they walked the aisle together, with Krista and her men forging ahead.

Summer ran a quick count, figuring there were almost twenty stands. Most had men milling about, some in front of the tables with gunny sacks over their shoulders. Others stood behind, looking attentive. There were a few women and children, too.

The place had an eerie feel to it, almost like nobody wanted to move too fast or say the wrong thing. It was strange to see everyone on their best behavior, but at least she didn't see any Scabs. That was a plus, though the armed cowboys watching the area made her skin crawl.

She wondered how long it took for the men, women, and children to get through the security station. Nobody had a bandage around their arms or legs, so no dog attacks. "Place is busier than I thought."

"Seems to be increasing each month. Word must be spreading."

"But how did all they all survive?"

"Necessity is the mother of invention," Edison said as they cleared the last booth.

"Desperation would be more like it," Summer quipped.

"That too," Edison added.

Summer noticed an old backhoe parked beyond the next building near the fence line, its fading yellow paint easy to spot. Several fifty-gallon drums sat next to it, not far from the front bucket. Fuel, she assumed.

Edison stopped his feet when an old cowboy stepped out of a building dead ahead.

"Here we go. Look sharp, men," Krista told the members of Team One.

CHAPTER 32

Krista Carr stood behind Edison as Heston, the leader of the Trading Post, walked toward them with two of his guards following behind. She didn't know the other men's names, but they were the same pair from the last several meetings. Both were tall and bearded, their thick hips carrying a pair of revolvers, dual-holster style.

Heston wore a tan-colored cowboy hat that had been evenly rolled up on each side, with a cloth hatband around the base of the crown. It was a white wrap and carried a buckle set on the left. The crown had a slight dent on each side and a well-formed crease down the middle, looking both purposeful and meticulous.

Heston wasn't armed, nor was he a lofty man, standing only an inch or two above Krista's height. He never seemed to change his clothes, either, wearing the same get-up for each of their monthly meets.

Perhaps it was superstition or Heston just preferred consistency. She couldn't be sure. Then again, maybe he only had one outfit.

His trademark jeans looked clean, though there was a light blue patch over one knee—something new and different. Everything wears out eventually, usually patience, but this man seemed to have plenty of that in reserve, especially when the monthly meetings with Frost became contentious and heated. That's when Heston's calm demeanor would step in and keep the peace.

Heston's pointed boots gleamed with polish, holding a steady black shine that seemed to be one of his trademarks. That and his dark gray dress shirt that never carried a single wrinkle, at least the part she could see under the heavy denim jacket.

Even his neck-wrapped bandana was the same—red and hanging loosely with a heavy knot on the front. It didn't serve much of a purpose other than to complete whatever message the man was trying to send with his choice of clothing and accessories.

His most noticeable features were his thin, ever-squinting eyes and thick brown mustache, like the whiskers of a push broom, obscuring both of his lips when they were pressed together.

She figured he spent most of the night picking food out of that hairy caterpillar, one that she assumed had been taking refuge below his nose since he first was able to grow facial hair.

"Good to see you again, Professor," Heston said in a Southern twang, taking off a leather glove. He held out his hand, thumb up.

"Likewise, Burt," Edison said, gripping and shaking hands with vigor, then pausing for a beat as he glanced back at the row of trading booths behind him. "Looks like business is up."

Heston let go of their shake, taking a new stance that included both thumbs pressing down on his silver belt buckle, typical cowboy style. "Can't complain. Though not everyone is here to trade."

"I imagine not. A lot of hungry people out there."

"Speaking of which, when we're done here today, I have two more families that I'd like you to consider. They seem willing. If you have the time, of course."

"Absolutely, I'll make the time."

"Excellent. One less thing I have to deal with."

Edison gave the man a single head nod, which Krista took to mean he was showing both respect for Heston's situation and the man's need for brevity.

Edison kept his tone steady when he asked, "Has the other side of the equation arrived?"

"Yes. Just before you. They're waiting inside, like always."

Summer leaned into Edison's ear and spoke in a whisper. "I don't know about you, Professor, but I would feel a lot better if we'd seen Frost and his men go through the same security check we did."

Edison gave her a long look, then said, "It'll be fine. Trust me. We do this every month."

Heston turned his attention to Summer and brought his eyes down to her tiny hands that were wrapped around Edison's elbow, then back up to scan her face. "And who might this fine young lady be?"

Summer answered before Edison. "I'm Summer."

Heston tipped his hat. "Pleasure to meet you, ma'am."

"I'm the professor's new assistant. Hope you don't mind."

"Not at all. We'll just need to rustle up one more chair," Heston said, his accent taking over the syllables. His eyes went to the bandages on her face. "Looks like you tangled with a critter or two."

"Yeah, you could say that. But it takes a lot more than that to keep this girl down. It's all about flashing and dashing, if you know what I mean."

Heston smiled, turning his piercing eyes to Krista. He finally acknowledged her with a slight head nod and a hat tip. "Carr."

"Heston."

The old cowboy turned sideways and held out a sweeping hand toward the building he'd just come from. "Right this way. Everything is ready."

The group traveled to the main door of the building, with Heston and Edison walking in stride next to each other. Summer was on the other side of the professor, clutching his arm.

Heston's guards had the lead, while Krista followed her boss, keeping watch on those in front of her. Her men were tasked with covering the group's six. Even though they were unarmed, except for their bare hands and tactical training, rear security remained their primary responsibility.

Other than Summer being involved, the rest of the greet had gone according to plan. Nothing much changes when you work for obsessive men who love their traditions. And processes.

All of it anticipated. All of it regimented, offering a calming respite from a world that was anything but calm. Or comfortable.

* * *

Summer took a step back as Krista assumed the lead, escorting their esteemed leader, Edison, through the door and into the foyer that led to what Edison had told her was called the Mediation Room.

Normally, this building was reserved for grievances and rulings, but the way Edison explained it on the ride over, the room ahead became the Negotiations Room once a month—on this day, at this time.

Edison told her that the meeting time and day of the month never changed, eliminating the need for communications between the two camps. Or advance reservations. She assumed the fixed date and time idea came from Edison, a man who preferred simplicity and consistency. Hallmarks of a great leader.

The members of Krista's Team One remained in the foyer with Heston's guards, leaving only Krista, Edison, and Summer to represent Nirvana.

When they cleared the threshold of the interior door, they were greeted by a wood conference table in the middle of the room.

It wasn't fancy, its four-foot by eight-foot plywood surface painted white, with a stack of bricks at each end serving as legs. One of the corners had been broken off, leaving a jagged edge of exposed layers running diagonally.

She wondered if the damage was from years of wear or from abuse. If this was a grievances room the rest of the time, then perhaps more than one scuffle had broken out.

It wouldn't take much for a couple of men to start fighting and break off the corner. Heck, it wouldn't surprise her if it happened more times than not, given the reputation of how Heston ran this place. Harsh rules and deadly consequences might not go over well with everyone, especially with the more desperate types.

Five folding chairs made of metal sat next to the table, three on one side and two on the other. A trio of sleeveless men stood on the far side, each one positioned behind an empty chair. All three had the same neck tattoo of interlocking chains.

The first was the handsome black man, Fletcher, the same guy who'd kept her safe from

Slayer and the others the first time they met. He'd offered her a gun for her defense before letting her go.

Fletcher stood farthest to the left, his chiseled face staring at her. His bald head gleamed under the overhead fluorescent light, its twin bulbs buzzing like angry bees. The generator chugging outside was obviously the source of the electricity.

In the middle was the man himself, Simon Frost. His blonde mullet, huge biceps, and scraggly beard were easily identifiable. So was the extra padding around his middle and the rugged look of his face, his eyes tight and watchful.

On the right was a younger guy with long, red hair pulled up into a ponytail. He was the trimmest of the three, his aura one of diligent underling.

His inquisitive eyes and prominent cheekbones made him stand out from the other two. While Fletcher was powerfully handsome, this guy was femininely pretty, looking like he might have been an underwear model back in the day. His arms were not bulging like the other two. Perhaps he didn't spend endless hours pumping iron or lifting engine blocks, both of which Summer had heard rumors about.

As Krista led Edison to their side of the table, Summer heard what sounded like a set of chains clanking together, then a run of pattering clicks.

When Summer looked to her right, that's when she saw it—a dog. A big, gnarly-looking blonde dog, coming straight at her in a sprint.

She backed up in a fast step, keeping her arms in front of her for protection.

"Stop! Come here, boy!" Frost yelled, but the golden-haired German Shepherd never changed course.

Summer's back hit the wall just as the dog reached her position. She screamed as the dog took a flying leap and knocked her down, twisting her sideways and onto her backside. She closed her eyes and sucked in a deep breath, expecting the dog to take a chunk out of her face, but that wasn't what happened.

A wet, slobbery tongue landed on her nose in a rapid-fire motion. She turned her head, trying to avoid the never-ending slobber maker. The dog's focus went to her ear, leaving a smeared mess of goo, licking her earlobe in an upward motion.

"Ugh, gross! Someone get this dog off me!"

A scarred hand came into view and snatched the dog's collar made of chain links, yanking the animal up and away in a blur of matted hair.

Summer rolled to her side, then pressed to her feet, wiping the drool from her cheeks, nose, and ear. It felt like she'd just taken an hour-long spit shower.

The animal's front legs were off the ground when Frost yelled at it with his face only inches away. "God damn it! I told you to stop!"

Frost made a fist and drew his arm back, then let it loose, landing a sharp punch on the animal's snout. The dog yelped with its legs still dangling, looking helpless. Frost brought his hands together and shook the dog hard in a choke hold.

A few seconds later, Frost let go with one hand and drew his fist back, readying another strike.

Summer ran and jumped on his free arm, screaming at him. "Stop it! You're hurting him!"

Frost let go of the dog and flung Summer loose with a sweeping arm maneuver.

She hit the floor hard, tumbling across the room, coming to rest with her back against the wall. The impact stunned her for a moment, knocking the wind out of her chest.

Summer gasped for air, while the dog ran to her, turned around, and stood in front, its teeth showing, snarling at Frost like an angry wolf.

"Don't you show me those teeth!" Frost snapped, his face red.

The dog took a slow step forward with its ears angled back and front shoulders low, growling with a foamy drool dripping from its mouth.

Frost started toward the pooch with fire in his eyes.

Krista jumped in front of him, landing a pair of stiff arms on his chest, stopping his advance. She was much shorter and half the man's weight, but she didn't seem to care. "That's enough! We've got business to discuss."

Fletcher never moved from his position behind the chair. Neither did the red-haired man, both apparently content to let Frost handle the situation on his own.

Edison hobbled past Krista and Frost, making his way to Summer. The dog let him pass, keeping its focus on Frost, who was engaged in a stare-down with Krista.

"Are you okay?" Edison asked, unable to bend over because of his back. He held out his hand to Summer, palm up.

"Yeah, just needed to catch my breath," Summer said after a painful grunt. A few more breaths came and went before she was strong enough to stand. She got up without Edison's assistance and went to the dog. The hound was still in defense mode, its attention solely on Frost.

Summer put her hand out, aiming for the fur across his back.

"You might want to rethink that. He doesn't like to be touched," Fletcher said.

Summer stopped her hand short of contact. "What's his name?"

"Sergeant Barkley."

"Easy there, Sergeant, everything's okay," Summer said as the mutt swung its head around and looked at her. She let her hand drift forward, watching for clues from Barkley. The dog didn't react, so she continued until she made contact.

Barkley's ears released the second she began to pet him, running her hand across the top of his back.

Frost and Krista separated.

"Now that everyone knows where they stand, how about we sit down like civilized human beings and take care of business," Edison said, his focus moving from one person to the next.

"Come here, boy," Frost said, snapping his fingers in the process.

Barkley never moved.

"I said come here!"

The dog planted his rear end on the cement with its tongue hanging out, panting like a freight train.

"I don't think he likes you very much," Summer said, wrapping her arms around the canine's neck, giving him a hug. "Do you, boy?"

"Yeah, well, screw that dog. Fucking turncoat," Frost said, turning away from Krista and returning to his side of the table. Frost sat in the middle chair, with Fletcher and the red-haired guy taking their respective seats as well.

Summer gave Barkley a few more rubs, ignoring the odor. She wasn't about to complain. It wasn't the dog's fault. He just had a lousy owner.

Right then, Heston came through the door, carrying an extra folding chair. He must have sensed the tension, his eyes running a quick scan of the room. "What the hell did I miss?"

"Just a little misunderstanding," Edison said. "But it's all under control."

Heston put the chair on the side of the table opposite Fletcher. Summer planted her butt in the new seat, assuming it was hers since she was the reason for it.

Krista sat across from the red-haired guy, giving him a smirk and shooting her eyes at the top of his head. "Still rocking the red, hey Dice?"

"And you the black. Nice headband, by the way. Bad hair day?"

She laughed. "Bad hair week. Been a little busy."

"Aren't we all."

Edison shook Heston's hand. "I'll take it from here, Burt. Thank you."

"Just yell if you need my guards. They'll be right outside."

"Thanks, but I think we can handle it from here," Edison answered as he sat down across from Frost. "We all want the same thing."

Barkley nestled in next to Summer and sat down, his neck pressing into her hand. She understood what he wanted and went into petting mode, scratching and rubbing, while keeping an eye on everyone in the room.

CHAPTER 33

Stanley Fletcher sat quietly next to his boss as the monthly meeting continued, his ears tuning out all the dick-measuring, testosterone-filled rhetoric.

Edison and Frost were engaged in a temper-charged battle for the lead moderator position, discussing today's exchange with sharp words. None of this was a surprise. It happened each month.

Fletcher's focus was on what would take place in a few minutes, when the meeting was about over. At least, that was the timing he expected.

The two leaders seemed content to put the altercation over the girl and the dog behind them. Fletcher figured Heston and his well-earned reputation had something to do with that, his men stationed outside with the only rifles in camp.

The girl sitting across from Fletcher was obviously nervous, her eyes giving away her emotions. He remembered those eyes—amped up and wary—from their encounter. It was only moments after she'd been rescued from the rogue Scab gang his team had hunted down and eliminated to restore order.

Her name was Summer, the same name that Slayer and crew had found on the back of the necklace recovered at the defunct cannery. Not a common name to be sure, but it did seem to fit her.

Granted, Fletcher had only met her once before today, but somehow his gut knew the name fit. Perfectly. Not for some mythological reason. More along the lines of a name matching the intellect hiding behind the eyes. A unique name for a unique person type of thing. She wasn't pretty by classical standards, but there was something endearing about her.

Perhaps it was her cleverness. Or her wit. Not many her age could have given Frost's patrols the slip—twice. Men who'd gunned down plenty in recent years and could hunt with the best of them.

Her ability to escape against overwhelming odds indicated she had plenty of guts and a set of balls bigger than his. More so since she'd accomplished those feats while traveling alone and unarmed. Impressive.

Summer was no slouch, that was for sure. The girl had skills. Yet, despite her smarts, he got the impression she was a bit off center from the short conversation he'd had with her. Not an obvious choice for Edison to drag along to an important exchange like this.

So why the girl? Why today?

Fletcher assumed the frizzy-haired young woman recognized him as well. The obvious tension in Summer's face and her random glances indicated she did, appearing apprehensive in this high-pressure summit.

It's an obvious conclusion when you see someone sitting with rounded shoulders and slumping in her seat. Even if you missed those tells, an astute observer would spot her trembling fingers, laced together on the table.

So far Edison hadn't introduced her since his group had arrived in the room. Probably a good thing, since Frost didn't know who she was. Not yet. A minute ago, Fletcher had considered informing his boss about her true identity but decided to wait to see where this was going, especially with what was planned for the rest of the day.

There are times when a subordinate should keep his comments to himself. More so when the comments are undiscovered facts. Facts that might escalate the bloodshed and ruin a perfectly laid plan.

He could always bring her identity up later, if need be, but once she was outed, there was no way to walk back the reveal. His tactical awareness skills were screaming at him to keep his mouth shut, so that's exactly what he'd decided to do.

Fletcher was sure his trusted friend Dice would agree. He leaned forward and looked past Frost, catching the attention of the former craps dealer sitting at the other end of the table. Fletcher raised an eyebrow, knowing Dice would understand the inference.

Dice gave Fletcher a nod back, then adjusted his flaming red ponytail, indicating he was ready.

"Everything looks in order," Edison said, his eyes scanning the last of the inventory list that Frost had given him on paper only a minute before.

"Like I said, we've completed our end. Now I need to see yours," Frost said.

Edison turned to Krista, who'd been quiet since the meeting started, and held out his hand. Krista gave him a folded sheet of paper.

Edison opened it, spun it around, and slid it to Frost with a tentative look on his face.

Frost took a minute to review it before he slammed his fist on the table. "You must think I'm a fucking idiot!"

"On the contrary—" Edison said, not able to finish his sentence before Frost spoke again.

"There were supposed to be six battery packs. Not five."

"I was just about to explain. We had a small problem with production. The last pack didn't test out as well as we'd planned."

"That's not acceptable."

"I understand, but sometimes these things happen."

"Don't break your word to me, Edison. A deal is a deal," Frost said, leaning forward.

"My apologies. We should have it replaced for you next week. We didn't want to provide you with something that wasn't up to specs."

"Apologies are for pussies," Frost said before turning his attention to Krista. "I'm sure your second would agree."

Krista didn't hold back her response. "Agree with you? Never."

Edison cleared his throat, his voice turning deeper and more intense, no longer looking or sounding the part of lowly professor. "You should know by now that we'd never come here without being prepared to offer additional compensation."

"As well you should," Frost replied.

"I'm prepared to negotiate, Simon. What's it going to take?"

Frost took a few seconds before he answered. "For starters, we're going to hold back half of the fuel we brought."

"For a battery pack? That seems a bit steep."

"Not just for that, old friend," Frost added, snapping his fingers at Fletcher in a hurry-up manner.

Fletcher dug into his pocket, pulling out the paper item he'd brought along. He gave it to his boss.

Frost unfolded the map and slid it forward to Edison. "I believe this belongs to you."

Edison took the paper in his hands, his eyes scanning it for a few seconds. "Where did you get this?"

"On our side of the No-Go Zone. My men cornered one of yours."

Edison swung his head around and shot an angry look at the girl slumping in her seat. He held up the paperwork. "What is this, Summer? Why didn't you tell me about this?"

"I knew it," Krista mumbled, though Fletcher heard the words.

Frost stood in a flash, pointing a finger at the girl. "That's Summer?"

"Yes, she's my new assistant," Edison said, his focus returning to Frost.

Frost fired his eyes at Fletcher. "Why didn't you tell me?"

"Honestly, I didn't recognize her. Probably those bandages on her face. Plus, she was all wrapped up yesterday. Never got a good look at her."

Frost squinted with his forehead creased, bringing his lips together in a thin, tight line. His faced beamed red, looking as though he was about to shoot a bolt of lightning from his eyes.

His expression vanished a moment later, then he put a hand into his pocket and took out the necklace that Slayer had found, shortly before he was gutted and killed.

Frost held it up, dangling it in front of Edison. "We found this, too."

Edison peered at Summer once again, clearly looking for answers.

Summer shrugged but didn't respond, scooting farther down in the chair, looking as though she wanted to disappear under the table.

Frost tossed the necklace at Edison. "You broke the treaty, Professor. Now there will be penalties to pay. Steep ones, otherwise there can never be peace."

Edison looked pissed, but Fletcher wasn't sure if that anger was meant for Frost or for the girl. Probably both, he guessed.

"I'm listening," Edison said.

Frost looked at Summer. "Her, for starters."

"Huh?" Summer said, sitting up in a flash. She looked at Edison. "What does that mean, Professor?"

Frost answered instead. "It means you're mine, bitch. You cost me two good men. Now get that skinny ass over here, next to me."

"No! No! No!" Summer said, shaking her head at Edison.

Krista stood with her shoulders back and chest out. "Nobody is touching the girl."

Fletcher did the same, matching Krista's stance and posture.

Edison put his hands up as a stop sign indicator. "I'm sure we can come to some arrangement, but Summer is off the table."

"The hell she is," Frost said, motioning to Fletcher to retrieve the girl. "It's my right to demand compensation as I see fit. Those are the rules, Professor. Your rules, or have you forgotten them?"

"I'm well aware of the rules, but we're not going to start peddling flesh," Edison said as Fletcher walked around the end of the table, taking a step to their side of the room.

Krista met him, her eyes staring into his.

Fletcher could feel the heat from her breath washing over his face.

Frost slammed the table again. "Bullshit. You must have known I'd demand this; otherwise, why did you bring her along?"

"I brought her along to teach her something."

"Well then, I'd say she's learned all she needs to. Failure is never an option."

"Professor, please! Do something!" Summer said.

Frost continued, "We need someone to handle the cooking and cleaning. Plus, provide a little entertainment for the men. Since she's the one who broke the treaty, she's the one who should pay the price."

"Entertainment?" Summer snapped. "No way! I'm not cleaning up shit, either."

Edison rose from his chair, his hands in scramble mode, moving air in a panic. "We can work this out. But first, I need everyone to remain calm. There's no reason for this to escalate."

"We're way past that, Professor," Frost said, his eyes sending a command to Fletcher to move ahead.

"Stand aside," Fletcher told Krista in a firm tone, his jaw clenched.

Krista never moved. "Not a chance, asshole."

Summer flew out of her chair and backed away, her feet taking her to the wall behind. The dog went with her, remaining at her side, its ears back and fur standing on end.

"I'm not going to ask again," Fletcher said to Krista, planning to eliminate the dog next.

Krista clenched her teeth, pushing air through them as she spoke. "Then you'd better take your best shot because I'm not letting anyone put their hands on that girl."

"Please, Simon. We can work this out," Edison said in a frantic tone.

Before his next heartbeat, Fletcher heard a long string of pops outside. They were random and at a distance. Gunshots. Dozens of them. They were followed by a chorus of commands. Frantic. Amplified.

Edison whipped his body around to face the door. Summer and Krista did the same. All eyes were now in the direction of the noise beyond the door.

Fletcher followed suit just as Heston broke through the door, his eyes wide and breath short. "We have a situation. I need everyone to follow me."

Nobody moved. Only stunned silence.

"I said, let's go! Now!"

Krista collected Edison and led him to the door. Summer followed and so did Sergeant Barkley, his paws pounding at the floor.

Fletcher looked at Frost, waiting for orders.

"You heard the man, let's move!" Frost yelled, his feet moving first, following the others out of the door and into the foyer.

Fletcher closed ranks behind Frost, as did Dice, the two of them coming together.

Dice sent his fingers into the knot of hair that made up his bushy ponytail. He pulled out a cylindrical tube about the size of a Chapstick. They'd hidden it inside his thick mop, where they knew Heston's guards never checked.

Dice gave it to Fletcher, who promptly tucked it in his hand, while everyone's focus was on Heston leading the way.

Gunshots continued, growing in number and intensity. Some of the verbal commands outside had been replaced by screams, raising Fletcher's heartbeat in the process.

Heston, Edison, Krista, Summer and Frost were now outside the central building, being protected by a lineup of Krista's guards and Frost's men. The dog was there too, his legs moving in lockstep with Summer, never leaving her side.

They all stood together, unarmed, a few yards from the end of the booths marking Trader's Row. The vendors had all fled, leaving their trinkets and other valuables behind.

Fletcher and Dice caught up, stopping two steps behind Frost, who was bracketed by the remainder of his guards.

To the right, Summer stood on one side of Edison, Krista on the other, with her team holding position in front of her.

A skirmish line of Heston's guards stood in front of everyone, using a half-moon formation, firing with their rifles level to the ground. The barrels moved left and right as the gunfight continued.

Fletcher knew the signs—they were spraying and praying, each of the thirteen men hoping to take out the threats ahead.

"Everyone back!" Krista snapped, her eyes focused on the swarm of Scabs climbing over the fence line ahead. Her hand went for the holster on her hip, but it was empty. She looked at the cowboy closest to her. "Hey you!"

He peered back with a puzzled look on his face, his rifle still engaged and shooting one round at a time.

"Your sidearm," she said, motioning at the weapon on his hip.

He let go of his rifle with one hand, then pulled the revolver from his holster and tossed it to her. It floated with almost no rotation, much like a knuckleball from a pitcher. She caught it, flipped it around, and cocked the hammer, aiming it at the Scabs ahead. "Tell the others, too."

He did as she asked, spreading the word, bringing more pistols out of their respective holsters. The revolvers were passed from man to man until they were in the hands of both Krista's and Frost's men.

The Scabs were everywhere. Hundreds of them, maybe thousands, flooding the compound in waves, their hands and feet scaling the switchback fence line with the dexterity of tree monkeys. Some of their heads exploded in a burst of red after bullets made impact, but the rest of the throng kept advancing.

A flood of Scabs broke off and swarmed the two guard towers, climbing the struts like an army of ants. The men in the towers got off several shots, but there were too many coming at them. It only took seconds for the horde to overrun their position and begin their munching feast.

Edison and company shuffled to the rear while the bullets and commands continued from the guards standing firm in front of them. Some of the orders were issued by Heston. Others were from Krista and Frost, each leader invested in repelling the attack.

Fletcher opened the tube Dice had given him with a twist of its cap, then put a finger over the spout to control how much fluid would leak out. He flicked it at Dice while Frost was turned away, sending drops of the pheromone solution onto the redhead's shirt.

Fletcher did the same to himself, then raised an arm to sample its odor. It wasn't strong, but it was noticeable, if anyone took a moment to sniff. He didn't think that was likely, not with the pandemonium unfolding ahead of them, which is why he waited until now to deploy the deterrent.

"There are too many! We gotta run!" Summer yelled.

"Isn't there a back gate?" Fletcher asked, already knowing the answer.

"Yes. Follow me," Heston said, pointing. "This way. Hurry."

One by one, their group peeled off and followed Heston's lead, passing close to Fletcher. Frost was the first, pulling a rush of frigid air with him.

When Summer scampered by with Edison, Fletcher applied the elixir to both of them in a covert splash.

Then he did the same to Krista, who followed behind Edison and the girl, walking backwards with her gun at waist level, firing two rounds at the Scabs.

Krista must have felt the liquid hit her skin, her eyes turning fierce. "What the hell is that?"

"No time to explain. Just trust me," Fletcher said, his voice barely audible over the barrage of gunfire. "We gotta go! Now!"

Krista lowered the gun, then turned and ran after the others.

Fletcher put the cap on the tube and stuffed it inside his pocket before he and Dice followed behind Krista.

Their group turned a sharp corner along the back side of the main building and jogged past the backhoe, eventually running into a stampede of Scabs coming from the right. They were packed together and snarling.

Fletcher saw one of Heston's cowboys climb the metal steps and enter the cab of the John Deere, then slam the door closed. He started the turbo-charged engine and spun the seat around before grabbing the control sticks.

A moment later, the hydraulic arm on the back of the dirt mover swung sharply. First, he brought it to the right, smashing into a collection of Scabs who were looking the other way.

The sudden impact sent them in the air as if they were hockey pucks heading down the rink. They landed on top of several more of their kind, knocking them down like pins in a bowling alley.

The operator brought the bucket back the other way with a jerking force, swatting three more cannibals, this time separating one of the meat-eater's legs in the process. Blood shot out in a wide arc as the bucket followed through, catching another Scab in the head. It, too, blew apart, sending brain matter and blood on the same trajectory.

The Scabs must have finally realized what was happening and turned their attention on the great machine, swarming it from all sides. Soon the yellow paint across the forged steel disappeared from view, fully engulfed in human scavengers.

The man inside the cab didn't stop what he was doing. He brought the backhoe bucket up about fifteen feet and then started to pound Scabs from above, stamping them flat like cockroaches. Strike after strike was made. Boom. Boom. Boom, each time the bucket compacting one of them into a pile of bones and goo.

It reminded Fletcher of squishing ants, at least until the horde ripped the door open on the cab and forced the driver out. He disappeared into a flail of revenge, his life now in pieces and part of their digestive system.

Summer must have seen all this, too. She took a quick step back and stumbled, as did Edison, both of them landing on the ground with surprised looks on their faces.

A quartet of Scabs closed on Edison's position, looking as though they were going to attack. However, that was not what happened. They scampered past the old man and Summer as if they weren't sitting there defenseless.

The four Scabs had eyes on Heston, taking a direct path toward him. The man turned and ran toward another building, this one smaller and made of wood instead of brick.

Krista ran to Edison's defense as more Scabs advanced. She took position in front of him, then unleashed two more rounds.

Summer worked the professor to his feet, while Krista's bullets hit the mark, liberating skin from bone in a dramatic spray of marksmanship.

Krista pulled the trigger again, but the gun only clicked.

Two of Krista's men joined her as a dozen Scabs descended on their location. Her troops fired their pistols, but soon their ammo ran out as well, leaving them no choice but to go hand-to-hand.

The men wrestled and punched, throwing haymakers, elbows, and jabs. They repelled a few Scabs, but it wasn't long before they disappeared under the weight of the pack, their limbs getting torn to pieces in a flurry of teeth.

Krista slipped away just as Heston's men arrived for additional support. The guards tried to stop the carnage in progress, but they were no match for the sheer number of targets.

Moments later, Heston's men became Scab food as well, their torsos shredded inside a bloody wrap of clothes.

Frost ran to the edge of the melee and snatched a sheath lying on the ground. It was still attached to a leather belt that used to belong to one of Heston's cowboys.

Two Scabs turned and noticed him, changing their focus. Frost didn't hesitate, letting loose with a sharp right, stinging the chin of the closest Scab. The barely human assailant went flying, tumbling sideways as if it had just been hit by a bus.

Frost brought his other fist around and under, nailing the second Scab with a powerful uppercut, landing a blow under its jaw. The punch sent the cannibal into the air. Like the first, its consciousness disappeared into the dark recesses of dreamland.

Frost made a hasty retreat, pulling the ten-inch hunting knife from its sheath. He dropped the belt and brought the blade up, its edge glistening under the burn of the sun.

The man held off another Scab by gripping his giant hand around its throat. He lifted the Scab off the ground, sending its eyes wide and skinny legs into a dangle. Its tongue flopped out of its mouth in a gurgle as its face turned a deep shade of red.

Frost brought the dagger up and gutted the meat-eater in an upward, slicing motion, starting at its navel and ending mid-chest. He tossed the dead

Scab aside, then took a step back, taking position in front of Summer.

Fletcher couldn't believe his eyes when Frost put his arms out with the blade in a defensive posture, looking as though he was prepared to defend the girl and the professor.

Then it happened.

Frost whirled around and jammed the knife into the side of Edison's neck. The tip entered the skin just under the ear, sinking deep.

Edison gasped.

Summer screamed.

Frost withdrew the blade with a quick yank, dragging tissue and blood with it.

Edison brought his hand up and covered the wound as blood shot out in spurts, squirting red between the gaps in his fingers.

Krista's attention came around. She froze with her face stiff as Edison toppled to the ground. A moment later, she ran to the professor, only to get decked by a swift roundhouse punch from Frost.

She flew sideways with her shoulder hitting the dirt first, then her body twisted, smacking the back of her head into the ground in a whiplash motion. She lay there stiff, her arms and legs no longer moving.

Frost bent down to Edison and readied the blade again, aiming the bloody tip at the man's eye.

Summer let out a roar as she jumped onto his arm, her hands latching onto his bulging forearm. She pulled and twisted, wrapping her legs around his neck, trying to leverage the weapon away from Frost.

Frost tore Summer off with a yank to her hair, making her scream as he swung his shoulders. His power and weight sent her flying like a ragdoll.

She hit the ground hard, her butt landing first, then her elbows and back, making her wince after the impact.

The dog joined the fight, running and leaping at Frost, its powerful jaw clamping down on his wrist. Teeth entered skin, making Frost cry out in pain.

Dice stood firm. So did Fletcher, both men watching the dog tear into their boss. Neither of them moved while Frost battled Sergeant Barkley, whose paws were off the ground, its entire body hanging from the man's arm.

Frost brought the knife around and let out a commando scream as he stabbed the dog in the hip.

Sergeant Barkley yelped, causing him to let go and fall to the ground in a twisted lump of fur. The dog squealed and whimpered, its head looking heavier than its body as it looked back at Summer.

When Fletcher saw Frost take a step toward Summer with the knife in a striking position, he took action. He used a flying leg kick, nailing Frost in the center of the chest.

The collision altered Frost's course, sending the goliath stumbling backwards, his feet trying to regain their footing. He fell on his ass about ten yards later, landing in front of a knot of Scabs approaching from the rear.

The hunger gang surrounded Frost as he got to his feet. He managed to fight off several, landing punches to their heads and blade strikes to their necks.

He outweighed them by a hundred pounds each, but soon there were too many. They dogpiled, gnawing at him like a pack of wolves, ripping the man's clothes from his body, then tearing into his skin.

Fletcher went to Edison and scooped him up, carrying the senior in his arms. "Hang in there, Professor. We're going to get you out of here."

Dice shook Krista, rousing her from her dirt nap. She pushed to her feet, looking dazed.

"You okay?" Dice asked.

"Barely," she answered, her dazed eyes scanning the scene. She rubbed her jaw, then opened and closed it, obviously testing to see how badly she was injured.

"We need to go!" Dice said, nudging her forward. He looked at Summer. "You too."

Summer ignored the man and ran to Sergeant Barkley, her face smothered in tears. The animal lifted its head to greet her, then tried to stand but couldn't, its hind legs covered in blood.

"Come on, I've got you," Summer said, scooping the animal up in her arms. She turned in a flash and ran to join the group, all of them heading at an angle to the left—the only direction free of Scabs—for the moment, anyway.

CHAPTER 34

Krista jogged alongside Fletcher as her adversary carried Edison in his arms. She matched Fletcher's stride, step by step, allowing her to keep her hands pressing on the wound in the professor's neck. "We need to pick up the pace, Fletcher."

"I'm trying, Carr, but he's heavy for an old man."

She smirked. "He does like his pancakes in the morning."

"Here, let me," Dice said to Summer, the two of them following ten yards to the rear.

Krista glanced back to see Dice holding his arms out, motioning to take Sergeant Barkley from Summer.

"Nah, I got him," Summer said with strain in her voice. The animal's head hung loose, bobbing as she fast-walked. So did its legs, flopping like cooked spaghetti. "Come on boy, stay with me. Please."

"I guess that answers that question," Fletcher said in a sarcastic tone, bringing Krista's attention forward.

Fletcher motioned with his eyes, directing her gaze to a slew of body parts littering the area to the right. Some had been cleaned of flesh down to the bone, others were partially intact. Heston's cowboy hat sat on top of the mess, its brim covered in a run of gooey tissue.

"Poor bastard," Krista said, her mind flashing a violent scene of Heston's death.

"Is that—" Summer asked, her tone charged with angst.

"Look away," Krista said, hoping to save the young girl from a visual she would never forget. "You don't need to see this."

"Seriously," Dice said to Summer, as if he'd been cued to distract her. "Let me take the dog. He's too heavy for you."

"I said no. Don't you understand English?" Summer snapped in a strained voice, turning to avoid the man's reach.

Fletcher carried Edison to the narrow gate at the back of the Trading Post, angling sideways to open the latch and squeeze through the opening.

Krista lost contact with Edison's neck when they went through. Blood shot out again, spraying more of Fletcher's clothes before she caught up and was able to resume her triage.

"Hang in there, Professor," she said, wondering if her mentor could hear the words. His eyes were no longer open, but at least his chest was still pumping air.

Fletcher brought his eyes to Krista. "I don't know; he's lost a lot of blood."

"He'll be okay. He's a lot tougher than he looks," she said, not wanting to admit the man was right. She motioned to the left with her head, taking an extra gulp of air to recharge her lungs. "The trucks are that way."

"He's not gonna make it that far."

"He doesn't have a choice. We have to get him back to the s—" she said, stopping herself in mid-sentence, before she revealed that Nirvana was in an underground silo.

"I'm sorry, the what?"

Krista changed her words in a panic, using a stutter to buy time to adjust. "—the station. Doc will fix him up. No problem." She scanned the area ahead in a noticeable fashion. Probably too noticeable, but then again, that was the idea to draw attention away from her near-reveal.

Fletcher took the bait. "Is something wrong?"

"I don't know. Maybe," she said after an eye squint, pausing her words for effect. He needed to think her sudden caution was the reason she stopped her sentence short a few seconds ago. "Where the hell did they all go?"

"The Scabs?" Dice asked, his voice landing on her ears from behind.

Summer spoke next in a breathy voice, almost as if she could read Krista's mind. "It's like they all went home or something."

"Or gave up," Dice said.

"Something obviously drew them away," Fletcher said, sounding indifferent to the discussion.

"Or someone," Krista mumbled without thinking, her mind pondering the tone Fletcher had just used.

Fletcher continued, his chest pumping harder than a minute ago. "No telling what happened. But I wouldn't worry too much about it. All that matters is they're gone. We've got more important things to deal with."

"He's right," Dice said.

Krista's mind latched onto a recent memory, one that took place a few minutes before. She kept her legs moving as she sniffed her shirt. A strange odor caught her attention. "What the hell was that stuff you threw on me back there?"

Fletcher hesitated before he spoke, looking as though he was debating whether or not to answer her. "Something we've been working on."

Krista pondered the recent events in her mind, digesting some of the more curious aspects about the attack. The Scabs had run past a defenseless pair of easy meals in Summer and Edison, only to attack Heston. It didn't make sense. Predators never ignore the easy prey. Not when they have a choice.

Her vision changed again, this time showing the dogpile of Scabs on Team One after they had come to her rescue. She was there, too, with her troops, in harm's way, but the Scabs left her alone, only tearing into her men. Her heart twanged with grief, thinking of their brutal deaths.

Right then, a new idea popped into her head.

She leaned forward and took a whiff of Fletcher's shirt. It smelled mostly like iron from the professor's blood, but she was able to detect a different odor. One that matched what she smelled on her own clothes. That's when it hit her. "It's some kind of Scab repellent, isn't it?"

"That's as good a term as any," Fletcher said, glancing at Dice while the group continued its scamper to the trucks.

"It must not work very well, since Frost still ate it," Summer said, laughing and wheezing for air, the dog's body bouncing in her arms as she ran. "So did the rest of your guys."

"We only put it on you three," Dice said, his chest hardly moving at all.

"And the two of us," Fletcher added.

Krista didn't buy his answer. "Why not everyone?"

"There wasn't time. We had to act fast."

"Well then, I guess we should thank you," Krista said, wondering why Fletcher would do that, especially against his own team like that. Tactically, he should have saved his men first. Not to mention his boss, Frost.

Summer groaned, no doubt due to the canine's weight taking a toll on her back. Yet she hadn't slowed down, not a lick, keeping up with Fletcher as the group motored along the fence line at a pace just short of a sprint. "Could've used it yesterday when I was out doing my thing."

"We didn't have it yesterday," Dice said.

"That's hard to believe."

"It's brand new," Dice said, pushing his legs forward another stride. "Are you sure you don't want me to take over?"

"Dude, I got this. Back off."

The transport trucks came into view three steps later, bringing newfound energy to Krista's legs.

"Which one?" Fletcher asked her.

Only two vehicles were parked in front of the main gate, instead of three as expected. She pointed. "The one in back."

"Are those your men?" Fletcher asked with concern in his voice, as a slew of bodies came into view. They were shredded into pieces, lying about the trucks along with several hundred spent bullet casings.

"Must have been a huge firefight," Dice said.

"That's disgusting," Summer said when she arrived with the unconscious dog. She pointed with her elbow. "But at least they hit their targets."

Krista followed her eyes, seeing a blanket of dead Scabs. Most with bullet holes and torn limbs. Blood everywhere. Nothing moving.

"Well, not all of them," Krista said in an emotionally torn voice, stepping over what remained of her men. Bits and pieces of flesh dotted the landscape, as if they'd been fed through a wood chipper, white camo uniforms and all.

Dice stepped forward to help Fletcher load the professor into the back of the truck, taking over for Krista with one hand on the neck wound.

Krista shook off her emotions and flushed the pain in her heart. She had a job to do. There wasn't time to grieve for her men.

She dug deep and found the stronger version of herself, then took a few moments to survey the Scab carnage. Some of the body parts weren't torn or shredded at the ends as she expected. They'd been sliced clean, with precise edges.

Summer must have just noticed the same fact. "Someone chopped through them like butter."

Krista agreed with the girl's assessment. "With something sharp."

Summer's voice tensed. "Oh my God. The Nomad? He did this?"

Krista nodded, surveying the casings and other evidence. "Must have tried to rescue our men."

"A minute late by the looks of it," Summer said, standing by the back of the transport, shifting her weight between legs.

Krista realized the missing truck held the goods they'd brought for trade. "Took our supplies, too."

Summer raised an eyebrow. "Or the Scabs did."

"I doubt Scabs can drive," Krista said in a terse voice, watching Fletcher and Dice move the professor forward, obviously making room for Summer and the dog. She noticed the professor's breathing was shallower. "Come on, Summer. Hurry up. The professor doesn't look so good."

"A little help?" Summer asked her.

"Yeah, right. Sorry," Krista said, stepping forward in a lurch to assist the girl into the truck with both hands.

Summer climbed the bumper and into the covered area of the truck, then put Sergeant Barkley down with a waist bend. She sat cross-legged next to the mutt, rubbing his neck with one hand, while pressing on his knife wound with the other.

Krista watched the girl bring her gaze to the professor, staring at him with tears falling from her eyes, looking as though someone had stuck a knife in her, too.

Krista figured Summer was torn between tending to the ugliest German Shepherd on the planet and Edison—a man who always had Summer's back.

Granted, both the dog and the professor were fighting for their lives, but how could that girl prioritize an animal she barely knew over a person who had kept her safe and fed all these years? It didn't make sense. At least not to Krista.

When the animal woke up with a whimper, Summer turned her attention to the canine, her face running a ghostly white when their eyes met. "I know it hurts, boy. But we'll be home soon. Just hang in there."

"Can you drive this thing?" Fletcher asked Krista, sounding more like a demand than a question.

"On it," Krista snapped. But before she turned and completed a step toward the driver's door, the professor sat up and gasped.

Everyone flinched in a startle.

"Krista? I need Krista?" the old man asked, his eyes glazed over.

Krista flew up the tailgate and into the cargo area, shoving past Summer. She knelt down next to Dice, nudging him to the side, then took Edison's wrinkled hand in hers, squeezing it between her fingers. His skin was cold, terribly so, as if he'd been sleeping in a walk-in freezer. "I'm right here, Professor."

His voice turned weak, almost to the point of a whisper. "Promise me something."

She leaned in close. "Sure. Anything."

"Stand by her," he said in a fading tone.

"Who?"

"Summer," he said, struggling for air to fuel his words. "She needs a loyal council."

"For what?"

His words became even more choppy and weak. "To take over."

"Take over?"

"Yes. Nirvana."

Krista hesitated a few beats, not wanting to admit that she'd just heard those words. "She's not ready, Professor."

"Rules of Succession," he said, the words arriving with mostly air. "Promise me."

"Okay. I will. You have my word," Krista said, feeling her heart break into two.

Edison took one last massive breath before the air in his lungs ran out. His head flopped back and tilted to the side, his eyes still open.

"Do something!" Summer screamed, tears flooding her face in waves.

Fletcher laid the old man back on the floorboard, resting his lifeless body on the cold steel.

"No! No! No!" Krista said, leaning forward and putting her hands on Edison's chest to start CPR. She pumped and pumped, but the life in his eyes never returned.

The blackness had him.

CHAPTER 35

Krista finished dressing the dog's wound with a wrap of cotton and medical tape from the vehicle's first aid kit. It took eleven stitches to close the hole, but the dog took the pain like a champ, just like he had for the past half hour.

Summer never stopped stroking the animal's fur the whole time, her eyes vacant with tears, even after her long bout of sobbing that seemed to have lasted forever.

Right now, Summer's attention didn't appear to be on anything specific, her stare aimed at a point somewhere off at the distance, beyond the back of the truck, far past the carnage littering the area.

Krista knew why. She felt the same way, staring at the blanket covering the professor's lifeless body, fighting back the shock of his death.

Summer had done enough wailing for everyone, but it still didn't lessen the grief squeezing Krista's heart.

Tears are for the weak, Krista reminded herself, forcing the anguish from her heart.

"That should do it," Krista said, finishing the wrap on Sergeant Barkley. She flashed a pair of tight eyes at Summer. It was obvious the girl needed a diversion, something to free her mind of the tragic, bloody death of her mentor and friend.

Krista knew the best way to do that was to grab Summer's attention with something unexpected. Verbal, that was—an emotional redirect—part shock and part awe—or simply callous. Either would work, if she delivered the words in the proper tone and with the right inflection. Just enough to engage, but not so much as to hurt. "But I still think this was waste of supplies."

Summer's empty, watery stare vanished in a heartbeat, as she turned her eyes to Krista. "I'm sorry, what?"

"You heard me. Our medical supplies should be saved for two-legged creatures, not four."

"How can you say that?"

"Simple logic. We must have priorities."

"No way we're letting Barkley die like the professor."

Krista felt an emotional stab slam into her chest, but she wasn't going to allow it to gain a foothold. Not entirely, otherwise she'd lose her status as Nirvana's toughest SOB. "Jesus, Summer. I didn't let him die. I did all I could."

"She did," Fletcher added from just beyond the tailgate, looking resolute, even though he wasn't technically part of their team. "Edison lost too much blood. There's wasn't any more anyone could do."

"Not what I meant," Summer said, making eye contact with Sergeant Barkley. "Someone has to survive today."

"You mean like the four of us?" Dice quipped in a matter-of-fact way, flashing his attention at Krista, then Fletcher and Summer.

Summer patted the dog on the neck. "Five."

Dice nodded, looking as though he'd just surrendered. Or he was trying to be supportive. Hard to tell. "Sure, five. That's something at least."

"We should get moving," Fletcher said to Dice, both men standing a foot apart, only inches beyond the rear of the truck.

"You guys aren't leaving, are you?" Summer asked.

Krista put a hand on Summer's arm, giving her an eye flare and a subtle head shake, hoping the girl would understand the gesture. Their enemies, or former enemies, needed to leave, but Krista didn't want to utter the actual words. Fletcher and Dice couldn't be allowed to follow them home, not without compromising something Edison held most dear—the location of Nirvana. "They have their own people to think about, now that Frost is gone."

"She's right," Fletcher said. "I'm afraid this is where we part ways. We've all got new responsibilities. People to think about."

Krista took her time, scooting a path to the rear of the truck, while her mind went into deep analysis mode.

She wondered what life in the silo would be like now that the professor was gone. She wasn't happy about Edison putting Summer in charge, but the Rules of Succession were clear.

So was her duty to fulfill her pledge to the old man, even if anointing Summer as Nirvana's new leader went against all known logic in the universe.

Krista hopped out of the truck, realizing her job as Security Chief was about to challenge her in ways she never expected—all of it propelled by an emotional young girl with no experience as a leader.

Fletcher took a step forward, meeting Krista with his chest out. She did the same, then craned her neck up to make eye contact—man-to-man, so to speak.

The last time they'd taken the same stance in front of each other, the two of them were about to go to war in Heston's meeting room.

She put a hand out. "I never thought I'd say this, but it's been an honor working with you, Fletcher."

Fletcher grabbed her hand. "Likewise. I've stood in battle with my share of warriors, but none braver."

"Or more stubborn," Dice added, his face under the control of a full grin.

Krista laughed, though it was forced with the anguish of the day still smothering her heart. The professor. Her men. So much loss. Yet, Summer needed a role model to follow, one that wouldn't show weakness, despite all the death. Otherwise, Nirvana had zero chance to succeed now that Edison was dead. "We are who we are. Those that can, step up."

"Roger that," Fletcher said.

Krista let go of Fletcher's hand and shook Dice's as well, then looked around before she brought her eyes back to the rugged black man. "We've got a long road ahead of us. Hopefully, we can continue to work together, like today."

"Leave everything in the past," he replied, his tone confident.

"A new beginning," Dice added.

Fletcher nodded. "First up, we'll need to figure out a replacement for the Trading Post."

"What's left of it," Dice added with a sneer on his mug.

Krista agreed with Dice's terse assessment. "We've both got a lot of dead to bury."

"And notify everyone back home about what happened," Summer said, wiping the tears from her face, her tone no longer filled with grief. At least, not entirely.

Krista was impressed with the new leader's sudden shift, though the girl had no idea how difficult the task would be. "You need to prepare yourself, Summer. There will be a lot of questions. Some of them won't be easy."

"You'll help walk me through it, right?"

"Sure," Krista answered, knowing what was coming. Casualty notifications are never easy. More so, when it's about the leader of a team.

"Need to start thinking about a complete rebuild, too," Dice said. "Probably fortify a few things while we're at it."

Fletcher scanned the area with his eyes for a few seconds. "Agreed."

"I'll bring a team back to collect our men as soon as I can," Krista said. "I'm sure we can spare a few to help with the cleanup efforts, too."

Fletcher nodded.

"Hey, wait a minute," Summer snapped. "I should be the one making these decisions. Edison put me in charge, Krista. Not you."

"You're right. My mistake," Krista said after a pause. It wasn't going to be easy keeping her take-charge self in check. Or taking orders from this grubby-faced youngster.

The tense look on Summer's face vanished. "We should ask for volunteers to help guard the Trading Post. Once it's cleaned up and all."

Fletcher looked at Krista, then back at Summer. "Some from each camp?"

"That's what I was thinking. Seems fair." Summer changed her focus to Krista. "Anything else?"

Krista looked at Fletcher. "Maybe next month you can bring some more of that Scab Repellent. I know we could use it."

"I'm sure we can work something out."

"Speaking of fair," Summer said to Krista, "we should probably replace the supplies that the Nomad stole. You know, live up to our end of the deal. The professor would have wanted it that way." She looked at Fletcher. "You wouldn't happen to have a spare needs list, would you?"

"No. Frost took care of that personally. But I'm sure I can work up a new one. How's a week from today sound? Give me a chance to settle in first. See what's what?"

"High noon?"

"That'll work," Fletcher said in that deep voice of his.

A subtle grin took over Summer's face. "I'll make sure Krista is here with bells on. Right Krista?"

Krista nodded, but didn't appreciate Summer's showboating—apparently at her expense. She'd just earned Fletcher's respect and now this snot-nosed girl was rubbing it in. It was all she could do to stop the eruption of harshness lining up in her throat.

It took every ounce of her self-control, but she managed to flush the anger, then replace the words with a response more fitting to her new role as Summer's bitch. "You ready to head back, boss?"

"Yeah, just take it easy," Summer said, leaning forward to give the dog a gentle hug. "I don't want anything to happen to our new friend."

Or anyone else, Krista thought to herself, thinking of all the possible threats still ahead of them. There were so many unknowns. So many possible outcomes.

She'd studied the Nirvana Code of Conduct well, but wasn't sure what the Rules of Succession would be if a newly-minted leader didn't have time to appoint someone new before her sudden and unexpected demise on the way back to the silo.

In truth, there were a million ways to die in a world like this. More so while traveling across an unsecured area with minimal firepower or backup.

Or witnesses.

Everyone knew that losses could occur on any mission and at any time. Some couldn't be helped, even if they happened to a popular young girl who was just anointed as the chosen one and entrusted with the lives of many.

TO BE CONTINUED in
Silo: Hope's Return
Book 2

I Have a Big Favor to Ask

I am an independent author who doesn't have the marketing budget of a big publishing house. So I rely on Amazon reviews and star ratings to help get the word out about my books.

If you could leave a review, no matter how short, I would appreciate it beyond words. Not only will it help me know what readers like and want to read, you'd be helping one of the little guys stay afloat in a crowded marketplace.

Thank you in advance for your help! Reviews are the lifeblood of independent authors like myself.

Want a free book?

All you need to do is sign-up for my VIP Newsletter on my website at **www.JayFalconer.com** and I'll send you a free copy of the all-new *Bunker: Origins of Honor* eBook.

Find out what happened in the days just before the unstoppable Jack Bunker got on the train and ran smack into the middle of an all-out invasion of the USA.

There's plenty of action in this prequel story, so get over to my sign-up page right now and join my VIP Newsletter.

BOOKS BY JAY J. FALCONER

New Blockbuster Releases
> *Bunker: Road to Redemption*
> *The Last Outpost*

The *SILO* Series
> *Silo: Summer's End* (book 1)
> *Silo: Hope's Return* (book 2)
> *Silo: Nomad's Revenge* (book 3)

The *BUNKER* Series
> *Bunker: Born to Fight (book 1)*
> *Bunker: Dogs of War (book 2)*
> *Bunker: Code of Honor (book 3)*
> *Bunker: Lock and Load (book 4)*
> *Bunker: Zero Hour (book 5)*

Time Jumper Series
> *Shadow Games* (book 1)
> *Shadow Prey* (book 2)
> *Shadow Justice* (book 3)

Narrows of Time Series
> *Linkage* (book 1)
> *Incursion* (book 2)
> *Reversion* (book 3)

American Prepper Series
>   *Lethal Rain Book 1*
>   *Lethal Rain Book 2*

Other Recommended Books
>   *Ashfall Apocalypse* (book 1)
>   *Ashfall Apocalypse* (book 2)
>   *Ashfall Apocalypse* (book 3)
>
>   *Highway* (book 1)
>   *Endurance* (book 2)

About the Author

Jay J. Falconer

Jay J. Falconer is an award-winning screenwriter and USA Today Bestselling author whose books have hit #1 on Amazon in Action & Adventure, Military Sci-Fi, Post-Apocalyptic, Dystopian, Terrorism Thrillers, Technothrillers, Military Thrillers, Young Adult, and Men's Adventure fiction. He lives in the high mountains of northern Arizona where the stunning views inspire his day.

You can find more information about this author and his books at www.JayFalconer.com.

Awards and Accolades:
2020 USA Today Bestselling Book
2018 Winner: Best Sci-Fi Screenplay, Los Angeles Film Awards
2018 Winner: Best Feature Screenplay, New York Film Awards
2018 Winner: Best Screenplay, Skyline Indie Film Festival
2018 Winner: Best Feature Screenplay, Top Indie Film Awards

2018 Winner: Best Feature Screenplay, Festigious International Film Festival

2018 Winner: Best Sci-Fi Screenplay, Filmmatic Screenplay Awards

2018 Finalist: Best Screenplay, Action on Film Awards in Las Vegas

2018 Third Place: First Time Screenwriters Competition, Barcelona International Film Festival

2019 Bronze Medal: Best Feature Script, Global Independent Film Awards

2017 Gold Medalist: Best YA Action Book, Readers' Favorite International Book Awards

2016 Gold Medalist: Best Dystopia Book, Readers' Favorite International Book Awards

Amazon Kindle Scout Winning Author

Made in the USA
Las Vegas, NV
29 August 2021

29092737R00256